The Reluctant Brides of Lily Court Lane

Susan Chan and Carol Polakoff

ISBN 13: 9780991343102
ISBN: 0991343107
Library of Congress Control Number: 2013957723
Franne M. Ficara, San Diego, CA

In memory of our dear friend
Barbara Fatheree
who brought us together

Acknowledgments

We'd like to thank the members of our reading group for their many comments and suggestions: Connie Ailshie, Jenna Benarba, Marilyn Mauer Brown, Pat Clark, Robin Goret, Alexis Inman, Bernice Michalec, Andrea Morse, Ginny Ollis, Norine Rose, Tammy Siemers, Lisa Strong, Steve Wall, and Pam Wasserman.

Special thanks to Jonathan Alston for sharing his knowledge of the Navy and his insights, and to Jacqueline Lipton, Esq. for her extensive review and many suggestions so helpful to new authors.

In addition, we are grateful to Sandy Bornstein and our other mah jongg teachers who introduced us to a whole new world. We also wish to thank our friends in book club and mah jongg—they inspired and sustained us throughout and never forgot to ask how the "book" was coming along.

Susan is most appreciative of her husband, Jay, for his unfailing encouragement and the many dinners he cooked while Susan was glued to the computer; Carol is very grateful to her husband Gary, for his love and unstinting support, and to her daughter, Melissa, who always enjoys a good story.

Lastly, we could not have readied this book for publication without the hard work and dedication of Franne Ficara. We are so appreciative of your editorial comments and business acumen.

Thanks to our readers—we hope you will enjoy meeting the women of Lily Court Lane.

We welcome your comments at *susanandcarol@yahoo.com*.

Susan Chan and Carol Polakoff

The Residents of Lily Court Lane

The Women

Maryann Croft	The bride at the New Year's Eve wedding lives at Number 1, the house with the red door.
Sarah Waterman	The widowed owner of *Sarah's Bakery* lives at Number 3, the house with the blue door.
Dallas Cruz	A recently divorced personal trainer lives at Number 5, the house with the yellow door.
Carolee Jensen	A paralegal and mother of an adopted daughter lives at Number 7, the house with the green door.
Jane Ellis	The beautiful, single travel agent and newest resident of Lily Court Lane, lives at Number 9, the house with the purple door.

Their Friends and Relatives

Alex Wolfe	The groom and Sarah's brother, owner of *Wolfe's Coffee Break*
Craig Waterman	Sarah's son, owner of the *Bayside Gallery* in San Francisco

Marvin Miller	An attorney officiating at the wedding, Carolee's boss
Simon Nordvahl	The wedding photographer
Cindy Jensen	Carolee's adopted daughter; works at *Sarah's Bakery*
Ming Sun	Manager of *Wolfe's Coffee Break*
Emilie Conner	An elderly French woman residing in Point Loma

Prologue: Paris, France, July 1942

A young man dressed in a precisely tailored elite German officer's uniform entered a ransacked house and noticed a painting hanging on the wall above an elaborate mantel. Earlier, a French
family had begun their day, just like any other day, believing that all
was well and good in their little world. Now they were gone.

The officer had obeyed his orders: clear out members of the
French Resistance and their families. Round them up quickly and
quietly, leaving no trace behind. His men had been ordered to strip
their houses of all valuables so they could be loaded on railroad cars
and sent to Germany.

He grimaced as he looked around him. He despised disorder.
His soldiers had been thorough, but careless. Draperies were torn
from the windows, tufts of stuffing wrenched from the sofa and
chairs overturned in search of jewelry and hidden money. Even the
silverware was gone, taken to be melted down to make German
armaments. Plants were upended and their earth spilled over the
highly polished wood floors.

His men left behind the one item that caught his eye—a lovely
painting of a mother and child. He stood before the painting for
a long time with a growing sense of elation. Such perfection, he
thought in awe. How had they missed this gem?

An inner light seemed to emanate from within the portrait,
caressing the cornflower blue folds of the mother's taffeta gown

and shining on the baby's blond curls. Both mother and child looked into the eyes of the unknown viewer, inviting the observer into their serene life. A small smile of contentment turned up the corners of the mother's lips and the infant appeared drowsy with bliss at being held so tenderly in her mother's loving arms.

The officer felt no concern for the family who had lived in the home as recently as this morning. They couldn't have known what a treasure they possessed, but he knew immediately.

He spoke aloud to himself, *"Mein Gott!* You are exquisite."

He felt the blood rushing hotly through his veins as he gazed at this masterpiece before him. No woman could compete with the lust he felt as he studied this treasure. Who could resist such beauty? Certainly not him.

In the dying light of the afternoon he removed the painting from the wall and turned it over to read the faded handwritten title on the back. *Mevrouw Van Bruggen Met Emilia.* Flemish? Perhaps. A Rembrandt or a Vermeer? He couldn't know for sure as it was unsigned, but all his art training told him he held in his hands something rare and very valuable.

During his youth, he'd studied at the Heidelberg Art Academy. There he learned, like his beloved Fuhrer before him, that he possessed a very minor talent. As a child, he'd dreamt of becoming a great painter but his professors instead guided him toward art history and taught him to become an expert art critic. Now he summoned all his training as he stood in the deserted house in the 14th arrondissement in Paris. This time he was glad his men had been so careless and overlooked the painting.

Suddenly, he heard a squeak from the floor above. Had someone been able to elude his men? *Ach,* it was probably nothing, a small pet, or a frightened servant. He considered searching the house himself, but he wasn't interested in making another arrest, especially not now. He looked back to the painting. There it was again, a sound from above.

He shrugged. No one escaped the Gestapo for long. He was sure whoever it was would be swept up later this evening. This painting was much more important. Muttering aloud, "I must have this," he crossed the room, pulled a section of the torn drapery from the window, and wrapped it carefully around the small painting. The package fit snugly beneath his arm. He quickly left the house, not even pausing to shut the door. He had the perfect hiding place in mind.

1

New Year's Eve—The Present

As the taxi turned the corner, Craig Waterman could see all of Lily Court Lane unfolding before him. It was a charming tree-lined street, only one block long, in the heart of downtown San Diego. On one side of the street, six houses glowed in the setting sun, their gardens overflowing with brightly colored flowers.

From his last visit at Thanksgiving, Craig knew where each of his mother's friends lived. Catering trucks and a florist van unloading wedding goods were parked in front of Maryann's house at Number 1 Lily Court Lane, the house on the corner with the red front door. She would be marrying his uncle tonight.

Next door to Maryann at Number 3 stood his mother's house, with a fragrant garden of the flowers she loved leading up to her blue front door.

Dallas, the women's personal trainer, lived in Number 5, the house with the yellow door and a barking dog in the front yard, eager for his run in the park across the street.

Craig did a double take—what in the world? Next door to Dallas at Number 7, the house was covered from rooftop to sidewalk with lavish holiday decorations—Christmas lights glittered everywhere and Santa's sleigh and eight reindeer crossed the roof. Lighted candy canes, bells and snowflakes graced the front porch while a huge inflatable snowman stood filling the yard. This festive house with the green door belonged to Carolee, the fourth member of his mother's group of friends. She'd added even more decorations to her display since he'd seen it at Thanksgiving.

His mother described Carolee as wildly flamboyant, with an "interesting" eye for design. Craig confirmed this for himself when Carolee came to their Thanksgiving dinner dressed as an Indian princess—not native American Indian mind you, but all aglitter in an iridescent green sari with bells around her wrists and ankles. What a character!

Noticing a car in the driveway of Number 9, Craig wondered if someone had moved into the vacant house with the purple door.

After he paid the taxi driver, he turned to see his mother flying from her doorway to greet him. She was wearing her baker's white coat with *Sarah's Bakery* embroidered in navy blue on the pocket. He was surprised to see she'd lost a few pounds and was looking younger. Her hair was now colored a flattering auburn, no longer the natural grey she wore for many years.

When she hugged him, he inhaled the familiar scent of gingerbread cookies and the floral perfume that always clung to her clothes. Ah, it felt good to be home with his mom, far away from the busy art scene in San Francisco.

"Hi, Mom, you look great!"

"And you look wonderful, sweetheart. I'm so happy to see you."

Arm in arm, Sarah led Craig into the house and seated him on a comfortable overstuffed sofa in her living room where many of the cherished mementos from his childhood were proudly displayed. Craig smiled at the photos, drawings and even a ceramic candy dish he'd made at camp one summer gracing the top of the baby grand piano. The dish didn't look half bad, he thought.

"Craig, I'm sorry, dear, but I have to go back to the bakery and finish the wedding cake we're making for tonight. Make yourself comfortable, and enjoy the light dinner I set out for you in the kitchen," she said, kissing him on the cheek.

"Your room is ready for you upstairs. Why don't you relax and I'll be back as soon as I can," she called as she rushed out the front door.

"Okay, Mom, I'll be fine," he said to her back.

As always, his mother was a whirlwind. Nothing seemed to slow her down, Craig thought, walking into Sarah's cozy kitchen. Spread out on the table before him were platters of cheeses, cold cuts, freshly baked bread, and a crispy salad. He smiled at the display. This was his mother's idea of a light supper.

Meanwhile, preparations were reaching a frenzied pitch at Number 1 Lily Court Lane. The bride, Maryann Croft, stood in her living room surrounded by a flurry of people, amazed she'd found so much happiness after the cruelty she'd suffered in her past. She tingled with anticipation. By this time tomorrow she would be at sea on her honeymoon cruise, locked in the strong, loving arms of her new husband. Her heart beat faster at the thought. At last she would become Alex's wife. Tonight, everyone she cared about would be with her to celebrate this special moment.

The wedding was only hours away and Maryann knew her friends were making certain all would go well. One by one they called to tell her their progress.

"We're putting the final touches on your wedding cake. You'll just love it," Sarah said.

Carolee was in charge of the wedding finery. "Your veil is here and it looks beautiful."

It had given them several anxious hours when it arrived at the bridal shop much later than expected. The antique lace wedding veil, worn by her grandmother, was to be Maryann's "something old."

Carolee also arranged for her boss, Marvin Miller, an attorney of some note in San Diego who occasionally served as a judge pro-tem, to perform the actual ceremony.

The final member of the quartet of friends, Dallas, was working with the caterer to make sure the food would be perfect and ready on time.

Maryann restlessly wandered from room to room through the chaos. Everywhere she went she was shooed away by the busy staff seeing to the decorations, moving the furniture about, and setting up chairs for the guests.

"Oh, sorry. I'll stay out of your way."

After saying that yet again, Maryann finally went upstairs to shower and try to rest but her stomach was a fluttery mess, butterflies bumping into knots. She was much too nervous to rest or even eat the dry toast and tea she'd made earlier.

As she sat in a chair by the window, all she could think about was Alex. She'd been so afraid to give love another chance after Michael, but now she was confident she'd made the right decision. She refused to allow the past to haunt her anymore.

Their guests would soon be arriving dressed in their New Year's Eve best. In addition to her friends, Maryann had invited a few of the other neighbors on Lily Court Lane and members of her self-defense class at the gym. Sarah's son, Craig, would also be there. He was to be his Uncle Alex's best man. The other guests included Carolee's daughter, Cindy, and Alex's employees from his coffee shop, his friends from his rowing club, the catering staff, and the photographer. In all, there'd be about thirty people in her small living room, just the right number for a room that size. An intimate and perfect wedding.

Maryann closed her eyes and pictured the beautiful gown she would wear, the candlelit staircase and the moment when her eyes would meet his. Her beloved Alex.

While Sarah was at her bakery and Maryann was trying to rest, Craig poured himself a second cup of coffee and continued to worry about a problem at his gallery on Sutter Street in downtown San Francisco. Earlier that day, unable to settle down to his paperwork, he kept making excuses to go outside to study the painting of the mother and child prominently displayed in the gallery's front window. Each time he looked at it he found himself transfixed by the beauty of the piece.

But something about this painting set off warning bells for Craig. He must discuss his unease with Jack, his partner in the gallery, when he returned from his buying trip in Russia.

The crated painting had arrived the previous afternoon on consignment from a client in Düsseldorf, Germany. Rodney, one of the sales associates, told Craig about the phone call he'd overheard between Jack and the painting's owner, Herr Schmidt.

"I don't know exactly what was being said because I only heard one side of the conversation, but I gathered the man is liquidating some art he's inherited from his grandfather. He plans to open a bed and breakfast in Germany and needs to raise funds for the project. He met Jack last summer, so he consigned the paintings to our gallery. They set the price for one of the paintings at forty thousand American dollars."

Craig was especialy surprised Jack agreed to the price without having seen the actual painting. The amount got Craig's attention and he made a mental note to discuss with Jack how he and the owner had arrived at the offering price.

Rodney continued, "Herr Schmidt seemed unable to provide a provenance for that piece. He told Jack it had been in his grandfather's private collection for a long time but he knew little about it.

A missing provenance for such a pricey work? Something else to discuss with Jack. A written document called a provenance typically accompanies each artwork, describing where the item is from, who the artist is, and who the previous owners had been. In other words, it is the history of the piece.

Getting ready to close the gallery for the day, much earlier than usual because of the holiday, Craig walked by the painting one final time. A memory tugged at him, something about stolen art from the past. Craig wanted no part of art fraud which had become such a common crime in the art world. He couldn't dwell on the painting much longer, though, if he was to make his flight to San Diego.

"You can leave now, Rodney. I'll close up. I'll see you when I get back. Call me if you need to."

"Thanks, Craig. Enjoy your trip and Happy New Year!"

Before setting the alarm, he took several photos of the painting and downloaded them to his laptop. Then he removed the small painting from the gallery window and locked it in the office safe. He felt more at ease. The painting was safe for now.

"Good night, Charlie, and Happy New Year," Craig told their security guard.

"Night, Mr. Wolfe, the same to you."

Once outside, Craig felt the cold winter wind blowing off the bay. Early New Year's Eve revelers were already finding their way into trendy bars and restaurants close by. It was chilly in San Francisco, the air fresh with a hint of frost. In the distance he could hear the famous cable cars as they clanged over the metal tracks. The faint bells and cheers of the tourists echoed as they "oohed" and "aahed" over the hilly ride through the city.

Wrapping his burgundy cashmere scarf tightly around his neck, Craig caught the bus back to his loft South of Market Street. His had been a quiet Christmas holiday, just a few evenings spent with friends, no special lady to warm his bed or kiss beneath the mistletoe.

Now he packed his bag quickly, placed his evening clothes in a garment bag, and then changed into a pair of comfortable jeans, a black turtleneck sweater, and a black leather jacket. He seemed totally unaware of the dashing figure he cut. Tall, loose limbed, with black hair and sparkling green eyes, he never lacked female companionship.

Leaning back in his seat on the taxi ride to the airport, Craig thought of his lucky Uncle Alex, fortunate to have met a wonderful, loving woman. Craig was looking forward to being the best man at the wedding tonight. He liked spending time in sunny San Diego. It was a welcome change from damp and chilly San Francisco.

Finally on the plane, Craig closed his eyes and tried to relax as they taxied down the runway. In his mind he again saw the painting, but for now, he needed to put aside his obsession with it. Tonight was his uncle's wedding and he was looking forward to it.

2

Something Borrowed, Something Blue

Candles lined the pathway to the open front door, leading the guests through the garden onto the porch where dozens of lacy icicle lights framed the doorway and hurricane candles flickered on pedestals. It was a crisp, dark New Year's Eve in San Diego, as always no snow or ice to challenge the evening's pleasure. The women in their long gowns looked elegant and the men handsome but uncomfortable in their seldom worn tuxedos, pleated white shirts, and black bow ties.

"Why Eleanor, you look lovely this evening. Jim, good to see you. Welcome. We're very happy you could join us this evening."

"Wouldn't miss it for the world, Alex."

The groom, standing in the doorway, was tall and proud, his hair jet-black with just a hint of silver at the temples. His striking blue eyes surveyed the activity surrounding him. This was no nervous groom. Rather, he was filled with a sense of anticipation of what was to come.

Tonight everything would be perfect for Maryann, Alex thought with satisfaction. And tomorrow his bride would get her wish to go on a romantic cruise to Hawaii. Ah, he sighed, as if he needed another cruise after all his years at sea. But anything for Maryann. He smiled watching the caterers and florists rushing to complete the buffet tables in the dining room. The harpist, seated next to the glowing fireplace, was playing soft romantic music.

It was strange, Alex thought now, how life could throw you a curve. Here he was back in San Diego, the city of his childhood, after all those years away. He'd graduated from the Naval Academy at Annapolis, and immediately married his roommate's sister. As they walked under the crossed swords held aloft by his friends and classmates, their future had sparkled with promise.

Alex had easily risen through the ranks to commander. After so much time apart from his wife while serving his country, he decided to take retirement as soon as he could. They'd travelled the world together and finally decided to stay in Seattle where they planned to open a coffee shop in the neighborhood where they lived.

But it was not to be. Alex had to face the tragic news of his wife's sudden death in a car crash. He felt lost and alone, until his older sister, Sarah, convinced him to join her in San Diego. He'd be near both the ocean he loved so much and Sarah, who'd lost her husband as well. They were partners in grief, he thought, basically cheerful people who deeply mourned the loss of their mates.

Sarah had found such happiness in the Lily Court Lane neighborhood, she'd finally persuaded Alex to move and open his coffee shop nearby. He'd lived comfortably alone above his coffee shop, but meeting Maryann had changed Alex's plans to remain a widower.

One look at Maryann and he'd fallen instantly in love. Plenty of women sought his company and his bed, but this one touched his heart. Something beyond her dark curly hair and perfect figure called to him. Her haunted look made him want to erase the pain he saw there.

A little brown sparrow with a wounded wing, he mused, when his sister had first introduced them at the coffee shop.

Tonight all of Lily Court Lane would be celebrating the wedding between Maryann Croft and Alex Wolfe. Maryann's living room was resplendent in silver and white; the fragrant boughs of evergreens perfuming the air already warmed by the crackling fire. Tiny white lights were strewn everywhere amongst the vases filled with calla lilies, gardenias and white roses.

Even the wide, curving staircase was festooned with ivory velvet bows and pine garlands, illuminated by the tea lights flickering on each step. The overhead lights had been dimmed in the living room and candlelight shadows danced on the ceiling. Joyous laughter and murmurs of conversation filled the room. Anticipation grew while everyone awaited the entrance of the bride.

Moving across the room, Alex approached Marvin Miller, a highly-respected attorney who would be officiating at the ceremony. Marvin had helped Sarah establish her thriving bakery and he'd become a friend to all the women on Lily Court Lane.

"Hello, Marvin. Hi, Craig. Happy New Year to you both! Marvin, Maryann and I are very grateful to you for agreeing to marry us on a holiday evening."

"Alex, I'm very pleased to do it. There's no place I'd rather be this evening."

Alex and Craig bore a strong family resemblance, both tall and handsome men, with the same sensuous mouth, gorgeous eyes, and muscular builds. It was difficult to see their family resemblance to Sarah. She took after the female side of the family, petite and comfortably rounded.

Their conversation was interrupted by Carolee who for many years had acted as Marvin's paralegal and general office manager.

"We're almost ready upstairs. How about you gentlemen? Are you all set?"

Carolee was dressed in a lacy beige and cream gown, rather than one of her usual outrageous ensembles. The only reminder this was indeed the Carolee known and loved by all her friends on Lily Court Lane came from her numerous jangling charm bracelets. Tonight her platinum blond hair was swept back into an attractive coil at the nape of her neck. She looked every inch the elegant Hollywood movie star, just as she'd planned.

When Alex replied, "Yep, we're all just waiting for the bride," Carolee swept over to the harpist to give her last minute cues and instructions. The young woman smiled up at Carolee from her seat at her instrument.

"I'm all ready. I'll start the Mendelssohn in five minutes."

Now glancing at her watch, Carolee saw that it was almost nine o'clock and the guests were being urged to take their seats. She looked around the room one last time and noted everything was perfection. The time had arrived.

Hurrying upstairs, Carolee joined Sarah and Dallas as they admired Maryann who was checking herself in the full-length mirror one last time. The long ivory duchess satin gown was lovely, her tiny waist wrapped in a cream-colored bow like a Christmas present. Maryann smoothed the fabric across her stomach. Oh, how those wedding butterflies were dancing inside her!

She hoped she looked perfect for her beloved Alex. Her makeup was just as she planned, light and natural; her dark curls brushed her cheeks when she moved her head. Her lips and fingernails were painted a pale pink, the exact color of a ballerina's slipper.

As her friends fluttered around her, she recalled the promise she and Alex made to one another several months ago. Maryann felt her face flush as she recalled their ardent lovemaking the night Alex proposed. They agreed they wouldn't make love again until their wedding night, a promise which proved more difficult to keep than they'd anticipated. The couple realized this was an old-fashioned idea, but they both wanted their wedding night to be special, filled with pent-up passion.

Standing behind Maryann, Sarah, her matron of honor, peered over Maryann's shoulder and smiled at her in the mirror.

"You look absolutely lovely, Maryann. I'm so thrilled for you and Alex. Just imagine, you'll be my sister-in-law as well as my neighbor and good friend and I've vowed not to be an interfering sister-in-law."

They both laughed, knowing Sarah loved to meddle every chance she could. She would never be able to keep such a promise.

"I'm so glad we became friends before you met Alex." Sarah continued. "Meeting Alex made everything even more perfect."

She took a long strand of pale ivory pearls from her evening bag and held them out to Maryann, saying, "I'd be honored if you would wear my pearls. Our mother wore them on her wedding day so long ago, and I wore them when I married Harry."

Maryann was touched by Sarah's generous gesture, and placing the pearls around her neck, she turned so Sarah could fasten the clasp.

"Oh they're so beautiful, Sarah. Thank you," said Maryann softly, as she smiled at Sarah's reflection in the mirror, the pearls glistening against her creamy skin.

Brushing aside a tear, Sarah continued, "Now that takes care of the borrowed item. What are you wearing that's blue?"

Maryann laughed as she lifted the hem of her gown, kicked off her satin slippers, and revealed ten toenails painted a deep winter blue. As she wiggled her dainty toes, her friends joined in her laughter at the sight of the blue toenails, such a contrast to her sweet delicate face and formal wedding gown.

Sarah was the oldest of the group and tonight she had chosen to wear a flattering rose-colored gown. She had slimmed down these past weeks so she could easily fit into her new dress with its matching short jacket. She'd been careful to select a dress that didn't have a revealing neckline, no cleavage for her. Her scars mustn't show tonight. The whole ordeal of breast cancer was still a very private issue for her. She was grateful to have survived and be here tonight to celebrate this special moment, and she didn't want any reminders of her past suffering.

Dallas stood at Maryann's side adjusting the fingertip length veil for her. She refused to think about her own failed marriage. At her feet sat Jude, her golden Labrador, who accompanied Dallas everywhere. He'd be the ring bearer tonight.

Jude had proven himself a loyal friend to Dallas and the women of Lily Court Lane. His bark always warned them of strangers, and he'd guard them with his life if it became necessary. But they wouldn't think about that tonight either.

Dallas leaned down and tied both wedding bands to Jude's collar. He'd been groomed that morning to look and smell his best. When he tried to roll in the grass at the dog park earlier in the afternoon, Dallas quickly stopped him with the promise of a run after the wedding.

Dallas stood up, looking regal in a shimmering silver sheath, her perfectly toned and tanned body reflecting the many hours she spent training clients at the gym. The friends first met there when they joined Dallas's self-defense class. They'd each decided to learn ways they could protect themselves as single women in the city. Each had her own reason for taking the class, but Maryann needed it the most. There'd been a time when she felt totally defenseless.

Later, the women further cemented their friendship when they began playing the ancient tile game of mah jongg each week.

"Ladies, it's time for a last toast as single women. Tonight we're happily losing Maryann to Alex," Carolee said as she expertly uncorked the champagne bottle without losing a drop.

"Oh, no, you're not losing me. I'll still be right here on Lily Court Lane," was Maryann's smiling response. "The only difference is now we'll have a man living among us."

Carolee smiled as she lifted her glass.

"Here's to Maryann, our friend, who captured the eye of the best looking man in San Diego. We may resent you for taking Alex off the market but we love you and we wish you a hot spicy night tonight and for all the nights to follow."

Maryann blushed and tapped her flute against the others and they all took a sip of the bubbly golden wine.

Just then, the beginning notes of *The Wedding March* floated upstairs. The moment had arrived. The women put down their wine glasses and readied their bouquets of white roses and gardenias. Dallas went first, gliding down the stairs with Jude proudly bearing the ring box. Carolee followed, bracelets jangling, and then came Sarah looking elegant and a little teary- eyed.

There was a dramatic pause. The room became silent. The music from the harpist and the crackling from the fireplace were the only sounds to be heard as the guests stood, knowing the bride was about to make her appearance. Every eye was focused on the staircase.

Maryann paused at the top of the stairs and took a deep breath. She knew in her heart she'd made the right decision, and smiling, she slowly descended the stairs looking radiant. The beautiful veil covered her hair and touched her shoulders but didn't hide her dark curls and sweet face. An audible gasp swept through the assembled guests. She was breathtaking.

Maryann took her place next to a beaming Alex, their eyes clinging to one another as they recited their vows and committed to a future together. The ceremony was short and simple, the "I dos" brief and loving.

Alex's warm lips tenderly brushed Maryann's as he kissed his bride again and then whispered, "I love you, Maryann, with all my heart."

The ceremony concluded with Marvin turning the couple to face the room, announcing, "Please greet Mr. and Mrs. Alex Wolfe!"

Everyone burst into applause and rushed forward to congratulate the newlyweds. Friends gathered around Maryann and Alex as the photographer snapped photo after photo of them and their guests.

"Well done, Alex. You made it just in time to get your tax deduction for the entire year," joked Jim, Alex's accountant.

"Oh, Jim. No business talk tonight," his wife, Eleanor, scolded as she smiled apologetically and led him away.

Jim turned and rolled his eyes at Alex.

3

Champagne at Midnight

Across the room, Jane Ellis, the newest resident of Lily Court Lane, held back a little, feeling somewhat out of place, having known the bride for only two weeks. Dressed in a simple green gown with long sleeves and a high neck, she looked very demure until she turned to reveal the dramatic backless cut of her gown exposing her perfect alabaster skin and the rich luxuriant mahogany red hair cascading onto her shoulders and flowing down her back. Her lips were painted a vibrant red, and parted now as she smiled at the happy couple.

Craig glanced across the room at the guests chatting and laughing as they greeted the bride and groom when his eyes lit on a gorgeous woman. He couldn't take his eyes off her. He was mesmerized. Who was she, he wondered? He hadn't met her at Thanksgiving.

Catching her eye, he smiled and nodded a silent greeting. Jane's face lit up and she returned his look with a raised eyebrow and mischievous grin. He quickly left his mother's side and made his way across the room.

"Hi, we haven't met. I'm Craig Waterman. Alex is my uncle."

"Well, hello, Craig Waterman. I'm Jane Ellis, a new neighbor. I've only lived here for a few weeks but Maryann was kind enough to invite me."

Seeing Jane talking with Craig, Maryann was pleased she'd invited her new neighbor. She'd imagined how terrible it would feel to spend New Year's Eve alone when it was obvious the entire street was attending a wedding in the house only a few doors away.

Maryann knew little about Jane, only that she was a travel agent, single, beautiful, and appeared to be in her thirties. Such a gorgeous new neighbor, it's a good thing Alex had eyes only for her, Maryann thought with a possessive smile.

In the kitchen, Carolee's daughter, Cindy, put on a large white apron as she added the final touches to the top of the wedding cake made by Sarah at her bakery. It was a delectable vision topped with a traditional bride and groom standing between rose buds and green leaves. The five tiers of white cake with strawberry filling and a smooth fondant covering was decorated with a lace design piped in royal icing. Cindy hoped her wedding cake design would make this evening even more special for her mother's friends.

Culinary school had really paid off for her. Her mother had been right after all, Cindy was indeed a natural in the kitchen. Thanks to Marvin's encouragement and loans from Carolee, Cindy had been able to afford culinary school, where she discovered she loved the baking classes most of all. When she wasn't in school, she gained experience helping Sarah at the bakery. Cindy planned, someday, to open her own bistro where she'd be the chef/owner specializing in locally grown seasonal produce and delicious desserts. Right now, she didn't know how she'd do it, but she was determined to make her dream happen.

A young man entered the busy kitchen and stood quietly watching Cindy's every move. He was the manager of Alex's coffee shop but all Cindy knew about him was his name was Ming, he was Asian and terribly handsome. They rarely spoke to one another. Whenever she delivered Sarah's freshly baked goods to the coffee shop, Ming would curtly say "thank you" and little else. Not very friendly, she guessed.

"Can I help you?" Cindy asked politely.

She was feeling uncomfortable in his presence. She didn't want or need anyone managing her efforts tonight and she was just too busy for any distractions.

"I came in to ask if you needed help," Ming answered formally.

He'd felt awkward during the ceremony not knowing anyone very well, except for Alex and a few of the other coffee shop employees. Alex had insisted he come to the wedding and not spend New Year's Eve alone. Ming felt it was his duty to attend out of respect for his employer, but most of all, he hoped to see Cindy, his secret crush.

Looking up at him, Cindy gave him one of her best artificial smiles and briskly thanked him for his offer, but refused his help.

"No I'm fine, thanks. I've got it all under control," she said, hoping he'd take the hint and leave.

Reluctantly, she noticed again how tall and good looking he was with his high cheekbones, almond shaped eyes, and smooth shiny black hair.

Realizing he was being ignored and feeling somewhat embarrassed, Ming turned and left the kitchen. Nice try, idiot, he thought to himself. Why did he become so tongue-tied around that girl? She probably thought he was a dummy.

Cindy quickly forgot about Ming as she briskly turned her attention back to the wedding cake. It was almost time for her to present it.

The caterers had already passed around the silver trays carrying hot and cold hors d'oeuvres. They'd outdone themselves with Kobe beef sliders, bacon-wrapped scallops, chicken skewers dipped in peanut sauce and cheese puffs filled with brie. Everything looked and tasted delicious. The buffet tables were covered with steaming chafing dishes. The guests would dine on prime rib, garlic mashed potato, and a wide variety of other dishes. A veritable banquet.

Sarah and Cindy had worked long and hard at the bakery that morning to prepare the beautifully decorated petites fours, marzipan sweets shaped like tiny fruits, chocolate covered strawberries, small éclairs, and lemon tartlets. They made sure the wedding guests would have an extravagant selection of desserts to choose from.

Time moved quickly at the party. The champagne flowed and everyone enjoyed the food. Just before the stroke of midnight, the bride and groom cut into the beautiful cake.

"Congratulations! Way to go! All the happiness in the world!" the guests called out.

Sarah beamed to see her brother so happy. Both he and Maryann were so deserving of happiness after all they'd gone through. It had been Sarah's words of encouragement which had brought the couple together.

Cindy stood in the kitchen doorway wearily observing the scene, still wearing her white apron over her new dress. She was tired but proud she'd helped fashion the wedding cake.

As she looked around the happy group, her eyes met Ming's dark, intense stare and she felt her breath catch. What could he be thinking, she wondered, looking at her like that? She tried giving him a little smile but he just nodded in response and continued watching her. Cindy asked herself with some annoyance, what is it about this man that made her heart beat a little faster?

After the cake was cut, Alex and Maryann laughingly fed each other handfuls of cake and frosting. Suddenly from outside they heard loud noises and popping sounds. Midnight had arrived, the New Year was beginning. A few guests remained inside the house at the bay window while most others spilled out onto the front porch and down onto the walkway.

Amid the cheering, two friends turned to each other with the hope this would be the year they would also find love.

"We'll talk soon," Carolee promised Dallas. "I have an idea to help us find our own Mr. Right."

Inside the house, the groom toasted his bride before they moved outside to see the explosions in the night sky. In his eyes was the promise of private fireworks to come later after all the guests left.

When everyone came back inside, they joined in singing *Auld Lang Syne* and lifted their champagne flutes to toast the happy couple.

When the guests finally left, each carried a small white box tied with matching ribbon that held a sliver of wedding cake. A little note was tucked under the ribbon.

"Place this box under your pillow tonight and you will dream of the one you will love in the coming year. We hope it will bring you great joy and lasting happiness."

It was signed, *Maryann and Alex.*

Several miles away in Point Loma, an elderly woman was already asleep and dreaming. Tonight marked just another year, one of a long lifetime of years for her. She was dreaming of a New Year's celebration from her childhood when she'd crept down the stairs in her long ruffled nightgown to watch what she'd been told was a special party that only grown-ups could attend. At nine years old, Emilie Laurent was too young to mingle with the guests.

From her hiding place on the stairs, she saw Mama seated on the sofa looking very upset. Papa stood in front of the fireplace talking with a group of men. To Emilie it didn't feel like a party at all. Everyone seemed very worried. The painting of the mother and child hanging above the mantle was the only bright spot in the room that night.

When Papa solemnly held up his glass and toasted *"Vive la France,"* everyone in the room joined in the patriotic salute. Emilie felt reassured then that all was well. Maybe that's what a grown up party was like she told herself.

Now, so many years later, she understood the terrible significance of that long ago New Year's Eve when all was truly not well and her world was about to change forever.

4

Whispers in the Night

Stepping out of the shower, Maryann wrapped herself in a large fluffy white towel. She glanced down at the glittering eternity band on her left hand as she heard the grandfather clock downstairs chime three times. The furniture had been put back in place, the rental chairs were gone, and the caterers had packed away the last glass. The top layer of the wedding cake was carefully wrapped and stored in the freezer where it would stay until their first anniversary.

She should be totally exhausted, yet she felt so awake and alive, absolutely exhilarated. A married woman now, she smiled to herself, knowing she'd married the man of her dreams. Those flashing blue eyes, wide shoulders and narrow waist, the very scent of his skin, all called out to her. She'd fallen in love with him the moment they first met in the coffee shop, but for so long she tried to deny it. She was so frightened of love.

She'd learned through bitter experience love was dangerous and she still had the scars to prove it. She rubbed her right arm remembering those days, thankful everything had healed well, both on the inside as well as the outside.

What she thought was love for her first husband, Michael, had blinded her to his cruel nature. She should have known better, she scolded herself, when it became apparent she'd made a grave mistake in judgment. She realized later her inexperience had kept her from walking away from him in the days before their wedding.

She'd kept reassuring herself he was only a tiny bit jealous, and only a little too possessive. One slap didn't mean anything and he'd been so remorseful afterwards, tearfully begging her forgiveness, and later sending her flowers.

Right before their simple ceremony at City Hall, she'd felt a sense of foreboding but she'd ignored her instincts. She loved Michael, she really did, she kept reassuring herself and she trusted everything would be okay. After her father's recent death, her mother's health had begun to decline and Michael promised he'd always be there to help Maryann care for the older woman. But those years married to him had been a long terrible journey into hell.

What a wonderful unexpected gift she'd received—to find true love and to be loved in return. When she needed Alex the most, he'd rescued her from the violence of the past. She shuddered recalling those horrible days. She was determined to put away all the bad memories. Tonight belonged only to Alex. They would make a lifetime of wonderful memories together, memories she'd cherish forever.

The white lace peignoir lay across the bed. She knew Alex would love to see her in, and as quickly, out of it. Instead she put on the old pink terry robe she had worn the night Alex had proposed to her several months before, and the only night they'd made love. It just seemed like the right thing to wear.

She paused on the stairs and glanced around the living room. The flickering flames from the fireplace cast a romantic glow on the room. It looked cozy and inviting. She was pleased it now had some masculine touches and looked like their room, not just hers. A few days before, Alex had brought over several favorite pieces of his own furniture.

As she continued down the stairs, she hungered for his touch and she could feel her face flush with desire.

And there he stood, waiting for her at the foot of the stairs. In his eyes she saw a combination of lust and tenderness, a yearning that nearly took her breath away. Their eyes locked. This was the moment they had been impatiently waiting for.

He'd taken off his tuxedo jacket and tie, and his white shirt hung open to his waist. He led her by the hand to the cushions piled on the rug in front of the fireplace next to the glasses of champagne and a silver tray of Belgian dark chocolate truffles. Wordlessly, he handed her a flute and picking up his own, tapped it against hers. As their eyes met, they both said at the same time, "To us!" Then they laughed together as they sipped the bubbly wine.

Maryann noticed the soft romantic music playing in the background, and reaching out, she tenderly stroked Alex's cheek. He'd thought of everything to make this moment perfect for them. He was so strong and rugged, yet sensitive and intelligent. Best of all, he was all hers now.

"Let's get rid of anything that comes between us," he said, taking away her glass. He smiled when he noticed, "You're wearing my favorite robe."

With a lusty grin, he untied the sash on her robe and slipped it off her shoulders. Her nude body glowed in the firelight.

"You're so beautiful," he murmured.

He could feel the intense electricity of desire coursing through his body. Don't rush, savor this special moment, he ordered himself as he clenched his jaw, tightly holding onto his control. Her body was so lovely, dewy and fragrant from her shower. His eyes smoldered with such hunger that Maryann had to clutch at his shirt to keep her knees from buckling.

Alex's shirt quickly disappeared as he pulled her to his chest, her breasts pressing against his bare hot flesh. He tenderly crushed her in his arms as his lips met hers. They sank into a deep kiss, their tongues meeting in a timeless dance of love.

"Oh, Alex," she breathed between kisses. "I love you so much."

Her breath came in little pants as she pressed closer to him needing to feel his body against hers. It felt so right to be in his arms.

Pulling back, his eyes devoured her. "I love you more than my own life. I'm yours. I can't hold back any longer."

With that, he lowered her onto the waiting cushions. He was a man on fire and tearing off the rest of his clothes, he covered every inch of her body with kisses, stroking her smooth skin, adoring her breasts. Each peak stiffened beneath his lips. His tongue flickered over her pink nipples again and again, her breasts filling his hands.

Maryann moaned with pleasure beneath him as he trailed kisses ever lower, tasting every inch of her. She knew where he was heading, and she could barely wait for him to reach his destination. She parted her legs, urging him on, as he teased her with butterfly kisses on her knees and inner thighs. At last, his lips found her moist center and covering it with his open mouth, he drank in her very essence sending waves of pleasure spiking through her body.

"Oh, my darling, you taste so good. We've been waiting so long for this night." He looked up into her flushed face, "Open your eyes, I want to see you, and I want you to see me loving you."

Maryann gasped, barely able to breathe. Reaching out, she clutched his lowered head as he pleasured her. Wave after wave began rising within her, building to a fevered pitch. She felt herself spinning out of control, but still he was unrelenting in his quest. She moaned and writhed beneath his lips. Suddenly, she cried out "Alex" as a maelstrom of pulsations overwhelmed her. He still didn't stop, but continued relentlessly until she felt the same overwhelming tensions building within her again.

Now Alex paused before she could reach her release, and covering her with his body, he thrust himself deep within her. She was ready and wrapped her legs tightly around his hips pushing herself up to meet him, thrust for thrust.

This felt so right for both of them, better than any novel had ever led her to believe. He moved deeply within her, touching places that shot sparks through her as they rode the waves together toward a final explosion. The New Year's Eve fireworks they'd watched earlier were nothing compared to this. Feeling Maryann quivering beneath him, Alex cried out his pleasure and buried his face in her neck.

As they lay spent, Alex smiled contentedly and whispered, "Don't think you're going to sleep just yet, my love. There's much more ahead."

Reaching over, he selected a truffle from the tray and placed it between Maryann's lips. Licking a little smudge from the corner of her mouth, he slid his tongue inside, deeply savoring the richness of Maryann mixed with chocolate. Alex began to caress her back and legs with his long, gentle fingers and soon he was exploring her whole body again, like a hungry man yearning for a good meal. He kissed each finger, touched the tip of his tongue to the shell of her ear, and kissed the hollow of her throat where he could feel her heart pulsing.

"You're so sexy, and I can't believe you're my wife. I want to make love to you forever!"

Maryann had longed to explore his body but she'd felt too shy before this. Now her confidence surged and she ran her fingers over his smooth chest, taking in his masculine scent and kissing every place she could reach. Finally, she came to the warm velvet of his hardened shaft. It swelled even larger in her hand as she caressed him, so soft and smooth, yet so large and hard.

He groaned, the pleasure was almost too much for him to bear.

Maryann lowered her mouth onto him and took his hardness between her lips. She savored his special taste, salty and all male. He gasped as Maryann ran her tongue up and down, and yet again.

Before he was hopelessly lost in his own passion, he swept her on top of him, impaling her forcefully yet gently. As she rode him, Maryann threw her head back in full rapture. Alex ran his hands down her breasts and along her sides until he reached the soft throbbing bud near his thrusting hardness. He found the spot that most aroused her making her lose all control. Wave after wave crashed over them and then with a lusty laugh, Alex pulled his bride close to his body. She could feel his heart pounding next to hers.

It was nearing dawn, and in San Diego's harbor their honeymoon ship, *The Ocean Voyager*, waited, yet they were reluctant to bring this magical night to a close. Whispering softly to each other of their undying love, and lightly dozing in the early morning hours, they knew wonderful adventures were ahead.

Today, they would sail to Hawaii—to sun themselves and swim in the warm waters, make love at night on secluded beaches, and return home to San Diego sleepy-eyed and happy, truly married, husband and wife.

5

Freshly Brewed Coffee

Sarah had been the last to leave the wedding, stopping at the door for one final hug and kiss for her brother and new sister-in-law.

"I'll walk you home," suggested Marvin as he lingered on the porch waiting for her.

"Why thank you, but it's only next door," Sarah replied smiling, but Marvin seemed reluctant to part from her just yet.

All during the evening he'd been aware of this little dynamo of a woman rushing around seeing to everyone else's comfort. What a wonder she was. He'd liked her from the very start when he helped her set up her bakery, but tonight he noticed her as a woman. A very pretty woman at that, and someone he'd like to get to know a whole lot better.

Now, standing on her front porch at Number 3 Lily Court Lane, he started to say goodnight, but Sarah interrupted.

"How about a cup of coffee, Marvin?" she asked, inviting him in.

Her son, Craig, not yet ready to call it a night, told her she shouldn't wait up for him. He was taking Jane to the Gaslamp Quarter to continue their New Year's Eve celebration at one of the dance clubs.

Hours later when the sun rose over Lily Court Lane, Marvin found himself still seated in Sarah's kitchen, his wedding cake box resting on the counter next to hers. Looking out her window, Sarah noticed a familiar looking young man leaving Dallas's house. My, my, she thought, wasn't he the photographer from the wedding? She noted his disheveled look, his rumpled evening jacket, and his blond hair falling over his collar.

Sarah hadn't been the only resident on Lily Court Lane who'd had a late night male visitor. Was there some magic in a New Year's Eve wedding, she wondered?

Turning back to her guest, Sarah refilled his mug from a pot of freshly brewed coffee. She smiled at him as he sat comfortably at her antique pine table. He looked so right sitting there in her kitchen, just like she'd thought he would. He added two generous teaspoons of sugar and more than a splash of cream. Sarah took hers black today, priding herself on starting her New Year's resolution to lose those last five pounds that seemed so difficult to shed.

As the sun peeked through the curtains and sparkled off his eyeglasses, Marvin looked at his watch and started to rise.

"I can't believe we've talked all night, Sarah," he exclaimed. "This has been a real pleasure, but I don't want to overstay my welcome."

"I've enjoyed every bit of it, too. Stay and finish your coffee."

Pleased, Marvin sat back down.

How surprised Dallas would be to discover another overnight visitor on Lily Court Lane, and a man at that. It had been a different sort of night than the one Dallas probably enjoyed, as Sarah and Marvin only talked all night. She sighed to herself, wondering if she would ever again be held in a passionate embrace. Oh, well, that part of her life was most likely over for good, she thought a little sadly.

Sarah often reminisced with pleasure about the intimate moments she'd shared with Harry, her dear husband, who'd passed away the year before. She remembered how New Year's Day always started with a special breakfast in bed. Harry prepared French toast topped with powdered sugar and sliced strawberries, freshly squeezed orange juice, and a pot of steaming hot coffee. Usually

Sarah was the cook in the family, but on those holiday mornings Harry would pamper her. After they shared the last bite, he would take her in his arms and make love to her in the early morning hours long before Craig awoke.

Those memories would always remain sweet and special to her. She missed her partner so much. In the lonely months after Harry died, Sarah decided to move back to San Diego where she and her brother, Alex, had grown up. She felt the only way to get over Harry's death was to move from Seattle and the sad memories it held for her.

"Penny for your thoughts?" Marvin asked now, noticing her far-away look.

Sarah realized she'd been lost in her thoughts of the past. She wouldn't speak of Harry to this charming, balding man who was becoming such a dear friend.

"Oh, just how quickly the night passed, and how much fun it's been to talk with you," she responded.

"I can't remember ever spending a happier New Year's Eve, Sarah."

He'd loved officiating at the wedding ceremony, hoping Maryann and Alex would be happier in their marriage than he'd been in his own. Last night he'd confided to Sarah about his marriage and the ex-wife who had become so distant and even hostile toward him.

"I was fresh out of law school and she was the pretty brunette undergraduate from Buffalo when we met. You know, Sarah, I can't remember a single time during my marriage when we stayed up late just talking."

Marvin was too embarrassed to add she'd quickly begun to shrink from his touch, although she certainly enjoyed the luxuries he worked so hard to provide for her. After several years she'd finally left him for her tennis instructor. It was a cruel stereotype playing out in real life—his life. Marvin felt abandoned at first, but then one day he realized he'd been set free.

Ruefully, Marvin told Sarah, "The irony of that whole fiasco is my wife made me into the successful lawyer I became. Her sharp tongue drove me from her so often I ended up becoming a hard-working attorney but a lousy husband. Looking back, I would've been much happier as a modestly successful attorney with a warm loving wife to come home to."

"Why did you stay with her for so long?"

"Now that's a good question. I'm an optimist and I kept hoping she'd change. It was as simple as that. I duped myself into believing our sham of a marriage was better than being alone. Yet the day I moved into my own bachelor apartment, I realized I no longer felt alone. I'd turned a corner in my life and it was as if a weight had been lifted from my soul. Since then, I've stayed committed to my work and my friends and I've built a wonderful life for myself."

He smiled at Sarah as he said this, but to himself he admitted he was still lonely.

Sarah felt touched by Marvin's confidences. For a moment she was at a loss for words, so she said the only thing that came to mind, "Another brownie, Marvin?"

He smiled as he happily accepted another of her delicious brownies. Gazing at Sarah's bright blue eyes, Marvin admired the efficient way she bustled around the kitchen. She looked as fresh as a meadow flower even though they were both still wearing their now wrinkled evening clothes. Marvin wished he could find the nerve to say these things to her, then stand up and take her in his arms and share a kiss to start off the New Year.

But he was concerned neither of them was ready for this step and secretly he feared she might reject him. Old habits die hard. Such impulses were all so new to him; his desires had been buried for so long. Anyway, Craig would be returning soon and it wouldn't do for him to find his mother in the arms of a man he barely knew.

Sarah and Marvin smiled at each other as they heard the front door quietly opening. Craig entered the kitchen and was surprised to find Marvin seated at his mother's kitchen table.

"Hi, Mom. Hi, Mr. Miller. What's for breakfast? I'm starving!"

"I knew you'd be hungry. Sit down, dear, and have a cup of coffee while I make breakfast for all of us."

"Please, call me Marvin," he said as Craig joined him at the table while Sarah busied herself again at the stove.

Soon they all settled down to a huge meal of homemade raisin scones with blackberry preserves, scrambled eggs, applewood smoked bacon, freshly squeezed orange juice, and even more coffee. Marvin felt as though he might explode with happiness, thinking this is what a real family feels like.

Sarah beamed with pleasure as Craig bit into another scone. She loved seeing her men eat.

Her smile faded when Craig said, "It's too bad Jane's missing out on this wonderful breakfast. She was tired out from dancing so much." He didn't mention his promise to call her.

Although she was dying to tell someone, Sarah didn't mention what she'd seen that morning feeling it was Dallas's secret to share—or not. Well, she supposed, she'd just have to find out more from Maryann when she got back from her honeymoon. She sighed inwardly, hoping Dallas wouldn't get her heart broken again. Her first marriage had ended so badly.

Looking at her son now, Sarah wished with all her heart Craig would have a happy marriage. She was convinced a woman like Jane was fine as a neighbor but not as a daughter-in-law. She was just too old for Craig.

After helping Sarah clear the table, Marvin saw her stifle a yawn—a sure sign it was time for him to leave. He wouldn't wear out his welcome; he wanted to be invited back. So with some reluctance, he left the warm and friendly kitchen carrying two boxes, a slice of wedding cake and a box of Sarah's brownies to enjoy later in the day.

Pausing at the door, Marvin turned to Sarah, "Thank you for a really lovely night," and then he impulsively reached out and took her hand and brushed it with his lips.

She looked startled at first, but leaving her hand in his, her face lit up.

"Oh, me too, Marvin. The time flew by so fast," she added softly. Looking into his eyes, she reminded him, "Now don't forget to put the wedding cake under your pillow tonight."

"I promise," he replied, but he knew who he'd be dreaming about.

He turned back and waved to Sarah as she stood framed in her doorway in the bright morning light. She waved until he reached his car.

As he walked down Lily Court Lane, Marvin heard Craig calling after him. "Marvin, wait a second. I need to ask you about something."

The previous day when Craig had finally found a moment to tell his mother about the painting that concerned him, she suggested he speak to Marvin. She was sure he'd be the right one to advise him.

"It's a business matter concerning my gallery and I'd like to get your professional opinion on it," Craig said as he stood next to Marvin.

"If it can wait 'til tomorrow, stop by my office first thing in the morning. I'll be glad to help you any way I can," Marvin replied, hoping this would provide an excuse to see Sarah again.

"Yes, that's exactly what I had in mind. Thanks."

The two men shook hands and Marvin got into his car, looked back one more time to wave to Sarah and drove off.

A while later, mother and son yawned as they climbed the stairs to their bedrooms. Sarah carried her wedding cake box, hopeful she now had someone to dream of. Craig knew he didn't need his box at all. He was certain his dreams would be filled by a woman with long red hair wearing a green evening dress.

6

Memories

Leaving the wedding, Dallas Cruz and her dog, Jude, set off on a late night walk around the neighborhood. Jude didn't care about New Year's Eve or weddings, he just wanted his walk. He sniffed the grass and the sidewalks, and then happily directed Dallas back to their house with the yellow front door at Number 5 Lily Court Lane.

Jude barked as they approached their house and Dallas was surprised to see the wedding photographer sitting on her front step. Tall and rugged, with a shock of unruly blond hair, Simon Nordvahl looked a little sheepish sitting there.

He hadn't planned to wait for Dallas. Leaving the wedding, he'd strolled down Lily Court Lane toward his van. Tourists always marveled at this green oasis virtually hidden among the high-rise condos and hotels, only a few short blocks away from the Gaslamp District, barely twenty minutes from California's border with Mexico.

He would return one day soon and photograph this picturesque street with its view of the Coronado Bridge and Point Loma in the distance. That'd give him an excuse to see Dallas again, he thought, as he smiled at her and reached out to pat Jude.

Dallas could only stare at Simon, wondering why he was waiting for her. How long had he been there?

At the wedding she felt he was taking far too many pictures of her instead of the bride and at one point she'd even waved him off, reminding him he should point his camera at the bride and groom.

He'd laughed, saying, "I can't resist. You're gorgeous."

She was flustered by his compliment and didn't know how to respond.

Simon had immediately been attracted to Dallas, her shapely silhouette outlined by her fitted gown. He was not surprised to learn from one of the guests she was a physical fitness instructor at a local gym. Whenever Simon looked at her, he felt happier than he had in a long time.

He'd worked at a local newspaper before moving from San Diego to join the *Los Angeles Times*, and was sent to Afghanistan as a photojournalist embedded with the American troops. Meeting Dallas tonight felt like he was emerging from a bad dream.

Jude woofed hello to Simon, greeting him like an old friend instead of an intruder. Dallas was surprised at Jude's friendliness toward Simon. This was not her dog's usual reaction to strangers, especially men sitting on her porch very late at night.

"Well, hi," she finally said. "I'm surprised to see you here so late."

Simon stood, unfolding his tall lanky frame with ease. "I wanted to see you again, and I didn't want to wait until tomorrow."

Dallas blushed and trusting her dog's reaction, she invited Simon inside and closed the door. Turning to ask him if he'd like a drink, she suddenly found herself wrapped in his arms.

"I wanted to do this from the first moment I saw you," he said, holding her close.

Wordlessly she pointed at the stairs, and they kissed at each step and all the way to the bedroom door, kisses long and slow and deep. Their unbroken embrace filled with passion as Dallas was overcome by a wave of midnight madness. This feeling of urgency, of heat flashing through her body, was so new to her. Evenings with her former husband had been so different.

They stumbled in the dark toward her bed. The room was filled with night shadows as moonlight filtered through the filmy curtains. Simon sat beside her on the bed and stroked the nape of her neck with one hand while with his other arm he encircled her waist. Leaning back against the pillows, he gently pulled her on top of him, finding her lips in the darkness of the cool room. His kisses were lingering, arousing and infinitely sweet.

Dallas opened herself to his exploration causing Simon to groan with desire. He ran his hand up and down her back, and finally cupping her bottom, he ground himself against her. When he rolled her over, Dallas could feel the strength of his body pressing down on her, his obvious urgency, his hardness rubbing against her most tender spot.

Growing up in Mexico in a protective family, Dallas had little experience with men. She didn't date in high school and the boys she met at her local college were scared off by her father's stern questioning. Only Rey had been willing to court her in a manner acceptable to her family. He'd been her first and only lover. But after they were married, he showed little desire for her, and when he did, he quickly took his own pleasure leaving her unfulfilled. She'd desired him before they married, but his selfishness soon killed her passion.

Her parents had been devastated at the news of their divorce and shocked when Dallas finally told them why she couldn't stay with Rey any longer.

Tonight, for the first time in many years, Dallas felt herself being swept away by desire as Simon stroked her breast through the silky fabric of her gown. Finding her nipple he circled the tip with his thumb. It quickly peaked under his fingertips causing Dallas to gasp.

She was quivering as he tugged the top of her gown down. Her breasts spilled into his hands as he bared her to the cool night air. His lips quickly found the tip of her breast and pulled her nipple into his mouth. She trembled in response, wanting more, so much more.

He blew a soft breath on her damp nipple, sending shivers up and down her spine and causing liquid heat to pool within her. The pleasure became almost unbearable. So intense that Dallas writhed beneath him as his hardness became more insistent.

She moaned aloud, "Oh, Simon. Oh, my God."

How incredible this felt. She wanted nothing more than to feel his bare skin on hers. Suddenly, a New Year's firecracker burst on the street below.

Simon's body jerked. He lifted his head, stunned for a moment, totally disoriented. Where was he?

"Darla," he cried out.

Dallas was frightened by his reaction. What had just happened, and who was Darla?

Simon sat up, gasping for breath.

"Simon, what's wrong? That was just some kid with a firecracker."

He was shaking as she put her arms around him, smoothing his back and holding him until his breathing returned to normal.

"I'm so sorry, Dallas. The noise outside took me away to another place, a bad place. For a moment I was back in Afghanistan."

"I understand, Simon," she said trying to comfort him, although she didn't understand. Not really. She didn't know him at all nor what he'd gone through in Afghanistan. To her it was only a firecracker but he'd reacted as though it was something much more.

"It's okay. You don't need to talk now. Just rest for a minute."

Simon lay down again and allowed her to hold him but he seemed far away. Slowly his breathing deepened and his head felt heavier on her shoulder. He'd fallen asleep. Dallas's arm grew numb, but she didn't want to disturb him.

What in the world had she gotten herself into? What's wrong with this guy? She didn't know whether to be mad or scared. What happened to her night of passion, dammit? Dallas could feel tears springing to her eyes. She couldn't help feeling here she was again, in bed with a man who didn't want her.

When it was nearing dawn she heard Maryann and Alex leaving their house next door, laughing as they got into the taxi that would take them to their honeymoon ship. They sounded so happy. Another tear trickled down Dallas's cheek. Love was always for someone else, never for her, she thought. It took a while before she fell into a light sleep. Simon continued to sleep deeply, hardly stirring.

The moon still shone through the window on the two of them. Downstairs, Jude woofed in his sleep as rabbits ran before him in a field where he romped and played in his doggy dreams.

When sunlight brightened the room, Dallas awoke and realized she wasn't alone in her bed. Jude was scratching at the bedroom door whining to get in. She found a tousled blond head resting on the pillow next to her. Then it all came back to her in a rush, the wedding last night, finding Simon at her door, inviting him in intending to just give him a drink which turned quickly into something else. What exactly, she still didn't know.

Squirming out from under the arm resting across her stomach, Dallas slipped out of bed. She crossed the room to her closet, removed the now wrinkled gown she was still almost wearing and changed into her old sweats and sneakers.

What had she done, Dallas asked herself as she walked Jude up and down through the neighborhood? She must have been crazy inviting a strange man into her home, she chided herself. This wasn't like her at all. Wishing with all her heart she could erase last night, she recalled how Simon looked, so handsome and vulnerable sitting under her porch light. Again she asked herself, what was she thinking, taking this stranger into her bed?

Leaning over to pat Jude, she mumbled sadly, "I must've been bewitched."

She thought of her parents in Mexico. Her mother would have been shocked to learn of her daughter's behavior.

The figure in the bed still hadn't stirred when Dallas returned home an hour later and reluctantly peeked in the bedroom door.

Should she awaken him? How was she going to face him? He looked so peaceful lying in her bed, almost as if he belonged there.

Shaking her head, she told herself she needed a cup of coffee and then she would be able to decide what to do. She'd make breakfast and perhaps the smell of fresh coffee would wake him up.

Whisking eggs and mixing pancake batter as she used to do for Rey, Dallas thought about her failed marriage. What a sham it'd turned out to be. She'd discovered evidence in his emails he was involved with someone else. Yes, she had felt guilty about invading his privacy, but when he left his laptop at home, accidently or on purpose, she couldn't help herself.

Things had reached the point where they were barely speaking to one another, and they never made love anymore. He was rarely home, and when he was, he never spent a moment with her. He preferred to take his laptop into his home office and close the door behind him. She had no part in his life. She wondered if his construction firm was doing as well as he bragged. With all the lies he'd told her, she began to realize she couldn't trust him about anything.

Learning the truth about her marriage had been the most shattering moment of her life. There was someone in her husband's life, and it wasn't another woman. It was a man and his name was Robbie. She had to reread his e-mails several times before finally grasping what was going on between Robbie and her husband. The last e-mail finally convinced Dallas her husband was gay.

> "My Dearest Hot One,
>
> Lots of fun yesterday, especially last night in front of the fire!
>
> You sure are one hot boy. Keep it up, like I know you can!
>
> Looking forward to our new love nest and being together in Phoenix!

Have you told the bitch yet? Get to it, lover boy.
Kisses and mucho hugs.

Love you! Yours forever,
'Big' Robbie"

Dallas was in shock. All that day she kept asking herself if what she'd read was really true and who was this Robbie person who had written such very explicit love notes to her husband? The numerous photos of the two men embracing convinced her this wasn't a prank. One of the men was clearly her husband and he looked so happy, unlike the way he looked when he was with her.

When Dallas confronted Rey that evening, he didn't deny the affair.

"Now the truth is out, we can be good friends," was his calm response.

"Friends?" she echoed in amazement.

He didn't want a divorce, he told her, but he did want to live his life as he pleased.

"I didn't want to accept it, but I think I always knew I was gay. We can be friends now you know the truth," he repeated again. "When I married you, I thought I could change, but as time went by, I knew I had to act on my feelings. I really didn't want to hurt you, but now that you know, we can keep on going as we have. Nothing needs to change."

Dallas felt betrayed, humiliated, and furious. Rey could live his life as he wanted, but why did he have to involve her? If they were only friends, she would've been happy for him when he decided to come out. He must've known taking her as his wife was selfish and denied her the chance for the children she longed to have.

Feeling overwhelmed by her emotions—sorrow at her failed marriage, pity for a man who felt he had to live a life of lies—she spoke sharply to him.

"Rey, I want you out of here now and I want a divorce. I have plenty of friends. I don't need another one, and I won't live in a sham marriage. Maybe some other women would, like those politicians' wives, but not me."

Rey hurriedly moved out that night. Although he wanted to keep the pretense going, he finally agreed to an uncontested divorce when Dallas threatened to tell his business associates the real reason for their separation. Dallas chose to remain in the house where she'd lived with Rey and she fought to keep the dog.

The days and months following their split had been very painful ones for her. She cried herself to sleep nearly every night and found herself sobbing through almost every meal. She couldn't understand how it was possible for a human to shed so many tears.

She accepted Rey was entitled to live his life as he chose. What she would never be able to accept was his deception. The fact he became so distant toward her and began to live his separate life within a few short months after they were married convinced her he never really loved her. He chose her for her innocence and naiveté and then married her as a convenient way to set the stage for his double life.

Now a year later, she still felt a few unshed tears gather in the corners of her eyes. The divorce had become final just a few weeks ago and now here she was starting a new year with another man who rejected her. Just like old times.

She hoped she'd be able to bury the painful memories of her ex-husband, but last night certainly hadn't helped her recovery. She ferociously whipped the pancake batter as her thoughts returned again to meeting Simon at the wedding. Ending up in her bedroom had seemed fated from her reaction to his first touch while he was taking the wedding photos and …. Her thoughts were interrupted.

"Good morning, Dallas."

She turned from the stove startled to find Simon standing in the doorway. He looked pretty good in the morning light even wearing last night's rumpled suit.

"Good morning," he said again, looking sheepish. "Last night started great. I'm sorry it ended the way it did. That certainly wasn't what I had in mind."

His blue eyes seemed sincere and more than a little embarrassed, but something in his matter-of-fact tone told her he wanted to leave right away. Disappointment flooded through her, confusing her. She'd wanted him to go, didn't she?

She tried to appear cool, saying, "You don't owe me anything, Simon," and then turned back to the counter continuing to whip the batter.

Simon studied her with the eyes of a photographer. She was truly beautiful in the morning light streaming through the kitchen window. Reluctantly pulling his eyes away from her, he leaned down and patted the dog.

"Hey, pal, maybe I'll see you again sometime."

Jude wagged his tail in response. Dallas stood silently watching, holding the spatula in one hand and the bowl of batter in the other.

"I'll call you," he said.

"Sure," was all she could muster.

"I'll call you," was the famous kiss of death, she thought. That said it all. He'd never call her and she'd never see him again. He hadn't even asked for her phone number. But did she want him to call her? Her ego said yes, but her common sense said, maybe not. She turned back to the stove and the pancakes now sizzling on the griddle.

He'd made a lifetime of studying faces from behind his camera and he could see she was very upset. Simon knew if he stayed in her kitchen for two more seconds he'd engulf her in his arms again and sweep her back upstairs and that wouldn't be fair to either of them. He wasn't ready for any relationship. As he turned and hurried out the door, Dallas tossed the pancakes into the garbage.

Well, that's that, she thought, sweeping away the crumbs. He'd never call. She felt relieved Maryann and Alex had already left on their honeymoon so no one would see Simon leaving her house in the early morning hours.

Simon knew he hadn't handled the situation well. At the very least he should've had breakfast with Dallas. His stomach rumbled with hunger and he felt sick at heart. She was too desirable in every way, and he'd already failed her.

After his return from Afghanistan he avoided people, even brushing off his old friends when they called him. He thought taking bridal photos would be less stressful for him than riding in military vehicles through war-torn areas and so he changed the whole direction of his career. But the atrocities he'd experienced still kept him awake most nights. Last night a simple firecracker had ruined his plans to make love to a beautiful woman.

It felt so good to sleep in her embrace. He hadn't been with a woman since Darla died before his eyes on that bright and awful day, a day that began as a routine reconnaissance mission. But nothing was routine in Afghanistan. They were driving in a convoy through a quiet, barren area, rocks and rubble piled high along both sides of the dirt road when suddenly a roadside bomb exploded, overturning their vehicle, and throwing him into a ditch beyond the rocks. The blast deafened him. He cried out for Darla, the photojournalist from the *New York Times*, who was sitting next to him.

Crawling his way out of the rubble, he found her pinned beneath the overturned truck. Her body was crushed, her blue eyes staring sightlessly upward toward the sky. He knew immediately she was dead. He sobbed over her lifeless form, willing her back to life, rocking her in his arms, until help arrived. Help that could do nothing for her. The medics tended to the others and called for a helicopter evacuation back to the base camp hospital.

For weeks after the blast, he felt unable to take another photo and remained isolated in his hospital room while his eardrums healed. He'd known Darla for only a brief time but their wartime affair had been mutually comforting, a life raft in a dark and dangerous sea of violence. They hadn't loved each other, but they were good friends.

He still missed her company and agonized over the useless way she died. In many ways he felt responsible for her death; although he knew there was nothing he could have done to prevent it. There were many nights, when in a deep pit of despair, he wished he'd died instead of Darla.

He was relieved he hadn't burdened Dallas by telling her too much about himself other than his current work as a wedding photographer. He didn't need her sympathy, although this morning he still desperately wanted her. What he needed was to escape and not add to the embarrassment he could see in her eyes. He knew he'd been abrupt, even a little rude. He wanted to return and apologize, but that would be a mistake for both of them.

It was best she forget him. But could he forget her?

7

Wedding Cake Dreams

Carolee always told herself she didn't believe in magic, but still she took two boxes of the wedding cake when she finally left Maryann and Alex on New Year's Eve. Maybe this would double her chances of finding love. She'd had little luck finding true love, or romance, despite the fact she was a very attractive woman.

Maryann had tossed the wedding bouquet in her direction, but it flew over her out-stretched hands to land in Jane's arms. Could it be that placing cake boxes under her pillow would act as a crazy charm and lure a man to love her, or at least give her someone to dream about?

Cocooned in a mountain of down pillows and quilts, a sleeping Carolee murmured the name of her favorite movie star, handsome blond Daniel Craig, with his intriguing accent. Sweeping her up into his strong arms, he declared his undying love for her. His lips came ever closer to hers and he embraced her tightly.

She awoke suddenly, hugging a pillow tightly to her body. Restlessly turning onto her side, she opened one eye and squinted at the morning sunlight streaming through the window. She shut her eyes tightly. She wasn't ready yet to leave her dream lover and face a new year.

Reluctantly opening her eyes several hours later, Carolee replayed the beautiful wedding of the evening before and the memory brought sudden tears to her eyes. She felt a bit sorry for herself lying there all alone. Wrapped up in her downy quilt, she had no man to love and yet another year had passed.

On this New Year's morning, she reluctantly accepted the fact there would be no movie star escorting her down the red carpet. She would never be "wined and dined" in a famous restaurant. No limousines would take her wherever she wanted to go. No shopping on Rodeo Drive, no weeklong stay at an exclusive desert spa being kneaded by an expert masseuse. There would be none of that for her.

She wondered if she should just eat the darned cake and get it over with. Still tightly clutching the boxes under her feather pillow, she fell back to sleep once again.

Weddings and love stories seemed to be for others. But she wasn't quite ready to give up yet. As she told Dallas last night, maybe this would be their year to find love.

Down the hall from Carolee's room, her daughter, Cindy, slept cozy and comfortable in the room Carolee always kept ready for her should she want to spend the night. Although Cindy was now twenty-two and living on her own, Carolee had kept all her stuffed animals and toys, things Cindy insisted she had outgrown, but which were far too precious for her mother to throw away.

Deep in sleep, Cindy kept seeing the same face in all her dreams. It was Ming, the young man from the coffee shop who'd tried to help her last night. Whenever she saw him she always felt bewildered by his unwavering stare. That he rarely smiled or spoke much unsettled, yet intrigued, her. It wasn't that he was scary, just intense, and so darned handsome.

In Cindy's dream, Ming was waiting at the end of a long road with his arms opened wide to welcome her into his embrace. In one hand he held a small bouquet of wild flowers and with his other hand he beckoned her to come closer. It felt like late afternoon with the air perfumed by star jasmine, and the sunlight glinting on his blue-black hair.

She tried to call out to him but was unable to speak. She tried to walk toward him but her feet held her back. She knew she desperately wanted to be in his arms, to feel his heart beating next to hers. She felt a lump in her throat and pressure building in her chest. Sobbing out loud, she suddenly woke up and was disappointed to find herself in her childhood bed down the hall from her mother's room, with a stuffed Mickey Mouse clutched tightly to her chest.

This wasn't what the wedding cake was supposed to do, she thought furiously. Reaching under the pillow, she took out the cake box and tossed it into the wastebasket as if it were a basketball.

"Damn," she shouted, and with that, she pulled the comforter over her head and went back to what she hoped would be a dreamless sleep without Ming's face to disturb her.

Was she ever wrong. He was right there waiting for her.

When the subject of Cindy's dreams returned home from the wedding, he was happy to leave the noise of the New Year's Eve revelers behind him and get back his quiet apartment. Alex had been his next-door neighbor and landlord for the past year, renting him this small studio apartment above the coffee shop which fit his needs perfectly. It was sparsely furnished with cast-offs from his parents' home, except for the kitchen area which was proudly stocked with new appliances and a variety of herbs and spices. A rice steamer stood on the counter and a wok resided on the stove. Ming's apartment and belongings were sparkling clean and orderly.

Standing in the hot steaming shower, he was finally free to think about the girl who made his heart lurch every time he saw her. Cindy. She was unlike anyone else he'd ever met, with her nose stud, and the purple streaks in her black hair. He found her incredibly beautiful—her delicate oval face, her ivory skin and large dark eyes.

His mother wouldn't approve, making Cindy all the more desirable, he admitted to himself. He could hear his mother's command.

"Son, find a nice Chinese girl," she'd say in her carefully enunciated English. She was very clear in her wishes for him.

He particularly liked it when Cindy smiled and he could see her front teeth slightly overlapped one another. For some reason, that slight imperfection drove him wild and made him want to kiss her.

Every day he looked forward to seeing her come into the coffee shop, but whenever she did, he found himself tongue-tied and unable to say much beyond, "Hello," or "Thanks." He stuttered every time he tried to say her name.

Ming knew when the time came, his parents would want to choose his bride. He guessed her family would come from the small village in southern China which his family left before he was born, or from Hong Kong where his grandparents still lived. But he'd grown up in America and wanted to find real love and choose his own bride. Would he have the courage to defy his parents and select someone like Cindy? She seemed so open and outgoing, so different from the girls he'd met through his family. Could she ever be interested in him?

Hanging his suit in the closet, he was still thinking of Cindy as the box containing the wedding cake fell out of his pocket. At the last minute, someone had pushed it on him, telling him to sleep on it and dream of true love. How silly, he thought, looking down at it, but shrugging, he stuffed it under his pillow. It wouldn't hurt and you never know, he thought with a smile as he drifted off to sleep.

One face quickly appeared—Cindy's face, the girl with the large eyes and skin like an angel. In his dream, he ran his fingers through the purple streaks in her ebony hair and they smiled at one another in total bliss. His mother was nowhere to be seen.

When he woke up later in the morning, Ming made a New Year's resolution. "I'll speak to her, really speak to her. I will overcome this fear."

Famous last words, he thought, terrified she'd only laugh at him.

8

The Urn

Sarah told Jane her son would be attending the wedding, but Jane hadn't expected to find him so attractive and charming. She'd been swept away by the romance of the wedding and then she saw Craig standing tall and handsome next to the groom. When their eyes met for the first time, he nearly took her breath away.

It was obvious Craig felt the same. He quickly crossed the room and introduced himself, staying with her for the rest of the evening. They discussed art and music and when he stood close to her, she could feel the magnetism radiating from his body, and later the softness of his lips when he kissed her at the stroke of midnight.

Fleetingly, she wondered if he was too young for her, but then brushed this unwanted thought aside. It was only a New Year's kiss after all, not a lifetime commitment.

Jane became uncomfortable when she felt Sarah's unfriendly glances in her direction. Everyone, except Sarah, laughed and applauded when Jane caught the bridal bouquet. Craig, however, seemed oblivious to his mother's glaring eyes because he couldn't take his eyes away from Jane. He kept finding excuses to touch her and to stand ever closer to her.

As the evening was ending, he invited Jane to join him at *La Mancha*, a dance club in the Gaslamp where they danced 'til dawn. They had a wonderful time and when they reluctantly parted hours later on her porch, it was with a promise to get together soon while Craig was still in town.

Jane didn't dream of Craig. She hadn't even placed the wedding cake box beneath her pillow. Now when the box caught her eye, she opened it and dipped her finger into the strawberry filling. Licking her finger, she pictured Craig's lips. She shook her head. She had no real hope anything could develop from their friendship.

What she really wanted to do now was go back to sleep, but she still had too many boxes to unpack. It may have been the start of a new year, but there was still a lot to do in her new home. As she straightened her bedroom, Jane fondly recalled meeting the women of Lily Court Lane. They'd insisted she attend the wedding even though she'd only been living there for a few weeks. After her mother died, Jane decided she needed a change of scene from Los Angeles.

Calling a realtor friend, she announced, "I need a change of scene. I liked San Diego when I went to ComicCon last summer. What do you think?"

Once she saw pictures of the charming house with the purple door at Number 7 Lily Court Lane, Jane instantly fell in love with both the neighborhood and the house. Her new neighbors had been so kind, bringing her little welcoming gifts, and then inviting her to the wedding.

While taking her shower Jane thought about the invitation to join their mah jongg group. Overhearing their conversation last night that they needed another player while Maryann was on her honeymoon, Jane quickly stepped in.

"I play 'a bit' and I love the game."

She omitted saying she was an expert player who had won many tournaments and had started playing the game with her mother when she was only ten years old. She'd see how well this group played before she revealed her own expertise. She admitted to herself she was lonely and wanted these new friends to accept her into their group. But she feared if they discovered how well she played, they might not want her to join them.

Jane's life on Lily Court Lane seemed almost perfect, except for one thing. Downstairs on the mantle was a problem waiting to be solved—the urn holding her mother's ashes. Whenever she was making coffee, or eating her meals in her sunlit kitchen, or lighting the fire at night, the urn was always there, a sad reminder her mother was now gone.

It was a nice urn though, as such things go, deep blue with a gold rim, made of solid metal, much smaller than one would expect to hold an entire person.

Five years ago, her mother had moved to Florida. She loved condo life on the Gulf of Mexico and played mah jongg with her likewise widowed neighbors. Life had gone well until one day she was gone, having died unexpectedly in her sleep. Her wishes were to be cremated and so the ashes were sent to Jane, without any funeral or ceremony.

Her mother wanted her ashes scattered over the Gulf of Mexico near where she lived but Jane couldn't let go of her mother that quickly. She wanted to scatter the ashes herself over the Gulf waters. She could imagine standing waist deep in the warm waves as she whispered a personal farewell to her.

While they lived apart these last few years, mother and daughter remained close, talking on the phone nearly every day. Jane missed those talks and so she had kept the ashes nearby and talked to the urn as if her mother were in the room with her. She wasn't ready yet to bring the ashes to Florida, but when she did, she would hold a memorial service for her mother's friends.

Enough of these sad thoughts, she decided. She was planning to spend a good part of the day working, sending New Year's greetings to all her clients, tantalizing them with the wonderful travel packages available in the coming year. She was fortunate her agency had been willing to place a new representative in San Diego. With her computer, Jane knew she could keep in touch with all her clients no matter where she lived.

As Jane took a break from work later in the day she sat in her kitchen drinking her café latte and missing her mother. She wished she could call her one more time just to talk. She recalled her wonderful laugh and her solid common sense which had guided Jane throughout her life. Her only regret was her mother had died before seeing her daughter happily married, with grandchildren for her to enjoy and to spoil. At least she'd been assured her daughter had a good career and could take care of herself financially.

Jane counted her blessings on this first day of a new year. She loved her work, she had made new friends, and last night she'd felt the glow from meeting an exciting new man. He was the one she would think of today as she bit into the wedding cake. Jane was sure she'd hear from him. She knew it would be only a flirtation, pleasant and short lived, and then he would return to San Francisco. His mother would be pleased.

She might be a few years older than Craig, but she was no cradle robber, Jane firmly told herself as she rose to make herself another café latte.

9

The Search Begins

Emilie stood gazing out at the gray metallic ocean on this second day of the new year. Morning had dawned, unusually dreary, a rare gloomy day for San Diego where the sun shines almost every day. She slowly turned to find Pearl, her friend and neighbor of many years, lighting a fire to warm the living room.

"There, Emilie," Pearl said. "Come sit at our little table by the fire. We can warm ourselves while we eat our lunch."

Emilie smiled gratefully at Pearl. She saw a kind, warm-hearted woman with short grey hair whose pleasant face hinted at the beauty she'd been as a young woman. She still maintained her slim figure, although she had grown a bit more rounded.

Pearl, Jim and their children had lived a few doors away from Emilie and Bill for over 20 years. They'd become close friends when they found how much they had in common. Bill and Jim, both retired naval officers, had enjoyed one another's company, sharing their love of sports, especially golf.

Pearl met her husband in the Philippines during World War II. Like Emilie, Pearl spoke little English when she first arrived in San Diego after the war. And like Emilie, she learned the language quickly. Her children had seen to that. Without children of her own,

Emilie doted on Pearl's and was a willing babysitter whenever she was needed.

Emilie and Pearl's friendship deepened when first Pearl, then Emilie, lost their husbands in quick succession. With Pearl's children grown and moved away, the two of them consoled one another through their grief.

Emilie's bones were aching today as she sat close to the fire finishing her egg salad sandwich. Pearl stayed for a while after lunch but then she had errands to run. After she left, Emilie lifted the time-worn family album and placed it in her lap as she so often did. Each page and every photo held a story of the few precious years she'd shared with her beloved parents and younger sister in Paris during the war.

There they were in faded black and white, the whole family, Mama, Papa, dark-haired little Noemi and her. In one photo they were gathered around the Hanukkah candles and the children were playing with their dreidles. Ah, here was the photo that meant the most to her. It was her ninth birthday and the photographer posed the family in front of the large fireplace in the living room. Above the fireplace mantle hung a small painting, clearly in a place of honor in the center of the room.

Emilie stood in front of her parents holding her little sister's hand. Both girls wore their best pinafore dresses, freshly pressed by their housekeeper, Mathilde. Papa stood erect, his hand on Emilie's shoulder, dressed in a fine dark suit and a stiffly starched white shirt, his large waxed moustache almost hiding his smile. Mama wore her pearls and brocade silk dress with her hair falling in waves to her shoulders.

How young her parents looked then, on that day so long ago, so full of hope. The clouds of terror had not yet rained down on their house in the 14th arrondissement. The next year would tell another story.

Emilie couldn't know then this birthday photo would be the last one taken of her family together. She'd wanted to go outside to play instead of staying indoors on a sunny afternoon taking family portraits but Papa had insisted.

"You are a very important member of the family," admonished Papa. "You must be part of it and stand up straight and behave like a proper French *mademoiselle*. You can play with your friends after we finish."

French children were expected to be obedient.

"Emilie, *ma cherie*, this is our family picture marking your birthday," her mother had reminded her. "You must be here, not with your friends."

Settling down to obey their papa, the two sisters stood side-by-side just long enough for the photographer to capture the scene and then they ran off to find Mathilde in the kitchen where she was frosting the birthday cake. Little did Emilie know there'd be no tenth birthday family portrait.

With a sigh, Emily returned to the present, as she gently touched the old photograph. Even after all these years, tears gathered in her eyes. She loved and missed them still. Her eyes drifted back to the photo. It was the painting above the mantle that caught her eye. Even in the small faded photo, the painting seemed to leap out at her, a portrait of a young mother holding her infant child. Papa had a special place in his heart for this painting which he'd inherited from his father.

Emilie's papa had been the son and grandson of tailors, but he'd moved up in society by becoming educated. Then, instead of following in the family trade, he built his own successful publishing house. He became known throughout Europe for publishing controversial political works, and especially those of celebrated Jewish authors and scholars. But at home, being French was more important than being Jewish.

Mama was known for her great beauty, kindness, and acts of charity. Together they made a formidable couple. They built a loving and happy home for their family, and agreed on all important decisions, sharing the same political views and deep love of France.

They feared the approaching Nazi menace, and as Emilie would later learn, they were key members of the early French Resistance.

Emilie could still hear Papa's voice as he told her the story of how his grandfather accepted the cherished painting in payment for a wedding suit from a very poor young man. Freidrich Vandenseen wanted to marry the young woman he loved. She didn't expect him to buy a new suit, but he wanted to surprise her. Although he had a job, he didn't earn enough to pay for extra things like new wedding clothes.

The young man said he didn't know much about this painting or about any art, but he knew the painting came to France with his great grandfather from the Netherlands over 100 years before.

Emilie knew the story very well, but still she'd ask, "Papa, why did your grandfather take the painting?"

"Well, my sweet, he boasted many times it was his lost Rembrandt. But we knew he hadn't been concerned with the value of the painting. He'd been pleased to do a *mitzvah*, a good deed, and help the young man."

Then Papa would conclude the story by saying, "Ah, young love," and kiss Emilie on the forehead. "One day, *ma petite*, you too will find such love."

Papa was delighted with Emilie's interest in the painting and promised her one day she'd attend the Sorbonne, the great university in Paris, where she could study art or even become a writer whose work Papa would publish to great acclaim.

It had been such a happy household. Her little sister, Noemi, admired her big sister and followed her everywhere. Emilie would often complain to Mama that Noemi was a pest, but her mother only laughed knowing the two girls were inseparable. Now Emilie wished she could be reunited with the little sister who so often distracted her, but whom she'd loved beyond words.

Sighing, Emilie turned her attention back to her cozy room in her American home and thought she'd take a little nap to pass the dreary afternoon. The fire had warmed her bones and was making her feel drowsy.

Several miles away from Emilie's home in Point Loma, Craig awoke early in his mother's house on Lily Court Lane. His body was alive again with thoughts of Jane. She'd been so easy to talk to, discussing his job in San Francisco and her work as a travel agent.

Most important, she shared his love of fine art, and she was knowledgeable about collecting and selling art. These were all the usual topics of conversation he'd expect to discuss with new acquaintances, but when discussed with Jane, they took on a more vital meaning.

Craig learned Jane had worked for several years after college as an assistant curator in a Los Angeles museum. Even though she loved the museum world she found it hard to make a living.

"I love to travel," she'd told Craig, "and one day I had an idea. Why couldn't I combine my two loves, art and travel? I researched travel agencies and I approached one that had limited offerings and suggested they offer tours to famous museums around the world."

Craig was entranced by her story, her vibrancy and her lips as she spoke.

"I guess they must have jumped at the idea."

"Yes, and much to my surprise, I became a travel agent. I felt sad leaving the museum, but this new career allowed me to combine both my passions and still make a living."

With every fact Craig discovered about Jane, he was attracted to her more and more. Still thinking about how she felt in his arms as they danced, Craig groaned with desire as he reluctantly rose from his solitary bed. Maybe a cold shower would help? He had to see Jane again before returning to San Francisco. The only question was when—and the sooner the better.

At first he'd been drawn to Jane's stunning red hair, the long line of her back, the delicate aura of perfume floating around her. She had such presence. When she entered the candlelit room at the wedding his world seemed to stop for a moment. The sparkle in her eyes revealed her enthusiasm for life. They were a pure and piercing blue with a thin shimmer of green encircling the pupils. What a woman!

Toweling off after his shower, he stretched and turned his thoughts to his upcoming meeting with Marvin Miller later that morning. He was deeply concerned he could be involved with a piece of art that might spell real trouble. Everything about this painting felt wrong to him. He didn't know why, but it seemed out of place in his gallery.

Was there a chance it could be a Dutch masterpiece that had slipped through the fingers of ignorant collectors? Had it been, as he most feared, stolen and sent to the United States to be sold quietly? So many questions and no answers. Yet.

Craig hadn't met the seller, Herr Schmidt, who'd sent the painting from Germany to his San Francisco gallery. The painting didn't appear to be German in origin, and there was no information about how it came into the hands of a German collector. Craig was told only that it'd been in the family for many years.

He was reminded of stories of artworks stolen by the Nazis during World War II and hidden away in many locations in Germany, never to be restored to their rightful owners, most of whom had perished in the war. A few of these works were now seeing the light of day and finally being returned to the heirs.

Craig didn't want it on his conscience that he had any connection with art possibly mired in theft and death and he wouldn't allow his gallery's reputation to suffer because of it.

Prior to the quick French surrender to the German invasion, French museums and galleries cleverly prepared themselves for the worst. The French government feared German bombs could destroy the historical sites and ruin the beauty of Paris. They worried much of the fine art would be stolen and then transported to Germany. Long before the Germans arrived, valuable pieces from the museums were crated and secretly smuggled to locations outside of Paris. In many cases the art was hidden in underground caves.

Most Parisians were unaware of the impending disaster about to strike them and their beautiful city. No one realized just how much would be lost in the war. During the first few days of the Occupation, the French felt relieved the invaders seemed so friendly. That soon changed. A strict curfew was imposed, food was rationed and became scarce, and people began to disappear. French citizens learned the meaning of fear.

Craig realized he had many questions to discuss with Marvin, especially the lack of provenance, the documented history of the piece. Where had it come from? Who was this owner, Herr Schmidt? Was Craig's partner, Jack, somehow involved in something illegal? No, he dismissed that idea. He knew Jack well and trusted him. Yet there was so much he didn't know.

Seated in Marvin's outer office on the 18th floor of a downtown San Diego skyscraper, Craig put down a magazine and greeted Carolee who was on her way out to file papers at the courthouse for Marvin.

Seeing the bright, cheerful Carolee reminded him of the wedding and his restless thoughts turned again to Jane. He hadn't been completely blind, noticing his mother's obvious dismay at his interest in her. At some point, he'd have to air this issue with his mother. Her hostile reaction had taken him completely by surprise. His love life was his own business—had been for many years. He didn't need to answer to anyone about it, especially not his mother. The whole incident left him annoyed and angry.

He'd left a long voice message for Jane earlier that morning but she hadn't replied yet. Was he wrong about her interest in him? He hoped not. He couldn't resist thinking about her lovely face and how it would feel when he ran his fingers through her silky red hair.

"Mr. Miller is ready to see you now," said the receptionist, interrupting his thoughts. "Please come this way," and she led him back to Marvin's corner office.

Marvin was seated at a large desk facing the floor to ceiling windows. They overlooked the harbor showcasing the cruise ships lining the Embarcadero. The sunlit office was decorated in a tasteful traditional style, the carpet thick and lush in muted natural tones. Sets of matching law books filled bookcases lining one wall and a comfortable seating area was off to the right.

Marvin rose as Craig entered and came around his desk to shake Craig's hand. The two men stood making small talk, chatting about the wedding and their breakfast together the next morning. Craig looked around the office and complimented Marvin.

"How do you ever get any work done with such a beautiful view?" Seeing the many cruise ships docked along the bay, he added, "Alex and Maryann must be well away on their cruise to Hawaii by now."

Marvin cleared his throat. "How's your mother, Craig?"

"She stayed home to make me breakfast this morning. By now I'm sure she's busy at the bakery. I really want to thank you again for all the kindness you've shown her."

Marvin felt his face grow warm as he responded, "I was happy to help her. She's a very special lady."

"Yes, I'm proud of her. After my dad died, I wasn't sure she'd be able to recover. Yet here she is, proving me wrong with a whole new life. She seems so happy these days."

Marvin wanted to say more about Sarah, but this was not the time or place. Instead he asked, "Can I get you some coffee, Craig? Let's sit down while we talk. Make yourself comfortable," gesturing toward the sitting area.

Marvin walked over to a silver coffee service already laid out on a low table in front of the brown leather sofa. Settling into the soft leather chairs facing each other, the two men sipped their coffee and then began discussing the matter that brought Craig to Marvin's office.

Leaning forward and placing his coffee cup on the table, Craig began by saying, "I don't know if you're aware of my work in San Francisco. I've been a partner in an art gallery for the last year."

Marvin listened intently as Craig told him of his suspicions about the painting.

"To me, the painting looks to be of museum quality, too special to be sold in a local gallery. So I feel I need some legal advice," Craig concluded.

Marvin adjusted his reading glasses as he thought for a moment. "If I'm to help you, I need to have a thorough description of the work, including its title, the artist's name, and everything you know about it. I'll need photos as well. Even the smallest detail could prove to be important in our research."

Craig breathed a sigh of relief when Marvin said "our" research, and handed him the folder he'd already prepared with several photocopies of the painting. There was something about Marvin that reassured Craig he'd come to the right person. His mother had been right to trust this man. He could feel Marvin's solid reliability and intelligence.

Marvin quietly studied the photo. Like everyone else, he was struck by the beauty of the piece, even in a photocopy. He clearly understood Craig's dilemma. His reputation could be damaged forever by a scandal, and he could even face criminal charges.

"I'm no art connoisseur, Craig, but this painting is absolutely beautiful. It really does look like something you'd see in a museum." Marvin continued "You're right to be concerned about it given the circumstances of how it came into your possession."

"What do you think I should do?"

Marvin thought for a moment before responding, "I'd be happy to represent you. I'll have a representation agreement prepared while we finish our discussion. Once we sign it, we'll have a legal contract.

It could be expensive to do a thorough search," he cautioned Craig. "I'll need funds to hire an investigator knowledgeable in art theft to assist me."

When Craig nodded his assent, Marvin added, "Excuse me for a few moments while I speak with my assistant."

Craig needed to uncover the truth. Money could not be a matter of concern right now. If necessary, he would use the remainder of the inheritance from his father.

When Marvin returned, Craig asked, "Who will you hire to do this search?"

"One of my former investigators is now specializing in art fraud. He has contacts all over the world and he's just the person to help us. But he's not inexpensive and, Craig, please understand if we do discover the painting was stolen, the authorities will have to be called in. The collector would be investigated and the presumed rightful owner would have to be notified."

"I understand. Please go ahead. Contact your man. I want the truth."

Marvin was impressed with the younger man's strong sense of integrity. Sarah had done well raising her son.

"Craig, if we learn it's stolen and belongs to someone else, we are morally obligated to seek out the true owner and return the painting. Fortunately, we now have computers to help us, but it's still a daunting task to search all the thousands of items in the databases around the world."

"This will be a very exciting adventure for me," Marvin continued, "certainly quite different from the family and business law I practice every day. I must warn you, though, we may end up without any answers. But if we do, the person who sent the painting to your gallery might well be hurt by this search. The international police will become involved, arrests could result. You and your gallery could be in serious jeopardy."

Craig firmly responded, "I won't change my mind about the search, Marvin. I want to go forward. If the painting was stolen, we must return it to its rightful owner."

Marvin's assistant knocked and then entered holding some papers she handed to Marvin.

"Here we go, Craig. Take a minute to read this over and if it meets with your approval, sign above your name."

Craig quickly read through the straight forward agreement and signed it. Marvin did the same and Craig then wrote a check for the amount of the retainer.

With that, the two men shook hands, and Marvin escorted Craig to the elevator. Craig planned to call Jack Hillson, his partner at the gallery, and let him know why he'd taken the painting out of the display window and placed it in the safe. He was ready to discuss his suspicions with Jack.

After Craig left his office, Marvin sat at his desk staring at the photocopy of the painting. Life had grown so interesting for him. He hoped this venture would end well for Craig's sake. What would it be like to have a son like that, he wondered?

As Craig waited for the elevator to arrive, his cell phone rang. It was Jane returning his earlier call. Feeling a rush of anticipation and not bothering to say hello, he asked, "Can I see you tonight?"

There was a pause before she replied, "Craig, I'm not sure that's a good idea. I saw how your mother looked at me at the wedding."

"Don't worry about my mother. I have so much to tell you, Jane."

After a long pause, she simply said, "I want to see you, too."

10

A Romantic Voyage

The Ocean Voyager was pampering Maryann and Alex with its heated swimming pools, spa, elegant restaurants and attentive crew. Their beautiful stateroom was served by a young steward ready to fulfill their every request. Their clothes were hung securely in wardrobes, and each dresser drawer was held in place so nothing could fall out when the ship swayed from side to side. Maryann and Alex quickly became accustomed to being rocked to sleep each night.

They were certain no two people had ever been more in love. Even the ship's captain watched them when they were dancing in the ballroom, holding each other close, oblivious to everyone around them. Lucky honeymooners, he thought with some envy, thinking of his own sour wife at home who no longer seemed interested in him or his seagoing life.

Waking up each morning to Alex's caresses, Maryann felt loved and secure for the first time since she was in college. Today sunlight was pouring into their stateroom and Maryann lay there contentedly enjoying the calm and very blue ocean waves lapping against the ship beyond their balcony. Never had she seen so many shades of blue, from the darkest blue of the ocean to the bright shimmer of the cloudless sky.

Last night had been wonderful, starting with a gourmet dinner at the captain's table, then dancing at the disco, and later strolling on the moonlit deck with a champagne toast at midnight. They kissed their way from the door of their stateroom to the bed, shedding their clothes as they went. Alex was fully erect and Maryann was more than ready for him.

Their burning desire for one another hadn't lessened since their wedding night. No matter how many times they made love, their passion for one another was all consuming, stripping away all Maryann's memories of the past.

As he thrust himself inside her, Alex said, "I love you, Maryann. I want this moment to last forever."

He rose over her, supported on his hands as he gazed down into her lovely face, her eyes glazed with passion.

"Alex, my love, yes, yes," breathed Maryann as her body was flooded with rising waves of pleasure.

She reached up to stroke his chest and then pulled him down onto her, welcoming his weight as he pressed her into the mattress.

Alex began to move deeply within her. Each thrust was met by Maryann as she tightly surrounded him holding him within her, until he groaned and rolled to the side, taking her with him. He lay spent, with his head on her shoulder and her hand stroking his hair.

When he recovered, he smiled into her eyes, "Ready for more?" he asked.

And she was.

Now, slipping naked from the bed in the early morning light, she tiptoed across the room to the compact bathroom. Once in the shower, she soaped herself with the frangipani scented shower gel, feeling relaxed as she stood under the hot steaming spray. Wrapping herself in a fluffy towel, she went back to the bedroom where Alex still slept in their large bed. She could see his reflection in the vanity mirror as she brushed her hair.

Lost in thought, she jumped as Alex murmured, "Good morning, my darling," surprising her as he came up behind her.

He was naked and erect yet again.

"Don't turn around," he requested. "Stay right where you are and just let me do everything."

Still facing the mirror, she admired his tanned bare chest as he lowered his chin to her shoulder. Their faces were side by side as their eyes met in the mirror. He inhaled deeply.

"You smell luscious, my beautiful sexy wife," he said as his teeth tugged gently at her earlobe. "You're up rather early."

Maryann giggled as she responded, "I see you are too, love."

She realized this was the very first time she'd ever made a joke about such a natural thing as her husband's huge erection.

Alex pulled at the edge of her towel causing it to drop to the floor. Maryann still felt a little self-conscious being naked in front of him. She blushed in embarrassment, yet felt a wave of anticipation for what was to come. She'd come a long way in overcoming the fear she'd developed during her life with Michael, but she acknowledged to herself she still had a long way to go. She closed her eyes as a child might, believing if she couldn't see Alex, he couldn't see her.

"No, darling, open your eyes. I want you to see how lovely you are and how much you turn me on."

Fascinated, she watched in the mirror as his hands slid over her body. She grew hungry for him as he began to stroke her nipples. With both hands he lifted her breasts, his thumbs circling the hardening tips.

"Hmm, I love touching you. Your breasts are so perfect and they fit in my hands as though they were meant to be there."

Maryann felt herself unfolding like a flower opening to the sun. His insistent erection pressed against her as his hand caressed her stomach and then slid ever lower. Her body responded to his touch, wanting even more.

"Slide your legs apart so I can find you," he whispered.

And she did. She felt safe and very aroused by his gentle instructions.

The heat inside her was building, building. Here was the man she loved above all others, yet she shivered as her past rose unbidden to her mind again. This time she managed to push the thoughts away. She wouldn't let her past come between her and Alex.

Alex felt the sweet honey dripping from Maryann's core as it coated his fingertips. She was quivering with excitement as his fingers slipped inside her. His touch was relentless, pulling back a little and then moving forward, always finding her sweet spot of ecstasy. Again, and yet again.

He leaned her forward, her elbows resting on the vanity. She lowered her head to watch as his hand pleasured her.

"Lift your head up so you can see us come together," he murmured.

Their eyes locked on one another in the mirror, Alex held her hips close to him as he eased slowly and gently inside her, allowing her to accommodate his full erection. He stood perfectly still watching her face in the mirror. When he knew she was comfortable with his formidable girth, he began moving slowly in and out, in and out. They writhed in unison as he continued to fondle her pleasure spot. Maryann gasped with surprise as she experienced such pleasure she'd never known before.

"Alex, this is even better than last night," she gasped.

Alex groaned, "Maryann, I love you and I love being inside you, being one with you. I want you more than I ever thought possible."

He spoke with strained exaltation. He couldn't contain himself much longer. "Come for me, my darling. Now!"

Maryann couldn't hold back. The waves began to course through her body, like the powerful ocean waves rolling under the ship. As she shattered in a burst of blinding heat, Alex gasped, and cried out with the force of his release.

Maryann collapsed onto the vanity. The cool marble pressed against her breasts as Alex leaned over her, cradling her in his arms.

Breathing more evenly now, Alex kissed the sensitive place behind her ear and asked, "Again, please?"

She smiled and nodded, desire growing once again. He knew how to please her. He turned her around, and she could see he was still fully erect and obviously prepared for more.

Wide eyed, she breathed, "Yes, more please. Don't stop." She felt she'd never get enough of him.

He lifted Maryann to sit on the vanity, her back against the mirror, placing her legs around his waist.

"We aren't done yet," Alex said softly with a smile, as he pressed his hardness into her once again. "I've waited a long time for you."

"Oh, Alex, it was worth the wait," she sighed.

These were the last lucid words she uttered as they began moving together rhythmically. It was slow and smooth and tender.

She lifted her hands to hold his face and kiss his lips. Looking into each other's eyes, this time their groans were softer but no less intense.

"That was a hell of a way to start our morning, babe," Alex said later as they left the cabin heading toward breakfast.

When they were seated across from one another in the ship's upper lounge with its 360-degree view of the blue Pacific, Alex raised his mimosa and toasted her.

"To you, my beautiful, sexy wife. I know we'll be exhausted by the time we reach Hawaii."

Maryann responded with a mischievous grin, "Yes darling, it's my mission, but that's what beaches are for. I'll even let you nap for a few minutes in between, if we have the time."

She chuckled, watching his face sprout a toothy grin. Maryann herself was smiling from ear to ear feeling proud of herself for putting her fears aside and enjoying the beautiful lovemaking of the past few days.

She hadn't thought of anyone else but Alex all morning. Hooray! As they tapped their glasses together, Maryann knew she'd never been this happy before or felt so fulfilled.

They devoured an enormous breakfast at the buffet, freshly prepared Eggs Benedict with bacon, waffles garnished with blueberries and strawberries, chocolate croissants slathered with butter, English muffins with marmalade, and café mochas topped with whipped cream.

When Maryann joked they would have to be rolled off the ship from eating so much, Alex smiled with a knowing gleam in his eye.

"No need to worry, darling. Once we're back in our cabin, I'll show you another part of my special custom exercise program that guarantees we'll both stay fit and trim. Think of it as your dessert," he said with a twinkle in his eyes.

Maryann laughed. She could hardly wait for that workout.

Lounging in side-by-side deck chairs, they spent the morning breathing the salty sea air, watching the waves, and chatting about their wedding, fondly remembering all their family and friends who'd shared their joy. They were counting on Simon's photos to capture the beauty and emotion of that night.

As Maryann returned to the book she'd bought in the ship's bookstore, Alex thought a bit about his business and couldn't help but wonder how the coffee shop was going without him, but he knew his manager, Ming, was more than capable of seeing to the day-to-day operations. Alex had great faith in him.

Gazing at his new bride, he vowed to put aside all thoughts of business. For two weeks they'd forget the outside world and enjoy this special time together.

"Should we try to climb the rock wall now?" Alex asked, without much enthusiasm.

"Maybe later, Alex," Maryann replied. "I'm anxious for you to get me started on that new exercise program."

Giggling like teenagers, they made their way back to the cabin for a long impassioned afternoon. There'd be plenty of time to climb the rock wall, swim in the pool, visit the spa, and shop in the boutiques. Later—much later.

11

Looking for Love

The doorbell at Carolee's house chimed a cheery tune promptly at 1:00. It was mah jongg day and Dallas was ready to play. Sarah stood at her side holding a plate of freshly baked macadamia nut cookies. Today was Carolee's turn to host the game and the mah jongg tiles were set out on the table waiting. Jane arrived moments later dressed today in skinny black jeans, knee high boots and a belted red designer tunic.

"Welcome, Jane, to your first game with the Lily Court Lane mah jongg players. We're happy you could join us," Carolee bubbled as she greeted Jane with a hug.

Dallas looked up from the table. "Hi, Jane, we haven't seen you since the wedding. How was the rest of your New Year's Eve?" Raising an eyebrow, she added, "I heard you and Craig ended up in the Gaslamp."

Sarah spoke before Jane could answer. "C'mon, ladies, the tiles are waiting for us."

Sarah's tone wasn't unfriendly exactly; maybe just a little gruff and dismissive, certainly not like the sweet Sarah they were all used to. The others looked at her in surprise and wondered if something had happened between the two women.

Jane, not wanting to seem ungracious, chose to ignore Sarah's coolness and sat down in Maryann's empty chair. Turning to Dallas, Jane answered her, "I'm glad you asked. Craig's a terrific dancer. He nearly danced my feet off."

"Humph", Sarah muttered under her breath. "Yes, that's because you're too old to keep up with him".

Carolee sensed some tension in the air and quickly changed the subject. "I wonder how our honeymooners are doing."

"I bet they're locked in each other's arms, making passionate love, right this very moment." Jane sighed, sounding as though she were wishing it was her.

Sarah shot her a sharp glance as she said, "Really? Well, I just hope they're not seasick. You can hit a lot of big storms crossing the Pacific." Turning to Carolee, she reminded her, "You haven't passed me my three tiles yet. C'mon everyone, let's play."

Despite the apparent tension between Sarah and Jane, the game went smoothly. Sarah even cheered up somewhat when she won the first game and began acting much like her old self. Carolee and Dallas were pleased Jane knew the rules of mah jongg and played very well, even winning the next game. After the third round, they broke for a light lunch.

Handing Jane a plate with strawberries and sliced melon, crackers and cheese, Carolee told her, "I always try to serve a low cal lunch at my house."

Dallas laughed as she added, "I have to exercise for hours after a game at Sarah's house. Her cookies are so addictive you can't eat just one."

Responding to their questions about her personal exercise program, Dallas told them about the "Rock and Roll Marathon" in June she was training for. The scenic course covered the distance from Balboa Park to the East Village and Petco Park.

Sarah, returning from the bathroom, rejoined the group. "Carolee, I see your Christmas decorations are down. How in the world did you manage that all by your lonesome?"

"Oh, it was no problem, I just stayed up all night," she joked. "I know what you're all thinking. Every year I promise I won't over decorate," she explained for Jane's sake, "and every year I'm glad to say I fail to keep my promise. Taking it all down isn't much fun, but Dallas came over with a bottle of wine and somehow we managed to drink our way through it," Carolee chuckled.

"Next year, Carolee, you have to keep your promise to limit yourself. Only one tree, please. I had to wash my hands twenty times to get the sap off my fingers," said Dallas. "Well, maybe two trees. I have to admit what you did was really gorgeous, especially the tree with all the thousands of twinkling lights on your front lawn. And the miniature one with all the kitchen ornaments you made for Sarah's bakery was just perfect."

Sarah chimed in then, "Yes, my customers just loved it. Carolee, you could really go into business decorating people's homes and businesses for the holidays."

"I never thought of that," she said slowly. "Perhaps that could be my future. I might follow in your footsteps, Sarah, and become an entrepreneur."

Dallas agreed, "I was relieved you at least hired a handyman to remove Santa's sleigh from the roof and the snowman from the front yard. I had visions of you toppling off the roof in one of your sparkly dresses and now that everything's gone, maybe the traffic will ease up a bit on Lily Court Lane."

With Carolee's passion for decorations, the street had become a busy tourist stop for the duration of the holiday season. Lines of cars slowly snaked by just to see Carolee's Christmas fantasy.

Grinning Carolee replied, "Just you wait until you see what I'm planning for Halloween. I've already been researching online and I just found a giant black cat with blinking yellow eyes and moving body parts. I hope you like witches too, because all of us are going to dress up like witches and have a big party here at my house."

Carolee's eyes lit up at the thought of all her plans.

"Carolee," exclaimed Dallas, "it's only January and you're already thinking about Halloween?"

Dallas and Jane smiled, for this was the Carolee everyone knew and loved—a woman with a zest for life and the imagination to create a visual feast for every holiday.

Sarah was glaring at Jane thinking, she's the biggest witch of all but let's spell that with a "b" instead, and she snickered to herself. She knew the others would be shocked to know what she was thinking.

As the tiles moved around the table, Sarah avoided speaking directly to Jane. They played several "wall" games which no one won, and then Dallas and Jane each won a game with Jane ending as the big winner of the day. She drew the final tile she needed to mahj and as she didn't have any jokers, she earned twice the usual number of points.

The game ended at four o'clock with Sarah excusing herself.

"Girls, I'm sorry, I have to leave. I still have a few things to do at the bakery before we close for the day."

She said good-bye to Dallas and Carolee with a hug, but only nodded in Jane's direction.

Jane lingered after Sarah left, thanking the others for a fun time.

"I would love to play anytime you need me."

"We loved having you here," Dallas responded. "You should stay and have dinner with us one evening. We go out a lot."

"Yes," Carolee added, "We like to sit at an outdoor café and evaluate all the men passing by. Speaking of good looking men, when are you going to see Craig again?"

"Oh, I don't know. Sarah doesn't seem any too happy with me since I started seeing Craig."

"So that's what's bugging her. Every time she looked at you, the room got five degrees colder," Dallas said.

"Do you really think that was it? She doesn't like you? I don't get that at all," was Carolee's puzzled comment. "Well, Dallas and I think you're fabulous, Jane, and we'd welcome a new romance on

Lily Court Lane, especially since Maryann and Alex are married. We need another love story to talk about."

"You know, I really do like Craig, and I'd like to see him again, but I wouldn't ever want to hurt Sarah."

"Don't be silly. She'll get over it and Craig will be going back to San Francisco in a few days anyway. If things did work out between you two, you'll be making lots of trips to San Francisco. Whatever happens, Sarah will adjust. She's really a great woman."

"I was planning to see Craig again tonight," Jane confided hesitantly, "but now I think I shouldn't."

"No," both women exclaimed at once, "you must keep your date. If you don't, it might please Sarah, but you and Craig would both be disappointed."

Dallas and Carolee longed so for romance in their lives and didn't want to see Jane lose her chance for love.

Waving goodbye to Jane as she walked next door to her house with the purple door, Carolee remarked to Dallas, "No wonder Craig likes her. She's so beautiful and such a nice person. The way he looked at her at the wedding made me shiver clear down to my toes," she added, fanning herself with her hand. "Whooee, I sure wish someone would look at me that way."

Holding open the door, Carolee said, "So, Dallas, let's try to make something like that happen for us. We need some male appreciation too. Don't leave just yet. I have a plan to tell you about. C'mon, let's go inside."

Minutes later, they were seated in front of Carolee's computer in her small home office while she explained to Dallas what she had in mind. Ads on television promised that with the help of an online dating service, they'd meet their true love within six months and then live happily ever after, or their fees would be refunded, no questions asked. They'd nothing to lose except some time and a little bit of money.

Feeling brave, they reassured one another, "We're modern women, and we can do this."

"The only thing the wedding cake did for me was give me nightmares," Carolee said to Dallas's amusement.

Dallas nodded, thinking about the night with Simon. Nothing good had happened to her that night either.

"We can do this," Carolee repeated as she sat at the keyboard.

"We will do this," added Dallas in agreement. "This may be just the thing for us."

Carolee hoped with all her heart the advertising claims were true and the service would work for them, but Dallas wasn't so sure. She still felt the sting of the recent past, believing she had married "The One," the true love of her life, only to find out he was the one true love for someone else, and not for her at all.

Then there was also her recent unpleasant experience with Simon. It seemed he could hardly wait to get away from her the next morning. Well, it didn't matter. She'd never see him again. What did she have to lose anyway by trying this internet thing, except maybe put an end to her loneliness?

"I'll register first and then you can do the same," Carolee said, running quickly through the questions.

She read all the magazines and took all those little quizzes so she knew exactly the kind of man she was looking for.

"My perfect man is educated and serious and loves his profession. He has a great sense of humor. He likes to work hard and play hard, and I want him 'hard' at the right moments." She giggled and then went on, "He doesn't have to be really handsome, but he has to have some charm and style."

Not one of the men in her past fit this description.

Now it was Dallas's turn. She answered "yes" to the question, did she like to exercise? "The answer to that one is easy," she commented to Carolee.

When she got to the part where she had to describe the kind of man she was looking for, Dallas made them both laugh by saying instantly, "Not gay!" She quickly typed out the description of her ideal man and pushed the enter key.

She was shocked to realize her description pretty much matched her recent almost lover, Simon. She'd described a tall, blue-eyed, blond-haired man, with an exciting career and a zest for life, in his thirties, who was athletic and adventurous.

This was just the opposite of dark-haired Rey, her former husband, who preferred the dim lights of bars and nightclubs, and the secrecy of his locked office. She shuddered whenever she thought of Rey's deceit. She didn't condemn his lifestyle, but involving her in a web of lies was more than she could stand.

Her dark thoughts were interrupted by Carolee's gales of laughter, as she pointed out, "Dallas, you've just described the photographer at the wedding. I saw you talking to him for most of the evening. How did that work out?"

Dallas blushed in response. She hadn't shared the story of taking Simon to bed and the miserable aftermath, and she didn't plan to.

Noting Dallas's flushed face, Carolee said, "Why, you little devil! I bet you took him home, didn't you?"

Dallas tried to smile at Carolee. She'd been caught red-handed, or really red-faced.

"Well, how was it? Tell me everything."

"It wasn't what you think and definitely not worth talking about. It was a big mistake on my part."

Carolee tried to press further but Dallas refused to elaborate except to repeat there really was nothing to tell. Carolee guessed there was much more to the story but she respected her friend's obvious distress. She wondered if Sarah knew what'd happened between Dallas and Simon.

"I can't wait to see who I'll meet online," Carolee said, changing the subject. She had visions of Brad Pitt and Jude Law, or even better, Daniel Craig. "I'm so glad we're doing this together."

"Me, too," agreed Dallas, "it's much more fun with you. I'd never have done this by myself."

Closing down the computer they decided to have fish tacos on the patio of their favorite downtown restaurant, *Casa Pacifica*. The two women strolled along the quaint Lily Court Lane and a few blocks later turned the corner into the Gaslamp. There they entered the noisy life of the city where tourists filled the streets following their noses to the delicious aromas coming from the open doors of restaurants. Street musicians playing and singing for donations made an exciting atmosphere along Fourth and Fifth Avenues.

By midnight when the two friends would be back home alone in their beds, lines of scantily clad young women would be forming, waiting to get into their favorite dance clubs. They too were hoping to meet someone.

Enjoying the early evening air, Dallas and Carolee ordered a bottle of white wine and sat outside watching the crowds flow past their table. As they sipped their chardonnay, they enjoyed the night scene while their dating profiles were flying across cyberspace.

12

Getting To Know You

It was early Thursday morning and Ming was pacing back and forth behind the counter of the coffee shop. Alex was still away on his honeymoon and wouldn't be back for another week.

Ming was feeling frustrated as he muttered out loud to himself, "Where are all our pastries? Sold!"

A single customer had just come in and cleaned out their entire supply for an office meeting.

"I'm glad to have the business, for sure," he mumbled, "but now I have a disaster on my hands with nothing to sell."

Panicking, he called Sarah at her bakery.

"Sarah, I really need your help. We just got cleaned out of all the muffins and cinnamon rolls. Can you bring me something fast?"

"Calm down, Ming, It's good to hear you have so much business. I'll send over some right away."

Breathing a sigh of relief, he replied, "Thanks, Sarah, you're a lifesaver," and hung up.

He immediately began to watch the door, counting the seconds until the fresh supply arrived. Until then, he hoped the waiting customers would be satisfied with coffee and the few cookies they had left. His business classes at San Diego State hadn't prepared him for the practical reality of running out of food. His classes focused on how to lure customers into the store, but that certainly wasn't his problem today.

Was he going to fail his first test as a manager? Now he understood all those times when Alex would tug at his hair and pace his office in total frustration. Alex had taken such a chance hiring him knowing he had no experience. He said at the time, "You may not know it, but just talking with you I know you're the right person for the job. Everything you told me about your family's restaurant and all the years you worked there—Ming, it's in your blood. You'll do just fine."

"Thank you for your confidence. I won't let you down."

As Alex had turned away, Ming breathed a sigh of relief. He was glad he wouldn't have to work for his family anymore.

He was about to call Sarah again when he saw a figure rush into the store completely hidden behind a tray stacked high with pastries. Thank goodness! At last the order was here and even better, it was Cindy, not Sarah, carrying the tray. He'd hoped it would be Cindy.

"You're here," he said, stating the obvious, as he rushed to help her with the heavy load.

Smiling brightly, Cindy replied, "The cavalry has arrived. You're saved. Alex told Sarah you'd probably need more stock, so we were all prepared, waiting for your call."

Studying Cindy intently, he saw how her smile lit up her face. He momentarily forgot the customers waiting in the slow moving line behind him. Then the rising voices registered in his brain and he turned away neglecting to say thank you.

Cindy stood there for a moment, shrugged, and then hurried back to the bakery feeling a little annoyed with him. How irritating he is, she thought. He didn't even say thank you. He may be really cute, but so rude. He'll never be the guy for me, in spite of my New Year's Eve dream.

A few moments later when his nerves had settled down, Ming looked around to thank Cindy and was disappointed to find she was gone. She'd been on his mind since the wedding, but he hadn't yet worked up the courage to call her or look for her in the bakery. He felt like a donkey on ice skates whenever she was around—positively awkward.

"Hey, Ming," a barista's voice cut into his distraction, "need your help over here. This coffee urn's not working."

With that, Ming pushed aside all thoughts of Cindy. He'd make time to think about her later. As if he could stop himself, even if he wanted to.

As the morning passed, the replenished supply of baked goods sold well, the repaired coffee urn perked away, and the busiest part of the day came to an end. Customers still continued to come and go, some lingering over their computers, or playing chess, while others rushed back to work. A group of stalwart senior men took up their post outside at a round table, solving the world's problems as they did every day. It wasn't until well after the lunch rush that Ming was able to take a break and think about Cindy again.

He decided he'd walk to the bakery hoping Cindy would be there. He needed to thank her for helping him that morning. It gave him a legitimate reason, but best of all it gave him an excuse to see her again. As luck would have it, Cindy was the only one in the shop. She stood behind the counter and watched as Ming walked in.

"You saved me today," he said without any preliminaries. "Thank you very much."

"You're very welcome," Cindy said, hoping the shock didn't show on her face. "We excel at saving lives here at *Sarah's Bakery*."

"You sure did today."

"On Thursday the coffee shop often runs out by mid-morning. You didn't know because that's your day off. Alex prefers to order less, so if he needs stuff, it'll be freshly baked."

Ming was pleased Cindy noticed his absence on Thursdays.

"Let's plan on an extra delivery for tomorrow as well," he said. "We'll probably need it again. Will you bring it?"

Ming stopped himself from adding he was looking forward to seeing her again. He suddenly felt shy and worse, he ran out of words. This strange girl, with her pierced eyebrow, black hair with purple streaks and black nail polish, wasn't his, and certainly not his family's ideal girl. Yet there was something about her, a beauty and sweetness, making him want to get to know her better.

Ming's instincts told him to walk out the door before he got himself in deeper. Instead he blurted out, "Can we meet later?"

There was that smile again.

"That'd be great," Cindy answered immediately, "I'd like that a lot."

"I get off at five. Can I see you then?"

"Sure, that works out fine. Do you like burgers?"

"Of course. Everyone likes hamburgers!"

"How about if I drive? I'll pick you up at the coffee shop and we'll go to *In-N-Out*. They have the best burgers in town."

"I've never been there."

"Oh, you'll love it, everybody in San Diego does," Cindy assured him.

"That sounds great," he nodded, happy Cindy wanted to spend time with him.

He tried to look cool despite his pounding heart. A date, a real date!

Ming gave her a quick wave good-bye and went back to the coffee shop barely able to conceal his excitement. The other employees noticed he was in an awfully good mood that afternoon.

Cindy hummed as she pulled out the final tray of baguettes from the oven. She, too, could hardly wait for the end of the day. She thought about the wedding cake she'd put under her pillow and her dreams of Ming's dark, intense eyes, and she smiled to herself.

Ming made sure the coffee shop was ready for any late afternoon stragglers. His day was nearly over and the assistant manager would close up for the night.

"Ming, you've got a phone call. It's your mother."

Everyone knew her call came at the same time nearly every day. They thought about teasing Ming but they were warned off by his fierce scowl every time he took the call.

Picking up the phone, he said, "Yes, Mom, how are you?"

He listened to her long reply as he refilled the sugar canisters. When he tried to avoid her call by shutting off his cell phone, she just called the store.

"Don't forget, son, you're coming to dinner tonight," she said now.

His parents lived in Rancho Bernardo close to the popular Chinese restaurant they owned. He was glad they were far enough away from downtown San Diego to give him some sense of freedom from their kindly but oppressive control.

"Sorry, Mom, I told you before I wouldn't be coming to dinner tonight. I'm busy." Ming sighed in exasperation.

Darn, he said to himself, he shouldn't have said it that way. He should've lied and told her he was working late. She would've accepted that, or he had a class tonight, or had to study for a test. But Ming hated lying, and his mother would probably see right through it.

His mother ignored his response, reminding him someone named Oi Ling was coming to dinner especially to meet him.

"We were expecting you."

Here we go again, he thought.

"Mom, I told you. I want to pick out my own dates. No more fix ups, please! I can't come tonight. I gotta go, Mom. I'll talk to you tomorrow."

He quickly hung up the phone, not giving his mother a chance to argue further with him. Tomorrow it would be the same thing. Another girl, another family dinner, all to get him married. No way, not by a long shot, he thought.

There could be only one happy ending according to his mother— seeing him married to a girl of *her* choice, living right next door to her and after completing his studies, he'd take his rightful place next to his father and older brother expanding the family restaurant business. Those were her plans, her dreams, for him.

Ming loved and honored his mother but she could be very difficult when she didn't get her way. His father was much more reasonable about dating and marriage.

The last time they had talked about it, his father said, "Son, you marry a girl you love and who loves you. You are one hundred percent American, and you can make your own choices. Just don't tell her I said so. Your mother thinks the old way is the right way, but she may be wrong. She worries about you."

Ming promised himself he'd remember what his father said and put aside his mother's annoying phone call, as he walked out the door and stepped into Cindy's beat-up Volkswagen.

In Rancho Bernardo, his mother stood shaking her head in exasperation after she slammed down the phone. She was furious. Her son refused to come to dinner and meet a nice girl. "What is his problem?" she asked herself yet again. She knew what was best for him, just as her mother knew what was right for her when she got married.

When she married Lloyd Sun, both families celebrated the union, she mused, and just look how long they'd been married with three beautiful children. This romantic nonsense about love was not part of their heritage. Love comes later after a married couple gets to know one another.

She knew her husband had come to love her, although it was true he wasn't a demonstrative man, Dorothy thought, as she returned to the kitchen. Even as a young man, he was rather reserved and she feared he'd be a cold and distant husband.

Her mother told her he was a good match for her flighty nature, and all of her notions of romance had been influenced by silly magazines—and she was right. Dorothy didn't see how much her son was like her at the same age, longing for love.

She finished preparing the wonton for the soup she would serve for dinner. A dinner without Ming.

13

Burgers and Texts

Cindy's ancient Volkswagen chugged noisily along the evening streets of San Diego. She quickly put Ming at ease by talking about her job at the bakery and made him laugh at her description of some of the strange requests for cakes in unusual shapes and sizes and some with risqué themes.

"We've made shark cakes, lamp cakes, book cakes and even cakes shaped like beds, complete with sheets and pillows—and various body parts," she added with a snicker.

"But the real winner," she continued, "was the wedding cake we made last summer with a bride and groom figurine on top, where the groom was wearing nothing but a top hat and the bride was wearing only a veil!"

"You're kidding! That's unbelievable."

"Absolutely true," she said, noticing Ming's hearty laughter.

Ming was pleased Cindy spoke to him as if they were old friends and so he was comfortable answering her questions about his life and family.

"My dad's obsessed with World War II history and he gave my brother and me important historical names. My older brother's name is Wing which in Chinese means prosperity, and his English name is

Dwight after President Eisenhower. I was named Ming which means smart," he chuckled, "and my English name is Winston after Mr. Churchill of England."

Cindy paid close attention, fascinated by what Ming was telling her. This was a window into a whole other world different from her own. Most people she knew named their children after themselves or a relative, or used more traditional names like John or William.

"So why does everyone call you Ming and not Winston?"

"When my classmates teased me by calling me Winnie, a girl's name, I told my parents I wanted to be called Ming or I would stop going to that school. I was a pretty stubborn kid and they finally started calling me Ming."

He never knew his mother had been secretly pleased when he wanted to use his Chinese name, not knowing he'd been bullied about his American name. Instead she took it as a sign he wanted to embrace his Chinese heritage.

Listening as Cindy sang along with a love song on the radio, Ming thought about his mother and her old-fashioned ideas of love. She believed children must obey their parents' wishes above all else, and that meant marrying the partner their parents picked out for them. Love, whatever that was, could come later and grow gradually as the couple came to know one another. Work and family counted for everything.

According to Chinese tradition, the survival of the family was more important than the wishes of any individual within it, Dorothy often told her son. Every act in an adult's life was overshadowed by the question, will this be of service to my family? Does it uphold my family's honor?

Ming heard stories about political oppression and starvation in China and he knew how much his parents sacrificed to come to a new country so he could grow up in a place where he would have enough to eat, a good education, and the chance to make a good life. All things hard to achieve in the China of their youth. He could live an American life as long as he remembered he was Chinese and behaved accordingly.

But now, seated in the car next to Cindy, his heart soared as he heard her repeat his name. Spoken in her soft sweet voice, his name felt special. All thoughts of his mother's traditions flew out the window of the old Volkswagen.

Cindy realized she was no longer intimidated by Ming's serious dark eyes which now crinkled at the corners as he smiled at her. She was glad to see he was much more relaxed. She'd been worried this date might turn out to be a real dud.

Ming proved to be such a good listener Cindy soon found herself telling him much more about her life than she'd planned. She told him about culinary school and her hope one day she'd be the chef/owner of a restaurant serving locally-grown produce.

"Oh, like that famous restaurant in Berkeley?" Ming asked.

Excitedly, Cindy replied, "Yes, exactly! You do understand."

He was pleased to hear her ambitions so closely matched his own. They discussed their favorite restaurants and food for a while longer and then, to her surprise, Cindy found herself telling him her secret, one she never shared.

"My mother adopted me when I was a baby. It was really gutsy for her to raise me as a single mom."

"Wow! I've never known anyone before who was adopted."

"I was really upset and angry when I first found out about it a couple of years ago. The truth is my mother didn't tell me until I found out by accident."

"Really?"

"Yes, I found a letter in my mother's desk with a picture of my birth mother. I look like her. Now I've been thinking about trying to find her and any other family I might have."

"What does your mother think about that?"

"I just hope she understands, but I need to do it. You're so lucky, you know exactly who you are, Ming. I want to feel the same way," was Cindy's emotional reply.

"Yes, but you're free to be whoever you want to be," responded Ming.

Not like me, he added to himself. Sometimes he felt trapped by his family's expectations, and he was envious of Cindy's freedom.

His tone was so solemn, Cindy wondered what he meant, but they'd reached the yellow and red banners of the restaurant drive-thru and their talk quickly turned to food. The night was cool so they decided to park the car and eat inside.

As they waited in line to place their orders, Ming stood close to Cindy while he studied the menu. He couldn't think of anything to say but he was happy just being with her.

When they reached the front of the line, Cindy said, "I really like their burgers because everything is so fresh."

"May I take your order?" asked the cheerful girl in the red and yellow uniform.

"Please make my burger 'animal style' and 'protein style.'"

Seeing Ming's puzzled look, she explained, "It's not listed on the menu but everybody knows that 'animal style' means extra sauce, and 'protein style' means wrapped in lettuce instead of a bun."

Ming requested, "I'll have 'animal style,' please."

"Strawberry," they both responded together when they ordered their shakes. Then they decided to split a large order of the special crispy fries.

The restaurant was busy tonight, filled with families and groups of teenagers with a long line of cars snaking along the drive-thru window. They were lucky to find a semi-quiet corner table and they were soon busy with their juicy burgers and drowning their fries in ketchup. Just a regular American date.

They soon lost track of everyone around them, and became the only two people in this noisy, crowded place, enjoying their first meal together. Their knees touched under the table as each shared their plans for the future.

"Oh, I'd love that," Cindy agreed when Ming suggested, "Maybe you'd want to use one of my recipes in your restaurant."

An image of the two of them kissing as they stood by his stove flashed through Ming's mind. He pushed the thought away feeling it was too soon.

Walking back to her car, Cindy asked, "Ming, are you going home or back to the coffee shop? I'll drop you off wherever you like."

"Oh, I live above the shop. You can drop me there."

"I never realized that, Ming. I'll bet it's really convenient for you."

Ming wanted to invite her up, but he was unsure of himself. He thought it was too soon, and besides, they both had studying to do for classes tomorrow.

Before Ming got out of Cindy's car, they exchanged cell phone numbers.

"Please text me when you get home, I want to know you arrived safely."

She promised she would, pleased he was concerned about her. Was that how it felt to have a caring boyfriend?

Less than an hour later, Ming got his first text: "Ming, I'm home. Thanx 4 dinner. Glad u enjoyed my fries!" This was followed by a smiley face.

"2 many fries 4 u 2 eat alone. Next time, we'll have a Messy Sundae @ Sammy's Pizza."

Cindy laughed, so there would be a next time. Maybe he likes me, she hoped as she texted back, "OK. Sounds fab 2 me!"

"C u 2moro."

In the following days, Ming made excuses to stop by the bakery just to see her and she'd drop into the coffee shop for a quick latte during her break, telling her co-workers, "I'll pass out if I don't get my afternoon caffeine fix."

That made Sarah smile knowing the real reason Cindy wanted to visit the coffee shop. How cute they looked together, she thought, watching Cindy rush out the door.

14

Chateaubriand for Two

That same night, another couple shared a very different dinner. They were seated across from one another in the elegant University Club above Symphony Towers. Marvin ordered chateaubriand for two after an approving nod from Sarah, and the sommelier poured a sampling of fine California red wine. Marvin lifted the stem of the glass and swirled the wine, examining its rich ruby color. He inhaled its bouquet and finally sipped it appreciatively, nodding his approval at the sommelier who then poured two glasses and quietly slipped away.

Sarah felt glamorous in her new black cashmere dress, especially since she'd lost some weight. Dallas's strenuous exercise program kept her moving and she'd stayed on track with her diet, despite her daily need to "taste" this cookie or that cupcake she'd just created at the bakery. She knew tonight her diet would be tossed out the window when she heard Marvin request the special chocolate soufflé for dessert. The waiter told them it was necessary to order the soufflé before the meal was even served so it would be ready in time for dessert.

"Sarah, you look especially lovely tonight," Marvin commented as he beamed at her across the candlelit table.

Lifting her glass to toast him, Sarah simply said, "Thank you, Marvin. You're looking pretty handsome yourself."

He was quietly relieved she approved of his appearance. He hadn't had time today to plan his wardrobe for dinner. Usually he went out to dinner with other lawyers and businessmen who were also still wearing their business suits after a full day at the office. He knew he'd be going directly from court so he'd had taken a moment this morning to select a fresh white shirt and his special red tie which was a departure from his usual dark stripes.

From the moment of Marvin's phone call the other day, Sarah had looked forward to this dinner. A tingle of excitement rippled through her, something she hadn't felt in a long time. The only cloud in the sky came from Craig when he called earlier to say he was spending yet another evening with Jane. He still had a few days left before his return to San Francisco and Sarah was disappointed he chose to spend so much of it with Jane. Weren't there other people in his world?

She wasn't happy to hear about his plans for the evening, but she tried to keep the disapproving tone out of her voice. Jane, again! Hadn't she seen enough of that woman this afternoon at the mah jongg game? Jane seemed to be everywhere she wasn't welcomed. Sarah just couldn't understand why everyone liked that woman so much.

Was her protective motherly instinct blinding her to Jane's good qualities?

"Don't wait up for me, Mom," Craig informed her.

"Don't worry about me, dear. I'll just warm up some leftovers. I'm used to eating alone these days."

Craig barely choked back a laugh. When he'd met with Marvin again earlier in the day to discuss his progress regarding the painting, Marvin said he was having dinner with Sarah that evening. She usually didn't resort to such little tricks trying to make him feel guilty, but she definitely had something against Jane.

Sitting across from Marvin, Sarah became lost in her thoughts about Craig as well as a secret she hadn't shared with Marvin. She still wasn't sure she should tell him. She sipped her wine and shuddered imperceptibly as she remembered her frightening experience.

It'd been five years since her cancer diagnosis. Five years was an important milestone for a breast cancer survivor. Although, she had to admit she was still a little nervous each time she scheduled a follow-up appointment with her oncologist.

Sarah was more reticent about her surgery than anything else in her life. Would Marvin still find her attractive if he knew about her mastectomy? She didn't know him that well yet, and she was afraid what his reaction would be. Being intimate with him meant she'd have to reveal her scarred body. She wasn't sure if she could.

Tonight was her first real date since her husband died. She hadn't planned to date ever again, but here was Marvin sitting across the table smiling at her. Was this the start of a different kind of relationship for them? Their time together before this had been all business, as Marvin helped her plan and set up her bakery and later agreed to perform Alex and Maryann's wedding. Then there was the New Year's Eve coffee and brownie marathon in her kitchen.

"A penny for your thoughts."

Startled, Sarah quickly replied, "I was just thinking what a lovely evening this is. Thank you so much for bringing me here. The view is simply spectacular."

Marvin felt a rush of joy at Sarah's words. Smiling with pleasure at each other, they turned to look through the large window next to their table, appreciating the twinkling lights of the city spread out thirty-four floors below. Above them shone a pale January moon that seemed close enough to reach out and touch.

The chateaubriand arrived at their table.

"Marvin, the steak is as juicy and tender as I've ever eaten and the vegetables are just perfect."

"I belong to this club because I can bring clients here, but this is the first time for a purely social occasion. Sarah, it's wonderful to share this first with you."

"That's so sweet of you to say, Marvin."

By the time the special soufflé and coffee were served, the wine bottle was nearly empty and conversation flowed easily. Over the melt-in-your mouth airy chocolate soufflé, Marvin toasted Sarah yet again, this time with his Irish coffee in hand.

"Here's to you, Sarah and a most enjoyable evening."

He reached across the table and gently squeezed her hand.

Sarah was surprised how the electricity seemed to flow between them. Whatever could have been wrong with his wife not to appreciate this wonderful man?

She lifted her cappuccino in response.

"No, Marvin, it's to us and our friendship. You've helped me in so many ways."

"I hope you'll let me do much more for you," was his quiet reply.

Her smile in return was mixed with equal parts hesitation and hope.

He wanted to say more but it was too soon to reveal his growing feelings for her. He acknowledged the truth to himself, though. He was unexpectedly falling in love with Sarah.

Sarah left her hand in his, and now Marvin lifted it to his lips and softly kissed it.

The rest of the evening flew by, and all too soon they found themselves in Marvin's black Jaguar driving across town to Sarah's house. Sarah sat quietly next to Marvin, surprised at how drawn to him she was. He stirred something in her she never thought she'd feel again.

When they turned the corner onto Lily Court Lane, Sarah noticed her porch light was on.

"Craig must be home already. Would you like to come in for a moment and say hello?" She really didn't want the evening to end.

15

Cupid's Bow

On this same clear cool January evening, Cupid still had a few more arrows left. Several blocks away on Fifth Avenue in the Gaslamp, a third couple was seated under the warming lamps at an outdoor table of a popular café. As Craig and Jane awaited their lobster dinners, they fell into an easy discussion of art.

"I have so many questions to ask about the gallery. I hope you don't mind."

"Not at all. I love to talk about my work, but promise you'll stop me if I start to bore you."

Jane took a sip of her wine and then asked, "What's a typical sale like?"

"When a potential customer expresses an interest in a particular piece, I remove it from the wall and take it into a showing room. The customer is seated in a comfortable chair and handed a glass of excellent Chardonnay."

"Then I begin the romancing. I like to ask the customer certain questions which will help him or her visualize the painting as part of their life."

Seeing Jane's questioning look, Craig explained further.

"I'll ask questions such as, will you enjoy this in your home or your office? Which room? Can you imagine telling your friends how you acquired this piece in San Francisco? Then I start the serious business of establishing the provenance of the piece. Clients love to hear about the fascinating history of the artwork."

Jane could see Craig enjoyed the selling process and finding just the right piece for a collector. She understood his belief that his clients' lives would be enhanced by owning original art.

Over their Bananas Foster dessert, Jane asked Craig how he'd met his partner at the gallery.

"When I first arrived in San Francisco, I went to art shows at various galleries as a way to meet people who had something in common with me. I enjoy the excitement of opening night and meeting new artists."

Jane nodded at this. She knew exactly what he meant.

"One evening I went to a showing of Russian art at the Bayside Gallery and I met the owner, Jack Hillson. He has a keen eye and knows how to buy art that will sell. After about six months we'd gotten to know each other very well and Jack asked if I'd like to be a partner in the gallery. He said he realized he needed a partner to share the workload, and I was a perfect choice with my dual master's degree in art history and business."

Craig studied Jane's face as she lifted her coffee cup. Should he confide in her?

"But now, I think we may have a serious problem on our hands."

At Jane's inquiring look, Craig told her about the problem at the gallery and his concern he might be selling a stolen, or possibly, fraudulent piece of art.

Jane leaned forward excitedly, "What an amazing story, Craig. I'd like to see it and help you if I can."

His description of the painting intrigued her and she could almost see the mother and child in her mind's eye.

Craig pulled out his phone and brought up an image of the painting.

Jane studied it carefully. "It's too small to make out all the details," she said in a disappointed voice, "but it does look lovely."

"Can I show you more after dinner? I have larger images on my computer back at my mother's house."

"So you're inviting me to see your etchings, huh?"

He laughed hoping she was thinking along those same lines. He wanted an opportunity to explore the powerful chemistry between them. Too bad he'd be returning to San Francisco so soon.

Thinking back to Sarah's stern treatment of her, Jane felt torn between a powerful attraction to Craig and a potential friendship with his mother. Would Sarah's disapproval keep them apart? Why did Sarah dislike her so much? She hadn't a clue.

The night air was chilly and Craig draped his jacket around Jane's shoulders as they strolled back to his mother's house. They walked past a café where Carolee and Dallas were seated at a table deep in conversation. Jane waved and called "Hello," when they noticed her, and then she and Craig continued on toward Lily Court Lane.

"I'm so glad we're doing this together, Carolee. After a marriage like mine, I need support from a good friend like you to encourage me. It's been such a struggle to relearn how to date, especially how fast things move now with computers and texting."

"But what about Simon? Did you ever hear from him again?"

"Oh, that whole thing was a big nothing."

"Too bad. Men can sure act like jerks sometimes. Who knows why they do what they do," Carolee added with a dismissive shrug of her shoulders.

Just then their waiter brought them the dessert menu. Looking at Dallas, Carolee said, "No dessert for us. We're dating and dieting!"

When Dallas nodded her head in agreement, Carolee urged, "Let's hurry home. I'm dying to see if we got any responses. And I'd rather read them at home than here in public."

As soon as they got to Carolee's home office, they went online. They were disappointed by what they saw. There were plenty of responses but they came mostly from senior citizens and attractive young hustlers looking for rich older women. There wasn't a single face or description they wanted to meet in person or even reply to online.

Yet, they weren't discouraged, it was still early in their search, and they were having so much fun. Then their hope turned to laughter as they read some of the responses out loud to one another.

One of Carolee's "possible" dates, named Big Joe, announced he was serving five to ten years for armed robbery and would be out soon ready to pursue true love and he hoped she would wait for him. Did she own her own home, he wanted to know?

Then there was the man who wrote to Dallas saying he'd once been a woman and asked if she had nice shoes. Just call me Eddie, but call me, was the opening line of his profile. They laughed so hard, tears began to flow.

After they recovered somewhat, Dallas continued reading to Carolee. Another man wanted to hire Dallas as his personal trainer in exchange for sexual favors.

At that, Dallas turned to ask Carolee, "Is it my picture that's getting me such weird responses?"

"No, it just looks like beautiful you in your workout clothes."

"Should I change the wording in my profile? No," Dallas quickly answered herself, "I was honest. That's who I am. There's got to be somebody out there for me. We'll just have to wait and see if Mr. Right joins this dating service."

By the end of the week, there were still no good possibilities, but there'd been lots of laughter. The two women could hardly wait to check their responses each night. Carolee made several coffee dates, but no one was interesting enough to see again. Dallas didn't make even one date for herself and was annoyed when she realized she kept thinking about Simon.

"Don't be disappointed, Dallas. Tomorrow will be better," Carolee promised her during their nightly call.

"You bet! I'm not giving up just yet, and hey, there's always Big Joe and Eddie."

They had another good laugh before saying good night.

16

A Kiss Goodnight

Jane glanced around the cozy living room as she waited for Craig to get his computer. Sarah had done a beautiful job decorating the room with all Craig's childhood mementos. Was it some kind of a shrine, Jane wondered? It seemed Sarah didn't want any woman coming into his life. Settling herself on the sofa she thought of the still unpacked boxes waiting for her at home.

"Here it is," Craig said, walking down the stairs.

Sitting next to Jane on the sofa, he placed the open computer on the coffee table. Leaning forward Jane studied the image on the screen.

"It's beautiful, Craig. Look how the artist used natural light to bathe his subjects," Jane said, pointing to the left side of the painting. "This certainly could be Flemish. You were right to be so concerned."

She took some more time studying the screen, holding it at different angles, enlarging sections to see them in greater detail. The longer she looked at the image, the more she became convinced she was looking at a masterpiece or at least a very good copy.

Thinking aloud, Jane continued, "There are a few things you've told me that seem suspicious. There's no documented history, it comes from Germany, and we don't know if it's ever been on the market before."

Jane stopped speaking for a moment, and then added in a low voice, "Craig, I wonder if this could be one of those paintings stolen by the Nazis during the war and hidden away for decades. Paintings of this quality seldom resurface in public."

Craig's eyes went wide, "Yes, that's exactly what I've been thinking, too. Paintings stolen by the Nazis are typically sold to collectors secretly and they never ever appear in public. I hope this owner, Herr Schmidt, has no idea what he inherited and that's why he sent it off so easily to us in San Francisco. My partner, Jack, settled the price at forty thousand dollars based on a photocopy and his casual friendship with this guy. Jack never saw it before he left on his buying trip."

"So low a price?" Jane was surprised. "Craig, that's chump change if it's a true Flemish masterwork. It could be worth millions of dollars."

Craig frowned as he answered, "Yes, I agree, but as I said before, I don't know much about this Schmidt fellow. He told Jack he found the painting in a special room in the cellar. When his grandfather died, he inherited the castle and everything in it. He plans to turn it into a high end bed and breakfast. You know, one of those places listed in *Relais and Chateaux*, where people can rent a room in a real castle. Selling the painting would give him some extra money to remodel."

"I wonder why he didn't have the painting appraised and sold in Germany."

"That's a good question and I have no answer for you."

"Do you think he could be hiding something?"

"That's definitely a possibility. Jack doesn't know him very well. They met when Schmidt visited San Francisco last summer and they hit it off. Jack's a pretty good judge of character. He did say Schmidt seemed very naïve about art. This is one of the paintings he sent us. The others are nice but nothing special and we should be able to sell them quickly."

"Do you think you should call San Francisco and make sure the painting is still safe? It would be awful if it were sold before we get to the bottom of this."

"Don't worry, I took it out of the display window before I left and put it in the safe with instructions it's not to be shown or sold until I get back. Jack is still away on his buying trip and I can't reach him. I left a message telling him I need to discuss the painting. He hasn't returned my call yet so he's probably still traveling and out of touch."

"In the meantime," Craig continued, "I hired Mom's friend, Marvin Miller, you remember the man who performed the wedding ceremony on New Year's Eve, to investigate the painting and try to locate the real owner if it turns out it was stolen."

"I remember Marvin. We had a long and interesting conversation and he seems like the right person to help you."

Jane turned to the computer screen again. "It's such a striking piece," she sighed. "I'd love to see it in person. What can I do to help you?"

"You've already been wonderful just listening to me and agreeing my suspicions might be true. Marvin told me he hired an investigator. Could you help me review the investigator's report?"

Craig smiled inwardly. Asking for Jane's help gave him an excuse to see her again.

"I'd really be delighted to help you," Jane replied sincerely.

Craig glanced away from the screen and looked deeply into her eyes. "Jane, I want ...."

Just then the front door opened startling both of them. Sarah and Marvin were returning from dinner. Craig stopped mid-sentence. He closed his computer and they both stood quickly to greet his mother and Marvin.

"Hi, darling," Sarah said warmly to Craig, giving him a hug. "Oh, Jane," she said in a much cooler tone. "What a surprise to find you here."

Sarah spoke more sharply than she'd intended, embarrassed Craig had caught her in her little white lie. It was obvious she hadn't eaten dinner at home alone. She was surprised to see her son with this woman again and she was wearing his jacket sitting so close to him on the sofa. What would have happened if she hadn't come home right then?

"Hi, Mom, Hi, Marvin," Craig said as the two men shook hands. "I was just showing Jane the painting," he said to Marvin.

"I'd love to see it again. May I? Has your mother seen it yet?" Marvin asked.

"What are you talking about?" Sarah asked, feeling a little left out.

"Mom, remember when I told you I had an issue at the gallery with a piece of art that seemed suspicious? You suggested I speak with Marvin and so I did. In fact I engaged him to help me and Marvin's hired a private investigator so we can determine if my suspicions are true. Since Jane has a background in art, I asked her to look at the painting."

Sara sighed with relief. So this was not a romantic tryst after all. It was just business. Her fears about a brewing romance were unfounded. This was just a neighbor helping her son.

While Marvin studied the picture on the computer screen, Sarah only glanced at it. She was happier just looking at the back of Craig's head as she daydreamed for a moment. It seemed like only yesterday he was her sweet little boy depending on her for everything. Listening to her son now, so seriously discussing the painting, she was proud of the man he'd become.

Standing up, Jane announced it was time for her to go home.

"Still unpacking," she added, heading to the door. "Good night, everyone. This has been such an amazing conversation. I never thought I'd be involved in something so mysterious."

Craig immediately got up and followed her to the door. "I'll walk you home," he insisted.

After they left, Sarah stood in the doorway with a troubled look on her face, silently watching them as they walked down Lily Court Lane.

Standing next to her, Marvin broke the silence, "I'd love a cup of coffee, if it's not too much trouble."

"No trouble at all, Marvin. How about a cookie to go with it? I have some cookies for you to take home."

They sat comfortably together drinking a final cup of coffee. Despite the dessert they'd eaten at the restaurant, Marvin devoured a few of Sarah's chunky chocolate chip cookies. When Sarah put their cups and saucers in the sink, Marvin came to stand beside her intending to thank her for the lovely evening. Sarah turned toward him and their eyes met for a long moment.

The air suddenly felt heavy, charged with expectation. For one breathless moment, everything stood still around them. Sarah's heart beat faster as she looked into Marvin's eyes.

Without thinking, or planning, Marvin leaned forward and gently pressed his lips to hers. It wasn't a long kiss, but it was infinitely sweet. As they drew back from one another they smiled with delight, and kissed again. This time he wrapped his arms around her, the kiss leaving them both breathless. It felt so right to have her in his arms. He saw an image of their future together and he could only dare hope she felt the same.

A few minutes later Sarah softly closed the door behind Marvin, dreamily touching her lips and smiling. Abruptly she frowned. What was keeping Craig so long? He should be home by now. The euphoric feeling evaporated.

Down the street, Craig was expectantly standing on Jane's front porch anxious to kiss the beautiful redhead. Their kiss on New Year's Eve had stirred his desires, and now he wanted more—to taste her lovely lips, to breathe her in and hold her in his arms.

She shivered.

"Chilly?" he asked.

"Just a little," she smiled.

"When can I see you again?" he asked, putting his arms around her, keeping her warm.

Jane placed her finger across his lips to stop him from saying more. He pulled her even closer. He could feel her warmth through her dress, the curve of her breasts and her long legs pressing against his.

She felt dizzy and weak as she seemed to melt into him. His body responded and he knew she could feel it, too. His heart felt like it would pound right out of his chest. He heard the sound of his blood thrumming in his ears, as his erection hardened almost to the point of pain.

"Good night, Craig," she murmured softly, feeling a flutter of something she chose to ignore. She moved to step out of the circle of his arms.

"I can't let you go just yet," he said and kissed her deeply, lingering to savor her sweet mouth. He wanted more, so much more.

When their tongues met again, he tasted a hint of the Bananas Foster they'd shared for dessert. As his physical need grew even more apparent and more urgent, Craig knew he had to let her go. He didn't want to but he could read the signs. She wasn't ready for anything more.

Reluctantly he took a step back saying, "Good night, gorgeous," and touching a bright red curl resting on her shoulder.

"Good night, handsome," she replied with a soft smile, her lips parted as though to say more.

Jane reluctantly entered her house alone and softly closed the door behind her, her heart pounding as she leaned back against it. It'd taken all her strength not to pull Craig into the dark hallway to prolong their kiss. She wanted him desperately. Should she call him back? How she longed to, but the thought of a stern faced Sarah waiting for her son stopped her cold.

Craig lingered on the porch for a minute trying to calm the fires that burned within him. Just then he heard the door open behind him.

"Get in here, lover."

"Yes, ma'am," he replied, swiftly entering the house.

"Make love to me," was all that could be heard in the darkened hallway. Their kiss was long and slow and deep. She needed him now, as her body trembled in anticipation of what was to come.

He cupped her rear, pressing her close to him. Her arms wrapped around his neck as he lifted her. She felt light and free as she wound her legs around him, her thighs gripping him tightly to her.

Their urgency was too great. They'd never make it up the stairs to her bedroom. Instead, they stumbled into the living room and collapsed onto the sofa.

"I'm glad I cleared all the laundry off the sofa this morning," was Jane's last coherent thought.

Hours later a very satisfied Craig turned his steps toward his mother's house. He was more than a little concerned about his mother's harsh reaction to Jane earlier that evening. He just couldn't understand what was eating her. He resolved again to discuss it with her and remind her he was a grown man. It was time to find out if she was just over-mothering him, or she had a serious objection to Jane.

When he opened the front door, the house was dark, and he could see his mother's bedroom light was off. There would be no answers tonight.

Undressing for the second time that evening, Craig tried to sleep. Jane's scent lingered on his skin and it took all his will power not to return to her warm bed.

Sarah turned fitfully in her bed hearing his footsteps down the hall. She stopped herself from knocking on his door to ask why he'd been so late. She wasn't ready for that conversation yet.

17

A Face in the Crowd

Maryann and Alex were thoroughly enjoying their honeymoon cruise. Enchanted by the Hawaiian Islands, they explored the unique sights on each island they visited—volcanoes waterfalls, and rain forests as well as delightful shopping. Maui would be their last port of call before sailing back to San Diego.

Breakfast today held little appeal for Maryann. As usual there was so much food, and in the past few days she hadn't felt much like eating. She'd often joined Alex at the gym, but today she felt an unusual fatigue creeping over her and she wanted nothing more than to sit down with her book, put her feet up, and take a nap.

How different this last week had been from daily life with her first husband, Michael, which had been filled with fear and dread. She never knew if he would he be pleasant on any given day or find fault with something she did and explode over it. A tremor ran through her at the memory of his touch.

Michael had been her high school sweetheart, the handsome captain of the football team, a good time jock, and a friend to all his buddies. He'd appeared so perfect in those early days, but once they were married, all the good times ended as he revealed his true colors.

Under his veil of charm, he was a violent sadist who took pleasure in giving her pain.

On a beautiful morning like this, she was grateful he was only a far distant ugly memory and nothing more. As Maryann dozed in the leather armchair bathed in the sunlight streaming through the ship's library window, Michael's unwelcome image faded. Maui drew closer and adventure awaited her on shore with her new husband.

Several hours later Maryann and Alex were seated on the outdoor patio of a flower-bedecked restaurant at the Waialua Mall. Maryann was hungry until the food arrived, but then she began to feel queasy and only picked at her food.

What was wrong with her, she asked herself? She'd looked forward to her mahi mahi sandwich, but now the odor of fish was just too much for her. She raised her plumeria lei and breathed in the fragrance. Ah, that felt better. She sipped some ice water with lemon slices and that helped, too. Maybe she'd take just a little bite from her sandwich.

Alex sat across from her, a look of concern on his face. "You're looking a little pale, darling."

"Oh, no, I'm fine, just a little queasy. Maybe I'm coming down with something."

"When we get back to the ship, let's take you to the doctor."

She patted his hand. How lucky to have a man who cares so much, she thought.

"I'll be okay," she responded. "It's probably too much sun and sea. Walking on land should do me good, and a little shopping therapy always helps," she added with a little laugh. "I have to buy some gifts for our friends and today's our last chance."

"Why don't you give Sarah a call while I pay the bill? I know Sarah would love to hear from you."

He was right, she'd been thinking about Sarah. It'd be nice to hear her voice.

Sarah's first question made her smile, "Are you two lovebirds having a wonderful time? Do you both have perfect tans?"

"Oh, Sarah, yes, the cruise has been wonderful, even better than I expected."

Maryann went on to tell her about some of the sights they'd seen and the luau they'd enjoyed a few days before. She, of course, omitted any mention of their favorite pastime.

"Did they really put the whole pig in the ground?"

"Yes, they really did and roasted it for hours and hours before we ate it."

"Well, I can't promise you a whole pig, but we'll have some barbecues this summer in my backyard."

"Oh, Sarah, that sounds so good," Maryann's voice was breaking a little as she nearly started to cry.

"What's wrong, sweetie? You don't sound like yourself."

"I'm fine, Sarah. I'm just a little homesick."

"Well, hurry home! We can't wait to have you back. Craig decided to stay for a few extra days and I have quite a story to tell you about some work he's doing with Marvin. We missed you at mahj but Jane tried to take your place. I have to admit she's a good player, Maryann, but she just isn't you."

Maryann was happy to hear she was missed, but wondered why Sarah had that odd tone in her voice when she mentioned Jane. Did it have anything to do with Craig? She was surprised to hear he was still in San Diego.

"Kisses and hugs, Maryann, and give Alex a kiss from his big sister. Have fun, you two," Sarah said as they ended the conversation.

When Alex came back to the table, Maryann had a broad smile on her face and looked a little less pale, ready to shop. The shaded mall felt cool after the bright sunlight of the restaurant. They strolled hand in hand, window shopping and stopping to buy gifts.

Maryann found some lovely Hawaiian print scarves for all her women friends. They also bought a carved teak salad bowl for Sarah, a matching bracelet and necklace made from seashells for Carolee and a beach wrap perfect for Dallas.

Next they stopped in front of a jewelry store window where Maryann protested, "No, Alex, I don't need a new watch. Mine is perfectly fine."

"Okay," responded Alex, reluctantly giving in. "But I'd like to find a new dive watch. I plan to do some diving at La Jolla Cove when we get back," and he led her into the store.

As a saleslady showed Alex several watches, Maryann wandered off to look at other displays. Then she saw something out of the corner of her eye. A shadow, the back of a man walking by the window. Oh God, was it him? She felt her knees weaken. Could he have followed her here?

She needed to sit down. Leaning on the glass showcase, she kept her eyes fixed on the window. She knew he was gone from her life, so how could it have been him?

"Maryann, come look at this one. It's perfect."

Turning toward her, Alex noticed Maryann looked upset.

"What's wrong?" he asked as he hurried to her side. "I thought you were feeling better."

"It's nothing," she said as she sat in the chair the saleslady provided. "I'm fine. You go ahead and I'll wait here for you."

Was she going crazy seeing things that weren't there? She knew she couldn't be right, but the man looked a lot like Michael. After Alex paid for the watch, Maryann pointed across the mall, "Let's go to that store next, Alex."

"Now, that's more like it. Enough of me. Let's find something you'd really like. Look at these," Alex said pointing to some designer handbags. "One of these would be a great souvenir of our time in Hawaii."

Maryann agreed they were lovely. It was hard for her to choose her favorite. Some of them were monogrammed with a familiar logo, but she preferred one with beautiful flowers painted on it. It would always remind her of the hibiscus flowers growing wild everywhere in the islands.

Alex insisted they also buy the matching wallet and checkbook cover. She was shocked when she saw the price tags, but Alex seemed so thrilled to buy them for her, she gladly accepted and gave him a peck on the cheek. Maryann was beginning to enjoy herself.

"There's one more thing. Don't you need an evening bag for tonight? The dress is formal for our last night on the ship and I know you'll be the most beautiful woman there."

Maryann smiled at the compliment and then chose a delicate, beaded, black evening bag. Alex heartily approved as he handed the saleslady his credit card.

Shopping with Alex was really fun. Maryann was coming to realize anything and everything was fun when she did it with him.

She gave Alex a bright smile, but then she tried to repress a shudder when thoughts of Michael flooded her mind. He'd always ask her to choose but he didn't mean it. He wanted her to answer he should choose for her. If she did select something herself, he would move closer and place his hand on her arm. Smiling directly into her eyes and speaking to her in a hoarse whisper, he'd pinch her arm hard leaving a welt that would darken into a bruise. If she showed any sign of discomfort, he'd laugh to cover it up.

Denying her any chance to make a decision for herself was his way of showing her he was in complete control of her life. His good looks and jovial manner always made everyone think he was such a charming man and a wonderful husband. They failed to notice her pained expression and the fearful look always on her face whenever he was nearby.

Maryann learned to wear long sleeves to conceal her bruises. As time went on, though, the bruises were less easy to hide, like a black eye, or a broken bone. She was trapped. She was sure no one would believe her if she revealed how abusive Michael was, and she was too ashamed even to try. Everything was her fault. He'd convinced her of that. She wasn't the perfect wife he was entitled to.

Breaking into her thoughts, Alex tenderly patted Maryann on the arm startling her. Quickly recovering, she smiled at her new husband as she took the filled shopping bag he held out to her.

Laden with all their packages, they took a taxi back to the ship. Alex was relieved to see Maryann was feeling better. She'd almost forgotten the fright she felt when Michael crept into her thoughts. She'd been sinking back into that state of fear, but she wasn't going to allow anything to interfere with her new marriage, she promised herself yet again.

Nothing was going to ruin her new life with Alex, she resolved, especially on their last day in Hawaii.

18

Loose Change

It was late one windy Thursday morning in January when Sarah stood in her kitchen frowning at the oven. Then she shook herself and began to slide the warm macadamia nut cookies carefully onto a silver platter, their nutty aroma filling the air. Her baking skills weren't the concern. That was the one constant success in her life, the thing that always turned out right for her.

She didn't care to admit it to herself, but she was more than a little miffed Craig was choosing to spend so much time in San Diego with Jane instead of with her. There was something about the way he looked at her that set off alarms in Sarah's head. Could her son actually be falling in love with that vamp?

There was no question in Sarah's mind. Jane was too old for her son. Why, she had to be at least thirty-five. Craig was only twenty-eight and still a boy, her boy. Yes, she knew there were couples for whom such age differences didn't matter, but Sarah was sure it wouldn't work for her son. Seven years was too much, she thought, as she angrily cut the crusts from the small watercress sandwiches before arranging them on the tray. Half the work of cooking or baking was in the finishing touches. If only she could arrange lives in the same way.

Next Sarah brewed the green tea for the mah jongg game she was hosting today. Jane would be taking Maryann's place again. She rolled her eyes at the thought. Thank goodness Maryann would be home soon.

"She's a cougar," Sarah mumbled aloud, repeating a phrase she'd learned from a television show describing older women who pursued younger men. A real predator. Craig should know better, but he certainly hadn't reacted well yesterday when she tried to caution him about Jane.

She thought a little mother-son talk would help. Instead he said he knew his own mind and it was time for her to cut the apron strings. Jane was his business, thank you very much. Imagine that, apron strings indeed! She was just trying to be a good mother. She knew what was right for her son—even if he didn't.

Sarah realized she was standing alone in her kitchen scolding her son when he wasn't there. He should be on his way back to San Francisco; instead, he was lingering here, saying he needed to meet with Marvin. He seemed in unusually high spirits, and she was almost certain it had more to do with Jane than with solving the mystery of the painting.

A few minutes later Sarah heard Jude barking outside her open front door announcing his arrival with Dallas. The food had been set out on the buffet, and the mah jongg table was ready with the colorful tiles. She smiled as she looked around the room. Everything was in perfect order. At least there were some things she could control.

"Hi, Sarah," Dallas said making her way to the living room. "Wow! Something smells good."

Sarah called out, "Thank you," from the kitchen.

"Have you heard from our Hawaiian honeymooners?"

"Yes, they called this morning from Maui. It's their last stop and they're seeing the sights on the island today. They sounded so happy doing all the things people do on ships. It sounds like the perfect honeymoon. I'm so happy for my brother and for Maryann as well, after all the difficult years she spent with that no-good first husband of hers."

"We can all agree with that," Dallas nodded.

Hearing the laughter coming from outside, Sarah and Dallas looked up as Carolee breezed in, arm in arm with Jane.

"Hi, ladies. Who's going to win today?"

They all answered at once, "Me!"

Sarah tried to greet Jane with the same enthusiasm she felt for the other women, but she just couldn't do it.

Taking a seat at the table, each of the four players began building their wall of tiles when Jane asked, "Are we playing for real money today?"

Sarah was irritated.

"Money? We've never played for money before. This is just a friendly game. I thought you told us you hadn't played very much."

"Oh, I used to play a little when I lived in Los Angeles. We never played for a lot of money, just dimes and quarters."

Jane could see Sarah was visibly upset and her cheeks had turned a bright pink. Could she be angry about something as small as playing for loose change? When Jane arrived she couldn't help but notice Sarah seemed her kind self to the others but cool toward her.

Oh, well, Jane thought, what can I do? I know what's really bothering her. It isn't the money, its Craig's interest in me. She sighed thinking she liked Sarah and if she was forced to choose between her friendship with her or a relationship with Craig, she knew what her choice would have to be. She lived in San Diego after all, and soon he'd be back in San Francisco and she'd be here on Lily Court Lane with Sarah. She wanted Sarah to like her but she couldn't get the memory of Craig's touch out of her mind.

She blushed hoping none of this showed on her face. It was a good thing Sarah wasn't a mind reader, she thought, as she finally turned her attention to the tiles in front of her.

Carolee was "east," and started the game. Anyone watching would have been surprised to see the different styles of the players. Sarah plucked at the tiles as though they were delicate cookies or delicious truffles, handling each one gently as though it might break. Dallas seized her tiles and swept them up as quickly as possible. Carolee toyed with hers taking her time to arrange them in an order only she understood. Jane handled the tiles efficiently as the pro she was, immediately selecting a good hand to play.

Mah jongg encourages players to find their own style. Sarah often chose the most difficult hands as she loved the challenge of trying tough combinations. Dallas played with intensity as she did all sports, and she was a clever and wily opponent. Carolee loved to win and was willing to take outrageous risks but she often made mistakes and was easily distracted. Jane knew all the possible winning combinations of tiles that would win and by watching which ones were discarded by the other players she was able to figure out which tiles they held in their hands.

Even Sarah forgot her animosity toward Jane and played her best, thrilled to win several times. Grudgingly she had to admit Jane was right. Winning actual money, even just loose change, was fun and when she lost, it wasn't that much.

During their break for lunch, Carolee and Dallas confessed to everyone's amusement they were searching for love online. Sarah was all ears. She shook her head in amazement, laughing at the strange stories the women told about the men they'd met so far. To her, this was a new use for the computer, one she was relieved not to need, as her thoughts strayed to Marvin.

Sarah felt a warm glow whenever she thought of him and the next time they had dinner together she was planning to tell him about her breast cancer. She was still worried how he'd react. She hoped it wouldn't make any difference to him but she needed to get it over with and move forward, one way or another.

Sarah's thoughts were interrupted by Jane asking Dallas and Carolee, "Have you considered speed dating? I tried it in Los Angeles and they have the same thing here. You won't have to wait for any more internet responses."

Dallas's eyebrows rose, "How does it work?"

Carolee added, "We're willing to try anything. There are too few eligible men and far too many of us gorgeous women out there looking around. We need results and we want them fast!"

Everyone burst out laughing.

Jane described the experience.

"You 'date' someone for five minutes in a safe place like a restaurant or a bar, and when the organizer rings a bell, you move on to the next man, and repeat it again until you've met everyone or the session ends."

"At the end of the evening," Jane continued, "you select your top choices, the men do the same, and the organizer of the event matches people up. If you don't get a match, you can go home to your cat and your TV. Sometimes you even meet someone who might be a good match for a friend, if not for you. It's kinda fun although it never worked for me."

Carolee and Dallas looked at one another, and exclaimed, "Let's do it!"

Sarah turned to Jane, and spoke directly to her for the first time that afternoon.

"Why don't you join them, Jane? Maybe you'll meet someone appropriate for you."

Jane just smiled.

"I'll consider it, Sarah. Thank you for the suggestion."

Carolee ignored the icy exchange.

"It sounds like a fun way to meet someone without spending a whole evening with a guy who turns out to be a huge bore. And besides," she added, "I don't have a cat!"

Eagerly leaning forward, Dallas asked Jane, "Do you want to come with us?"

"Thanks, but not right now," she said, looking directly at Sarah. Sarah rolled her eyes but said nothing more.

"The internet can be a dangerous place. You should use your head and make some rules to protect yourselves," Jane warned. "You need to be careful about making arrangements to meet your online dates in person. Be sure you meet in a public place you can leave and get home safely without being followed."

Jane had just put into words all the things Dallas had been feeling about online dating although she'd been willing to try it. Teaching safety in all her self-defense classes at the *Seaport Village Fitness Center*, she always stressed caution and instinct. "Street smarts" she called it, and urged the women to use their common sense.

All Dallas's mahj friends, with the exception of Jane, had successfully completed several of her self-defense classes and they were very vocal as they expressed how empowered they felt by her lessons.

"Dallas, I think I'd be interested in taking one of your classes. May I come by the gym and observe?"

"Sure, just let me know when you want to stop by."

Sarah looked up sharply from the table. That woman, she's everywhere! She felt a rush of anger, and wanted to yell "Go away, bitch," but she had the good grace to blush and keep her feelings to herself. Always act like a lady, she'd been taught. She knew she wasn't being fair to Jane but she just couldn't help herself. Her son's future could be at stake.

Sarah was relieved when the game finally ended and everyone rose to leave. She'd had enough of Jane for one day. She groaned silently when Jane expressed interest in joining the group permanently.

"I'd love to be your regular fifth player. While I'm sitting out, I can bet on the winner, and when the hand ends, I'd rotate in and take the seat of the person who was "east." That way everyone gets a chance to play, to bet and learn by watching the other players."

Dallas and Carolee agreed immediately. They were enthusiastic about Jane joining their game but Sarah, looking busy as she packed the tiles away in their box, said, "Let's wait and see what Maryann says first."

As Jane walked home, she pictured Craig's handsome face and gorgeous body. Must she give him up? Then there was the issue of the painting. She wondered if Marvin's detective had found anything yet. She hadn't heard about any progress. From her years at the museum, she knew there were several promising internet sites, one of which was the Art Loss Register and she wondered if the private investigator had checked into it.

Jane felt the painting spoke to her. The face of the child had touched her heart and Craig had touched her heart as well. She didn't have a child of her own, even though she'd always wished for one. She could understand a mother's love, even Sarah's.

She'd help Craig if she could, and enjoy the romance for the time being. She knew it would be very hard to give him up now they'd made love. Sadly, Jane admitted to herself, she'd found a man she wanted to be part of her life, but one she probably couldn't have.

19

A Chance Meeting

The following week the American Psychological Conference on Stress Reduction was meeting at the San Diego Convention Center. In one of the smaller conference rooms, Dallas sat alone in the front row waiting for the start of a presentation called "The Role of Exercise in Alleviating Stress and Anxiety in Returning War Veterans."

There's a huge military presence in San Diego, with Camp Pendleton, Miramar, North Island and Naval Base San Diego to name only a few installations. Thousands of active duty military men and women and their families make San Diego their home and many of them decide to remain in the sunny southern California climate after leaving the service.

Dallas had witnessed many young men and women returning from combat duty with missing limbs and disfiguring scars from the terrible conflicts. They returned with outward physical scars, while countless others looked whole but were not, their hearts and minds deeply disturbed.

Dallas had met and worked with quite a few veterans at her gym. She wanted to better understand the stress and anxiety they brought back from the battlefield so she could help them more effectively.

She glanced down at the pamphlet in her lap as she waited for the panel to begin and was just starting to read the biographical information about each of the speakers when the lights dimmed. The members of the panel filed in and took their seats on the brightly-lit stage. As the audience applauded, Dallas saw they wore their uniforms, except for one—a long-haired blond man dressed in casual civilian clothes.

Dallas strained forward with a jolt of recognition. Was that Simon, the photographer, her wedding night visitor? What was he doing here?

The moderator was a physician from the Veterans' Hospital. He introduced each panel member explaining they would be speaking from first hand traumatic war experience, describing what their assignments had been, where they'd been stationed and how they'd been injured in Afghanistan. Each speaker had a different story, one was badly burned in a firefight, another was injured in a roadside bombing, but they all had various levels of stress-induced problems arising from their experiences.

Simon introduced himself, not as a military man, but as a combat photojournalist. He talked about the searing blast he'd endured while riding with the troops, the tragic loss of his female colleague, the damage to his eardrums and the terrible stress symptoms interfering with his life.

Hidden in the darkness, Dallas was gripped by his story.

"It controls my life in so many ways and hurts all my relationships," he said as he went on to describe his return to the United States and the night terrors that had taken over his sleep and still continued to haunt him.

"I've had only one good night since I've been back when I slept through an entire night. It was because I met a beautiful woman who took me home."

The audience laughed in appreciation.

"But even that didn't stop my PTSD," he added, "and it ruined what might have become a wonderful relationship."

Of course no one could see her, and no one knew it was Dallas he was talking about, but still she blushed in the dark. Would he tell the whole embarrassing story? Dallas was relieved when he left out most of the details.

Simon ended by saying, "I let this woman down and didn't tell her the whole story. I let myself down as well. She'll never know how sorry I am and she probably thinks I was rejecting her, but it was me and my problems that interfered with a promising relationship. I felt like such a jerk, and I'm sure she'd see it the same way."

Dallas was struck by Simon's sincerity. Once he finished speaking, she understood why he'd called out Darla's name, and why he'd reacted so violently to the explosion of a harmless firecracker. If only he'd told me, she thought, I would've understood. Now seeing him, she experienced the same attraction as before, and felt a little better when she realized he hadn't rejected her.

Dallas was fascinated by the panel's discussion of an exercise and counseling program that had been established at a VA hospital in northern California. This could lead to a whole new program at her gym.

When the lights came up, the panel took questions from the audience. As the last question was answered, Dallas started to slip away without being noticed. She'd gone only a few steps when she heard Simon's voice calling after her.

"Dallas, stop! Is that really you? Please, don't go!"

Reluctantly turning, she saw Simon rushing up the aisle toward her. She'd been caught. "Oh, hi, Simon."

"I can't believe you're here," he said. "I wanted to call you."

Dallas stood quietly looking at him, uncertain what to say.

"Don't worry about it, Simon. It's no big deal. I wasn't expecting you to call."

She really wanted to say, it was a very big deal. Why hadn't he called her?

Instead she said, "Well, Simon, it was nice seeing you again and hearing your story. I hope things get better for you."

As she turned to leave, Simon kept talking. "I wanted to tell you more that morning but I acted stupidly. I was wrong not to tell you and I've been sorry ever since. You were terrific to me and I behaved badly. I hope you can forgive me. It's just so hard to talk about it. I hope you could tell I was really attracted to you, and I don't mean just physically. I had a feeling you were someone I wanted to get to know better."

"And then," Simon said sadly, "it all went to hell when the fire-cracker went off. I was frustrated and angry with myself for letting the PTSD take over. I just had to get out of there. Please, at least let me buy you lunch."

Dallas hesitated. Was that a good idea?

"Please Dallas, give me another chance."

So much went through her mind, but finally she quietly agreed.

"Okay, I guess," she replied uncertainly.

The pair sat in silence at an outdoor table in the afternoon sunlight and ordered a late lunch. As they waited for their food to arrive, Dallas thought of the previous evening when she and Carolee had taken Jane's advice and gone to a speed dating session at another restaurant just a few doors down the street.

When it was over, Carolee was frustrated.

"Damn all men. They were such duds. I'm going to be one of those old ladies with a hundred cats!"

Shaking off the thought, Dallas turned to Simon breaking the awkward silence.

"I was surprised to see you on the panel. You spoke so well, everybody did. It was important for the audience to hear your stories and it helped me, too. I got a lot of good information I can use assisting the vets I work with."

Simon looked at her as she sat across the table with the sun sparkling off her glossy black hair.

"I'm still in group therapy and my doctor suggested I get out more and tell my story so once I got home to San Diego, I began to travel around talking to different veterans groups about those three seconds that changed my world. Sharing the story's brought me a little more peace and it's helping me heal. Maybe it'll help others, too. But as you know firsthand, I still have a long way to go."

Dallas said in a soft, sad tone, "Oh, Simon, that sounds so awful. I'm so very sorry about what happened to you."

Putting his hand up to stop her, he spoke sharply, "I don't need your pity nor do I want your sympathy. The worst thing happened that day, a wonderful woman was killed, and I still feel responsible I couldn't save her."

He felt badly when he saw Dallas recoil at his harsh tone, so he quickly added, "I'm sorry, Dallas. I didn't mean that the way it came out. You did help me, more than you know."

Just then their lunch arrived. Dallas lifted her fork and began to eat her salad in silence. As he picked at his tuna sandwich, Simon thought about what he'd just said.

After a few seconds he continued, "I'm sorry if I upset you. I keep saying all the wrong things. It's so hard to be back in the real world while the same horrible things keep happening over there. I've kept replaying that day over and over in my mind."

His words touched her and several times she wanted to reach across the table and hold his hand to comfort him. Would he welcome the gesture? Did she really want to start something with this troubled man? She already had enough of her own problems with her ex-husband, but she couldn't stop herself from trying.

"It must be hard carrying so much guilt and sadness with you all the time" was her quiet response.

"Yes," he said and didn't say any more.

He just looked at Dallas with his bright blue eyes. Feeling himself intensely drawn to her again, he pushed back his desire. He wouldn't take the chance of hurting her again. Yet, he wanted to touch her, run his fingers through her thick black hair, kiss her lips, and much, much more.

He wasn't used to feeling like this, especially these days. He'd begun thinking he might never want to have a relationship again. It was too painful to lose someone you cared about.

As they finished their lunch in silence, Dallas glanced across at this damaged man who attracted her so much. What should she do about him? She stood up, starting to lay a twenty-dollar bill on the table.

"I have to be getting back to the gym."

Simon gently pushed her hand away.

"Please, put your money away. I asked you to lunch."

"Thank you" she said and turned to leave.

He rose and called after her, trying to keep her there a little longer.

"Would you like to see the wedding pictures?"

"Sure. Call me," she said over her shoulder, and kept on walking.

He stood there in the sunshine, feeling lost and sick at heart, knowing he didn't want to let her go.

20

Ching Ming

Ming and Cindy were standing in his kitchen several blocks from where Dallas and Simon were having lunch. That morning they'd gone to the Asian supermarket and shopped for the ingredients to make *moo shu* pork. This was Cindy's first visit to Ming's apartment and she was enjoying herself in his clean and bright kitchen. The fresh afternoon breezes wafting through the open window mingled with the spicy fragrance of the marinade he was teaching her to make.

Ming handed the mixing spoon to Cindy.

"Now stir all the ingredients together," he directed.

She'd already measured wine, soy sauce, garlic powder, sesame oil, hoisin sauce, and cornstarch into a small glass bowl. Cindy carefully stirred it.

"Yum, this smells so good."

"Add it to the fresh pork we've cut up," he said, handing her the larger bowl. "Later we'll steam the pancake wrappers we put in the freezer and chop the vegetables for a quick stir-fry in the wok with the pork. Let's go buy some wine for dinner while we're waiting for the pork to marinate," Ming suggested, placing the bowl in the refrigerator.

They joined the afternoon tourists strolling along Fifth Avenue, the sun warming their shoulders and glinting off the storefront windows. Ming considered taking Cindy's hand but he was too shy. They walked side by side, bumping shoulders on the crowded street, smiling at one another as they went.

Cindy spotted Dallas and Simon having lunch and pointed them out to Ming.

"There's my mom's friend, Dallas. You saw her at the wedding. Oh, she's with the photographer," Cindy said with some surprise.

They seemed deep in conversation and Cindy didn't feel comfortable interrupting them, so she and Ming passed by unnoticed, and turned their steps toward the Martin Luther King Jr. Promenade.

In the wine shop, Ming headed over to the red wine section and carefully looked through the shelves.

"Cindy, I hope you like red wine. This pinot noir would go well with our dinner."

"Yes, I do," she responded with a smile.

She was impressed with Ming's knowledge of wine. If she was going to own a bistro, she'd have to know a lot more about wine, too, she decided.

When dinner was ready, Ming placed a heaping spoonful of moo shu pork in the center of a steamed pancake, folded it carefully on the plate, and presented it to Cindy.

"Here you are."

She eagerly took a bite and her eyes lit up.

"Oh, Ming, this is really delicious!"

Ming smiled at her praise, pleased she liked his cooking. He was having such a good time, but then he always did when he was with Cindy. There was just something about her that made him want to smile.

Cindy looked at Ming seated across the small kitchen table, thinking wistfully he hadn't kissed her yet. How she wished he would. She could almost feel his lips on hers.

After helping to clear the table, Cindy wandered into the living room and noticed the framed photos on the bookcase. One in particular caught her attention showing a large Chinese family of several generations.

Ming came and stood behind her. "That's my family and there's me."

He pointed out his mother and father, his brother and sister, his two uncles and their wives and children. Seated in the center of the group were his elderly grandparents. Both his mother and grandmother wore a *cheong sam*, a beautifully embroidered traditional Chinese dress.

"You look much younger in this picture. When was it taken?"

"Five years ago when we visited our family in Hong Kong for the *Ching Ming* celebration."

"What's *Ching Ming*?" she asked with a puzzled look on her face. "I know about Chinese New Year, but I've never heard of *Ching Ming*."

"It's also called Tomb Sweeping Day."

"Oh," Cindy said, "that sounds like the Mexican 'Day of the Dead.'"

"You're right, it's very similar. The *Ching Ming* festival occurs every spring in China and Hong Kong. It's a time when families go to the cemetery to pay their respects to their departed relatives."

Suddenly Ming clapped his hands together loudly three times, startling Cindy.

"That's to call their spirits. We tell them we're here to pay our respects. We visit each of the graves, sweep away the old fallen leaves, and place fresh flowers and special paper money on the graves—not real money—which we burn there. We also bring food for them to use in the afterlife. We light joss sticks—what you call incense—and their fragrance fills the air and rises to heaven."

"We eat the sweet things at the graveside," Ming continued, "but take home the other food items and they become the centerpiece for a family meal. We exchange memories of the dead and the youngest members who never knew these relatives get to hear stories about their ancestors. That way, each generation has a continuing connection to the last and the celebration gives everyone the feeling the family will continue for generations to come."

"That's so cool," Cindy said wistfully. "I'll never have a family picture like that. There's only my mother and me and since I'm adopted I don't know if I have any family out there somewhere. I could even have brothers and sisters I don't know about."

"Have you given any more thought to looking for them?"

"Yes. I talked to my mom again and she's okay with my searching for them. I was really afraid she'd think I didn't love her, but she understands my need to know who I am and where I come from. She keeps suggesting I talk to Uncle Marvin and ask for his help again."

"That sounds like a good idea. Is that what you're going to do?"

"I'm not sure. Uncle Marvin couldn't find her before and sometimes I'm not really sure I want to find her. What if she doesn't like me or doesn't want to be found? After all, she did give me away once. Maybe she doesn't want to see me or be part of my life. I don't think I could take being rejected again."

"But, Cindy, for all you know, she may be looking for you right this minute. Have you ever thought about that? You should check out the websites that could help you reconnect with your birth family. They work only if both sides are looking for each other."

"That might be a good idea," she said doubtfully.

"I think you should try it," Ming said decisively. "It's a good thing to know your family."

One of the things Cindy liked most about Ming was his optimism. His advice made sense. He seemed so sure of himself and always so calm. It felt great to share her thoughts with him. Plus, he was so hot!

If only she knew how he'd agonized before working up the courage to call her and defy his mother's plans.

21

A Secret Revealed

⌒

Sarah nodded at her reflection in the mirror, "I will do it. I *must* do it. Tonight's the night. I am going to tell Marvin."

For this important night Sarah chose a classic tailored white blouse with her most slimming navy skirt—severe yet feminine. With her outfit matching her resolve, she'd finally tell Marvin about the breast cancer. She owed him the truth before things went any further. Then, if he wanted to make a quick getaway, she'd have given him the opportunity.

Of course, her son knew and she'd told her friends on Lily Court Lane about her surgery, but somehow, telling Marvin was making her very anxious, even her hands were clammy.

Sarah remembered the supportive sessions with the breast cancer group she'd joined after her mastectomy. Through the long painful months of chemotherapy, this wonderful group of courageous people had sustained her. Several women said their husbands no longer wanted to touch them after the surgery. Were they afraid of hurting their wives, or even worse, were they appalled by the disfiguring scars they saw? Some of the women added they were afraid to show their scars, or even look at them themselves.

This made Sarah realize how lucky she was. Her husband Harry had always found her desirable. He said he'd love her forever and find her sexy, even if she decided against reconstruction.

After her shower, Sarah faced the mirror head on and regarded her naked breasts with a critical eye. The surgeon had given her a new left breast, and made certain both breasts matched. But some scars remained and the tattooed nipple on the reconstructed breast had a slightly different look than her real one. Yet overall, they looked really good. Youthful, too.

The plastic surgeon told her beforehand even in the best of times no two breasts ever look exactly alike. Bodies are never perfectly symmetrical, he'd said, and then added she should be thankful things had turned out as well as they did. And she had been—until now.

What mattered tonight was telling Marvin. They were going to try a new Indian restaurant in the East Village. *Que sera, sera*, she thought. Oops, maybe she should say that in Hindi. Well, whatever language it was in, what will be, will just have to be. Tonight was definitely the night.

She planned to tell him straight out before they left for dinner, and not soften her words. She knew she wouldn't be able sit through an entire meal with such a burden hanging over her and she didn't want to tell him in the restaurant.

With that decided Sarah went downstairs and put the white wine in the refrigerator to chill. A little wine never hurt. It might even help.

Marvin called to tell her he was leaving his office, so Sarah took out the wine glasses, sat at her kitchen table and waited for him to arrive. She tapped her newly polished fingernails nervously on the tabletop.

Carolee left Marvin's office earlier the same afternoon. At the animal shelter on Morena Boulevard, she was greeted by several enthusiastic workers who led her along an aisle of cages holding the most adorable kittens, puppies, and even a few dozing reptiles. Although she adored Dallas's dog Jude, Carolee decided a kitten would be a better fit for her. A kitten would be loving but more independent. Men? Ha! The men she'd been meeting recently weren't very loving, just independent and not worth the effort.

She'd always wanted a pet, and the Humane Society was just the place to find the right one. As she walked along the aisles, she was falling in love step by step. She wanted to take all the kittens home with her. They were so cute but she was looking for the kitten that was the perfect match for her personality, really cute with tons of attitude.

At the end of the row, in the very last cage, sat a little black kitten with white paws who walked over to the bars and silently looked up at her. Lifting one paw up to the bars, she tilted her furry little head to one side and looked beseechingly up at Carolee.

"*Meow*. Please like me best," the kitten cried softly and Carolee's heart lurched. This surely was the one.

"Who are you, little darling?" she asked as the kitten stretched and reached toward her. "You have such pretty white socks, little one, just like a little lady wearing gloves. Would you like to come home with me?"

"*Meow*. Yes, indeed," responded the kitten as she rubbed against the bars of the cage to get closer to Carolee.

It was a case of love at first sight. An hour later, Carolee drove home to Lily Court Lane with a purring bundle of fur. The newly named Miss Mittens rode in her own carrier case right next to Carolee on the front seat.

It felt a little like having a new baby in the house, jumping and playing, and needing lots of love and attention.

"You're much better company than anyone I met at speed dating, my darling little Miss Mittens," Carolee told her when the little kitten curled up in her lap "And I bet you'll be less disappointing, too!"

⌒

By now it was late afternoon as Marvin walked by Carolee's house, strolled up the garden path to Sarah's blue door and knocked. Sarah opened the door instantly, as if she had been standing behind it waiting for him. He noticed the tension in her face. A little furrow had even formed between her eyebrows.

"Hi, Marvin, come in. Please, sit down."

Marvin had seen the tension on her face, now he could hear it in her voice.

She directed him to the most comfortable chair in the living room.

"I thought some wine would be nice" she said quickly and thrust a glass into his hand.

"Uh, white wine is a nice choice," he said slowly. "What would you like to toast, Sarah?"

After all his years as a trial lawyer, Marvin could read people's body language pretty well and Sarah's was screaming at him that something was up. He'd planned to give her a hello kiss but sat down instead when he saw how agitated she was. Something was brewing for sure, but knowing Sarah, she would tell him only when she was good and ready, and in her own way.

Sarah ignored the question.

"Marvin, I have something to tell you," she blurted out in a rush, standing barely a foot in front of him with a distressed look on her face. Without further ado, she launched into her story.

"Five years ago I found a lump in my left breast that turned out to be cancer and I had a mastectomy. I've had reconstruction and I look fine but I still have some scars. Even after five years, I'm still afraid the cancer might come back. I can't help worrying how people will react when they know I'm a cancer survivor. Harry was great about it, and the scars made no difference to him. But maybe that was because we were married for a long time before the surgery."

Marvin sat there stunned. It was the last thing he expected to hear.

Before he had a chance to respond, Sarah took a deep breath and continued, "I just had to tell you. I hope this won't make any difference to you, but I'll understand if you don't want to see me anymore."

With that, she turned away to face the empty fireplace, not wanting him to see the tears in her eyes. Her hands were cold and shaking. There, I've told him, she thought to herself, and now it's up to him.

Setting down his wine glass, Marvin quickly stood and went to her. He gently turned her to face him, and placed both hands on her shoulders.

"Look at me, Sarah. I see a beautiful woman standing in front of me. Haven't you figured out I've fallen in love with you? You, Sarah, all of you, just the way you are. I've been afraid to tell you how much I love you because you might think I was just a foolish old man. A scar means absolutely nothing to me. You are lovely with or without scars, because you're you."

Her eyes welled up and a tear rolled down her cheek as Sarah placed her finger over Marvin's mouth to silence him.

Indignantly, she said "You are not an old man, Marvin Miller. Don't you dare say such a thing and you're certainly not foolish either. You're my prince," and she smiled at him, barely holding back the full force of her tears.

Clasping her tightly in his arms, Marvin spoke in a husky voice filled with emotion, "Oh, my darling Sarah, to me you are perfect. Time has only made you better."

"No, Marvin, I'm not finished yet. Sit here and let me show you how I look now. I'm far from perfect."

Marvin was surprised at Sarah's response as she pushed him back into the armchair.

Although she was touched by his declaration of love, she knew she had to take this confession one step further. She felt frightened but was determined to continue.

She summoned all her courage and with shaking hands, unbuttoned her blouse and stood before him in her lacy white bra. Reaching for the clasp at the front, she opened it and pushed the bra aside to reveal her breasts.

"This is how I look now."

Marvin told himself to remain cool and not to react, but inside he wasn't cool at all. He carefully scrutinized both breasts like the serious lawyer he was. Seeing the scars, he felt deep sorrow for the pain she must have suffered as well as great admiration for her courage.

This was one gutsy lady.

Sarah was relieved there wasn't any sign of pity or disgust on his face. Only love.

Marvin spoke hesitantly, and with a little embarrassment.

"Sarah, I can't tell which one is the reconstructed one. They're both beautiful to me. In fact, I'm having trouble holding myself back from touching you," he added with a slightly wicked glint in his eyes.

Sarah was ecstatic at his reaction and allowed herself a small smile of relief. Reaching out she took his hand and placed it on her left breast.

"This is the reconstructed one. It has no feeling."

Marvin lifted his other hand and touched the real one that was sensitive to his touch.

"I love them equally," he said as he held both her breasts in his hands and lightly kissed the crest of each one.

He understood the significance of this moment and it stirred him. He wished it would lead to something more, but it wasn't the right time. He'd wait until he could take her in his arms and make love to her.

Leaning forward, Sarah kissed him softly on the mouth. "You are such a good man, Marvin. I love you, too."

There, she'd said it, but she was still feeling a little scared and unsure of herself.

Standing up, Marvin took her in his arms. He could feel the warmth of her bare breasts pressing against him.

"I can feel your heart beating and that's the real you. You're a very brave woman," he murmured into her soft hair and then kissed her again.

Marvin held her for a long moment. Then Sarah eased away and closed the clasp on her bra. Marvin tried to mask his heavy breathing as he helped her button her blouse. He knew he had to be patient, but hoped he didn't have to wait too long. She was some woman, with or without breasts. The love of his life! You don't have to be a twenty something to find the love of your life, he realized with a burst of happiness.

"If we didn't have reservations at the restaurant, I'd sweep you in my arms and carry you upstairs and make love to you all night long."

"Oh, Marvin," she said, barely suppressing a giggle, "You know, Craig could come in at any minute. We'll have plenty of time after he goes back to San Francisco."

Marvin agreed with her, an expectant twinkle in his eye.

A few doors away, a single but happy Carolee slept quietly in her bed that night with a little ball of purring fur under her arm. Miss Mittens warmed her entire body. In the morning when she awoke, a small tongue licked her cheek telling her it was time to get up and make breakfast for two.

22

The Phone Call

The next morning Marvin was feeling quite pleased with himself, having told Sarah he loved her. He was happy beyond belief she returned his love. Between their romance and helping her son uncover the mystery of the painting, his life had taken on a whole new meaning.

When he got to his office, he found a phone message from his private investigator. Marvin could hear excitement in the man's voice, and he immediately returned Terry McDonald's call.

"Terry, this is Marvin. What have you found?"

"Hey, Marvin. I not only found something, I struck gold!"

Marvin knew Terry sometimes exaggerated, but he was rarely this animated.

"Oh, really? What?"

"There's this Art Loss Register which lists thousands of items that are missing. I spent a couple of days going through the archives looking for '*Mevrouw Van Bruggen Met Emilia*,' the name you'd given me. Yesterday I found an item that might be the painting. The name is different, it's in French, and so I almost skipped over it but the description of the painting matches. It's a picture of a mother and a child and it sounds a lot like your painting. Then I realized that the title had the same girl's name, although it's spelled differently, '*Madame DuPont Avec Emilie*.'"

"Really? Well, that sounds very promising."

"You're never going to believe this! A woman named Emilie Connor listed the missing work and she lives right here in our own backyard, just five miles away, in Point Loma no less. Get this, her story is the painting was stolen in 1942 by the Nazis when they looted her family home in Paris. Can you believe it?"

"Her name is Emilie?"

"Yeah, what a coincidence. One of my contacts at the DMV looked up her driver's license and she's no spring chicken. She's about eighty. She must have been a kid when this happened. I even found a phone number for her. Do you want me to do a little reconnaissance in her neighborhood and find out more about her?"

"Hold off on that. It's terrific news indeed. You've done very well, Terry. Can you just check and make sure she's still alive and living at that address? In the meantime, I'll call my client and see how he wants us to proceed."

Terry's report was startling. A person living in San Diego had registered a claim for a painting missing since World War II that sounded very much like the one in Craig's gallery? Could it really be a painting from so long ago travelled through Europe, crossed the ocean, and then wound up in a gallery in San Francisco? Incredible! It was hard to believe, but as a lawyer, Marvin knew stranger things had happened.

Terry McDonald had also said the painting was registered with both Interpol and the ALR under the name *Madame Du Pont Avec Emilie*. The fact a version of the name Emilie appeared in both titles and was the name of the supposed owner led Marvin to hope this really could be the rightful owner of the painting.

Terry also explained the Art Loss Register, ALR for short, was a respected resource. It had been helpful to others searching for their lost artwork.

"The ALR," he told Marvin "is a cooperative effort among art galleries, auction houses, and insurance companies attempting to uncover fraud and return missing artworks to their rightful owners.

If this is our missing painting, then it's likely other agencies such as Interpol will become involved."

Marvin already knew Interpol was an association devoted chiefly to fighting international crime, but now he learned from Terry it also maintained a stolen art database. This was beginning to sound more and more like it might be a crime of international proportions.

Marvin looked at the name and address he'd jotted down on the pad in front of him, Emilie Connor, listed as living at 3389 Shawnee Lane, Point Loma. He called Craig.

"You won't believe this, Craig, we may have found her. The true owner of the painting."

A stunned silence. Then Craig said, "What? So fast? I can't believe it!"

"Me neither. I'm shocked. I just got the news not five minutes ago." Marvin was almost stuttering with excitement, "And you'll never believe her name—Emilie!"

Craig sat back in disbelief as Marvin retold the investigator's story.

"I wonder if the painting was named for the owner, or if she was named for the baby? Time will tell us more. Her full name is Emilie Connor. She was born in France but she's a naturalized American citizen and has lived here for many years. Here's the kicker, she lives in Point Loma."

Recovering from the initial shock, Craig exclaimed, "How amazing! This is absolutely incredible news. You know, Marvin, I never thought we'd get anywhere with this search, let alone get a result this fast. Kudos to you and your investigator."

Craig continued slowly, "Now, I have to decide what steps to take next. Even with all my suspicions, I didn't plan what to do if the search proved to be successful. Let me give this some thought and I'll call you back."

Marvin was a little disappointed, but he understood how Craig felt. He wanted to march right up to Emilie Connor's door and meet the woman claiming to own this painting. But, he would have to respect his client's wishes and wait for Craig's decision.

"Okay, Craig. You're the client and the decision how to proceed is up to you."

Now that his suspicions might be confirmed, Craig had to call his partner Jack and break the news to him. But before he did anything else, he wanted to call Jane. They'd spent every possible moment together since that first night at the wedding. They'd done all the usual things that new couples do--movies, dinner, strolling on the beach at La Jolla Cove, long walks on the pier in Pacific Beach.

But he hadn't managed yet to spend an entire night with her. Each night he returned to his own bed in the wee hours of the morning. Hours after he left her he could still feel her warmth and her taste remained on his lips. He was aroused just thinking of her. Even though he was barely managing a few hours' sleep after being with her, his energy was boundless.

Jane just finished a call with an East Coast client when Craig phoned. She smiled when she heard his excited voice, then gasped at his news.

"Do you mean she actually lives here in San Diego?"

"Yes, can you believe it?"

"Craig, this is just so incredible! She must be very old by now."

"Yes, and I don't want to waste any time."

When he said that, Craig realized he'd made his decision. He'd meet Emilie Connor as soon as possible and he wanted Jane at his side. Having that reaction told him how he felt about this red-haired woman. He couldn't kid himself; this romance was the real thing.

He'd have to deal with his mother's interference. She'd just have to understand his life was his alone and he'd live it as he saw fit. She could choose—be happy for him or not. He'd made his decision. He wanted Jane in his life.

Craig called Jack who had finally returned to San Francisco. He sounded excited about the new artworks he'd found in Russia. Craig let him go on for a while waiting impatiently for him to finish and then finally he had to interrupt him.

"Jack, please stop talking. I have something very serious to discuss with you about one of our paintings."

"Okay, but why are you still in San Diego? The gallery's been running fine without either of us here, but I thought you'd be back by now."

"Two reasons, Jack. One is a stunning redhead I met here and the other is the painting from Herr Schmidt."

"Yeah, what's up with that? You moved it to the safe."

"I have quite a story to tell you."

Craig proceeded to tell Jack about the search for the painting's owner and how he'd located Emilie Connor. Jack listened with a growing sense of dismay. He'd been looking forward to a healthy profit from the sale.

"How reliable is your information, Craig?"

"Look, Jack, the investigator was hired by a highly-respected lawyer here in San Diego who's worked with him before. Don't worry about the cost. I'm footing the bill for his services. I'm planning to call this Emilie Connor right away. What do you think?"

Jack paused for a moment before answering, "Well, do what you think is right. Do you want me to fly down there? If this woman is the true owner, we have a lot of work ahead of us and a very disappointed German client. We may not get a commission from the sale of the painting, but returning it to the true owner should enhance our reputation in the art world and give us lots of great publicity."

Maybe this could work for us after all, Jack was thinking. We could use it to our advantage.

Craig couldn't wait. He called the number Marvin had given him.

"Mrs. Connor?"

"*Oui*. Who is this please?"

"Mrs. Connor, my name is Craig Waterman. I'm calling you about a painting you placed on the ALR some years back entitled '*Madame Du Pont Avec Emilie.*' I may have some information as to its current whereabouts."

He could hear the excitement in her trembling voice when she responded in her heavy French accent. He was immediately charmed by her and quickly agreed to go to her house the next morning.

"I can't believe, *monsieur*, that you may have news for me. News I've been waiting my whole life to hear. Can you come at ten o'clock? I'll be at home with my friend Pearl and we can have a real French breakfast of coffee and warm croissants.

He agreed and said he would be bringing a friend with him.

"Be on time, *monsieur*, so the croissants will still be warm."

When Marvin heard about this, he didn't agree Craig should meet Emilie Connor without him. But Craig said he didn't want to alarm the older woman by bringing a lawyer with him. He wanted this to be a casual meeting to discuss the possibility the painting might belong to her.

The next morning Jane and Craig drove to Point Loma. It was a beautiful winter day in mid-January, sunny and breezy. They pulled up in front of a small charming wood frame house that looked lived in, yet immaculate. It was painted white with green shutters and a green front door. The well-tended garden was lovely and still had a few winter blooms.

It was a neighborhood of mostly older homes, each one built in a different style with its own personality, so typical of Point Loma. Despite the eclectic architecture, all the houses meshed together as they faced the calm ocean.

How lovely it would be, Jane thought, to live with Craig in one of these little houses by the sea and be lulled to sleep at night by the sound of the waves after Craig made love to her.

Jane compared this to her house on Lily Court Lane where she was lulled to sleep by the night sounds of the city—sirens, trains, and foghorns. She slept peacefully all the same, feeling quite relaxed in her cozy home. Craig was the only missing ingredient in her life.

He held Jane's arm as they walked up the front path to the door and rang the bell. It was precisely ten o'clock.

23

Remembering Paris

While waiting for Craig to arrive, Emilie Laurent Conner thought of her childhood home in the 14th arrondissement in Paris. It'd been steps from Papa's publishing business. He'd often return home early to greet his two girls as their housekeeper Mathilde walked them home from school. They'd find him seated behind his ornate rosewood desk in the study, his beloved painting in full view hanging above the fireplace in the living room.

The girls would burst in with their school bags and girlish laughter, and rush to greet him. He rose from his desk to lift both girls high in the air and twirl them around, his moustache tickling their faces as he kissed them. How Papa adored his children.

Mathilde would start the dinner preparation as Mama and Papa joined the girls in the study.

"How are my three prettiest girls in Paris?" Papa would ask teasingly.

"Oh, Papa, you are so silly!"

They'd giggle as they talked about their friends at school.

Sometimes Papa would show them art books with paintings by the great masters and they in turn would proudly display their childish drawings.

"Here you are, Papa, and here's Mama, and Mathilde, too," they said as they pointed to their most recent work of art.

"So beautiful," Mama would remark.

"I have the makings of two great artists." Papa would add.

They'd eagerly listen to the girls talk about their school day. They never ran out of conversation. Sometimes Papa would read them stories from the newspaper or they'd listen to the radio together. Most often the girls would do their homework for the next day while Mama and Papa helped them.

The sisters would delight their parents with their progress at the piano and play the latest piece they were learning. Noemi, at six, had just begun taking lessons but she already showed extraordinary talent. She'd easily surpassed Emilie who preferred to be outside with her friends. Emilie tolerated the piano lessons for her papa's sake. Those golden afternoons of their happy French family never faded from Emilie's memory.

Neither had the memory of that terrible afternoon in 1942 when she returned home from school to find an empty house—no Papa, no Mama, no Noemi. Not even Mathilde.

The Paris they loved was disappearing. German soldiers were marching into Paris with their shiny tanks and large guns. Emilie had been frightened to see the armed stern-faced soldiers marching along the Champs Elysée. When she became frightened and cried, Papa hid his own fears and reassured her they would not harm her or any of her family.

In succeeding months there were many changes and her parents seemed nervous and seldom laughed as they used to. There were many nights when Emilie overheard her parents' worried voices and the comings and goings of visitors long after she was supposed to be asleep. She often got scared and pulled the covers over her head when the voices grew loud and heated. It was then her little sister would crawl into bed with her and Emilie would pat her and tell her there was nothing to be afraid of.

But Emilie was very afraid and she could see the same fear on her parents' faces. Mama and Papa suddenly looked much older. Papa often stayed late at the publishing house, so their pleasant after school time together grew shorter and shorter, and then disappeared altogether.

On the morning of Emilie's tenth birthday she would walk to school by herself for the very first time. Noemi was being kept home with a sore throat and fever, and was resting upstairs in her bed. Mathilde had left earlier that morning, planning to spend the day with her sister on the family farm, so Mama would stay home with Noemi. Papa had scheduled meetings at home in his study and he was expecting his important visitors to arrive soon. He'd confided in Mama there was trouble brewing everywhere and not just in the publishing business. He looked very upset, his forehead crisscrossed with deep frown lines.

Papa sat at the table with his uneaten breakfast, drinking from his large coffee cup while Mama, trying to appear as if everything was normal, carefully packed Emilie's lunch. She enclosed a special marzipan candy shaped like a strawberry for her birthday girl.

Beckoning Emilie, Papa said, "*Ma Cherie*, tonight we shall celebrate your tenth birthday," and with that he kissed her on both cheeks and engulfed her in a big hug. "We have a special surprise for you," he said, hiding his worry from her.

He was determined his little girl would have a normal birthday celebration. He knew these were dangerous days for French patriots and his secret work with the Resistance was threatening his family. German soldiers and spies were everywhere and even a friendly neighbor could no longer be trusted.

"I can hardly wait," Emilie said as she danced from one foot to another in anticipation. "I've waited so long to be ten years old! Now I'm a big girl."

"And that's why we're letting you walk by yourself," Mama said kissing her. "Now, you must be careful crossing the street and come straight home after school. No playing outside today. We'll be waiting for you."

In all the excitement, Emilie left her school bag on the floor near the front door. Just as she reached the sidewalk, she realized she didn't have it. Her teachers wouldn't excuse her just because it was her birthday, so she turned back toward the house. She quietly opened the door, and crept into the front hall on tiptoe to make sure no one would see or hear her. She was too embarrassed to admit she'd left her schoolbooks behind.

After she picked up her school bag and turned to leave, she glanced toward the living room and was startled to see Papa taking down the painting from above the fireplace. He held a small knife in his hand and was lifting the brown paper backing from the painting. Emilie stood silently and watched as he slipped an envelope into the opening he'd made and then carefully resealed it with glue. She wanted to ask him what he was doing, but didn't want him to know she was there.

With one last glance at him, she quietly left the house. What was Papa doing? Was this to be part of her birthday surprise? She wondered, her excitement rising again. Feeling very grown-up as she crossed the street, Emilie walked down the boulevard toward school.

During art class that day, Emilie drew a special picture for her ailing sister. It showed the two of them holding hands as they strolled through the Tuillerie Gardens, where Mama and Papa liked to take them for walks on Sunday afternoons. If they were well-behaved they were taken to lunch at an outdoor café where they happily ordered *Croque-Monsieur* sandwiches of ham and melted cheese, along with tall glasses of *citron pressé*, the tart lemonade so popular with young French ladies.

The school day seemed to last forever. Papa would surely be at their front door waiting for her. She walked along cheerfully but when she turned the corner onto her street, Emilie was shocked to see the usually busy sidewalks were deserted and silent. Scraps of newspaper blew in the wind. Windows were broken and many of the house doors stood wide open. Emilie noticed cracked windshields on many of the cars parked along the street.

Where was everyone? Was this really her street? Had she turned the wrong way? She didn't think so.

There should be children playing on the sidewalk outside their homes, and women returning from the market with their shopping bags, ready to prepare dinner. Street vendors should be pushing their carts with flowers and vegetables, hoping to earn a few more francs before the end of the day. But there was no one.

She could see her house at the end of the block, so this was the right street after all. Emilie saw with growing horror her own front door stood wide open and broken glass from the front windows lay shattered in the flowerbeds. Mama's fine lace curtains were getting dirty as they blew in the breeze through the broken windows.

Mama would be so upset.

Emilie stood outside the open door, unsure of what to do next.

"Mama?" she called out as loudly as she could. "Noemi, Papa, where are you?"

She called out their names again and again. No one answered as she stood there on the front walk, confused and panic stricken.

At last Emilie worked up the courage to step through her doorway. What she found inside her house was even more terrifying. Everything was in shambles. Furniture was overturned, mirrors were smashed, and dirt from Mama's potted plants was spilled all over the floor and on her mother's best Persian rug, now covered with muddy bootprints.

She wandered through the house in a daze, still calling out for her family. Mama, Papa, Noemi, Mathilde! Silence.

She began to sob as she realized she was alone in the house. Where could she get help? She ran outside and looked in both directions but the street was totally deserted. Should she look for a policeman? He would know what to do, but not seeing a soul, Emilie rushed back inside and picked up the telephone. Then she noticed the phone cord had been ripped from the wall.

Turning, she slowly walked up the stairs in shock.

She found the usually cheery bedroom she shared with her sister had been turned upside down. She was alarmed to see Noemi's favorite doll tossed on the floor. Noemi loved that doll and would never go anywhere without the shabby little thing. Clothes were strewn everywhere, and even her little music box had been smashed.

She walked slowly to the other bedrooms. Again everything had been smashed or was missing. Emilie stood there frozen in fear, surrounded by chaos, not knowing what to do.

There was only one safe place she could think of. She ran back into her room and into her closet. Pulling the door shut, she slumped down into the shadowy far corner with her back pressed against the wall. Unconsciously, she put her thumb in her mouth for the first time since she was a baby and tried to stifle her sobs.

She'd left the house this morning a happy little girl looking forward to a birthday party. Now, she found herself all alone in a scary world, where nothing looked right and there was no one to help her.

It seemed like many hours later when she heard loud thumping noises coming from the living room. Someone was in the house and walking with heavy footsteps. She forced herself to lean forward and open the closet door a crack. It squeaked and her heart jumped. She heard a man's voice speaking in a language she didn't understand. It wasn't Papa.

Even though she was as careful as could be, the door squeaked again as she closed it. She froze holding her breath. Had she been heard? All was silent again. There were no footsteps climbing the stairs.

She breathed a sigh of relief when a few minutes later she heard those footsteps leaving the house but she remained frozen in her hideaway. More hours passed. Her stomach growled with hunger but she was too afraid to open the door. Was someone still in the house waiting for her to come out from her hiding place? Where was her family? Why hadn't they come home? Had they forgotten about her?

Later, more footsteps and this time a voice calling, "Emilie, Noemi." She cowed further back into the closet before she recognized the voice. Mathilde had returned!

With a thankful sob, Emilie burst out of the closet, ran down the stairs shouting, "I'm here, I'm here, Mathilde!" and flung herself into the comforting arms of their housekeeper.

"Oh, *Mon Dieu*, you poor child! Are you hurt, my little one?" Mathilde asked, holding the child close to her ample bosom.

"No, I'm fine, Mathilde," Emilie sobbed. "But where are Papa, Mama, and Noemi?

Shaking her head sadly and looking around at the awful damage, Mathilde was silent, still holding tightly onto the little girl who'd suddenly become her responsibility.

"I don't know, little one. I just don't know."

Mathilde rocked the crying child in her arms trying not to cry herself. But her heart was breaking. Emilie's papa, Monsieur Laurent, warned Mathilde of this very possibility, so she knew immediately what she should do. He'd told her of families who simply disappeared since the Nazi occupation. No one knew where those people were taken and no one had returned to tell their stories.

Mathilde immediately understood this child was in true danger if she was discovered. The Nazis didn't like leaving anyone behind who could bear witness to their horrific acts.

She would tell Emilie about her suspicions, but not yet. She knew in her heart these wonderful people were probably gone forever, taken by the Nazis to be tortured and executed. Her heart ached for the little girl and for herself. What was in store for the two of them? She grimaced at the possibilities. But then she realized she couldn't afford to let her fears take over, for her own sake and for Emilie's.

Mathilde insisted Emilie pack her school bag with a favorite toy and a few clothes. Her bag must be light enough to carry and not arouse suspicion should they be stopped by the Gestapo. They must leave immediately and go to her sister's farm outside the city. No one would look for them there. They must hurry to avoid curfew hours.

As they walked through the house for what was to be the last time, they both noticed that many things were missing or smashed—Mama's jewelry case from the top of her dresser, the candlesticks on the dining room table, the Hanukkah menorah from the buffet were all gone. Much of the fine crystal and china lay in shards on the floor.

The door to the wine cabinet hung from its broken hinge. The few remaining bottles of wine were broken, spilling blood red onto the floor.

The drawers in Papa's desk had been pulled out. The wall safe where Papa kept his important documents lay open and papers littered the study floor. Mathilde searched for the packet Monsieur Laurent had prepared for her with the family records and money. It was missing. She would have to manage without them.

Emilie turned back for one last forlorn look at her beloved house. It was then she noticed something else was missing, something very important.

"Papa's favorite painting of the mother with her baby, Mathilde, it's gone! He always said I looked just like the baby in the painting! He promised it would be mine one day."

Letting go of Mathilde's hand, she darted back to the fireplace and touched the blank wall where the painting had hung only a few short hours ago.

"It was here this morning when I left for school. I saw Papa...."

"Emilie! Come! We must hurry. Let's go, child. Tell me later."

As she hurried out after Mathilde, Emilie saw the family photo album among the papers and debris strewn on the floor, and scooped it into her arms. Papa always took pictures of their family celebrations and Mama carefully placed them in a red leather album along with their birth certificates. Emilie tucked the precious album into her schoolbag and placed her small trusting hand in Mathilde's. Together they left the house, the only place Emilie had ever called home.

The streets were still empty and eerily quiet. They were both terribly frightened.

Emilie lived with Mathilde's family on their farm outside of Nemours during the war years. Their kindness and determination saved Emilie's life. They became her second family, but in her heart could never replace her beloved Papa, Mama and Noemi.

Life on the farm was often very hard, without any of the comforts Emilie had always taken for granted, but she survived and with Mathilde's nurturing, eventually blossomed.

Whenever she was asked about her family, Emilie would retell the story of that day when she was a little girl who lost everyone she loved and was rescued by the courage and kindness of her loving housekeeper. An overwhelming sadness in her chest would choke her voice, and tears would run down her face unchecked.

Emilie never stopped wondering what happened to her family when they and the painting had gone missing. All she had left were her memories and a red leather album full of faded photographs.

The chiming of the doorbell roused Emilie from her reveries and she looked around her cozy living room in Point Loma. All that was in the distant past, she sighed to herself.

Her antique teacart awaited her guests. The white porcelain cups with the faded red roses and gold leaf edges were placed next to an inviting tray of croissants and pots of butter and raspberry jam. Emilie had been waiting for this moment for seventy years.

Gripping the silver head of her cane, she pulled herself from her chair and made her way to the front door. She was meeting a young man who claimed to know the whereabouts of the painting her papa had loved so much—the painting stolen so long ago.

24

Homecoming

The final days of Maryann and Alex's honeymoon drifted by as their ship swept across the Pacific toward home. The weather remained glorious and Maryann all but forgot the frightening incident on Maui. It wasn't Michael. She knew that.

They watched sunlight dancing on the waves and flying fish darting in and out of the ocean. They enjoyed afternoon tea in the ballroom and watching children cavort in the waves of the Lido Deck pool, romantic dinners, evening strolls on the deck followed by lovemaking in their suite.

Maryann seemed to lose her "sea legs" a day or two before they got back to San Diego. The motion of the ship defied her stomach's logic. Just when she was ready to take a motion pill, she would suddenly feel better. At other times, she'd rush to the open deck for a deep breath of fresh air. She thought she'd shaken off the cold, or whatever it'd been, from the previous week, but maybe she hadn't. She didn't feel she needed to see the ship's doctor. It was probably just a touch of sea sickness and she'd be fine once she got home.

Maryann and Alex danced until midnight on their final night on board ship, followed by a loving champagne toast as they leaned on the railing watching the moon overhead in a sky that seemed filled with millions of stars.

"Thank you, my darling Alex, for the most wonderful honeymoon any bride could wish for."

"You've made me so very happy, Maryann, and I promise we'll have many more wonderful times together."

They both took a sip of the wine and then hurriedly returned to their cabin where they made love into the wee hours and fell asleep locked in each other's arms. It was dawn as the ship docked in San Diego at the Broadway Pier.

Unbeknownst to the honeymooners, this was the very same morning Craig and Jane were scheduled to meet with Emilie Connor for the first time to discuss the mystery of the painting.

San Diego sparkled in the cool sunlight of a beautiful winter morning as Maryann and Alex disembarked and made their way home, just a brief taxi ride back to Lily Court Lane. Looking at his new wife seated next to him in the taxi, Alex felt a rush of pride mixed with tenderness. She was a wonderful, exquisite miracle who had entered his life.

She met his glance and smiled recalling their intimate moments. She still hadn't told Alex about her waves of nausea, hoping they'd stop but now she suddenly felt like hanging her head out of the taxi window. She kept the window open and breathed in the fresh morning air, hoping she could she make it home without getting sick. Wasn't sea sickness supposed to stop when you got off the ship?

As the taxi turned down her street, Maryann caught sight of the red door, Number 1 Lily Court Lane. Home at last! Alex unlocked the front door, turned toward her and kissed her deeply. Sweeping her off her feet into his arms, he carried her across the threshold.

"Welcome home, Mrs. Wolfe," he said with a broad smile.

Maryann fought off the urge to be ill right down the front of his Hawaiian print shirt. She desperately needed a cold compress and a soft bed. As he put her down, Alex studied her face noticing the pallor beneath her newly acquired golden tan.

"Darling, you look a little pale."

"Oh, honey, I'm just a little tired."

"Sit down and let me bring in the suitcases. Then I'll make you some coffee or tea and something to eat. I'll bet Sarah's stocked our kitchen with enough food to last us for a month."

When Alex said "food," Maryann clamped her hand over her mouth and made a dash for the bathroom. Alex stood in the middle of the living room looking puzzled.

"Did I say something wrong?"

He heard the sound of running water and a feeble reply, "I'm okay, just splashing some cold water on my face. Be right back."

Several minutes later, Maryann smiled weakly as she sipped the chamomile tea Alex made for her.

"Thanks for the tea, honey. I must have picked up a bug on the ship. Not to worry, I'll be fine. I just need some rest. Honest, Alex. You go to the coffee shop. I'll just rest and be perfectly fine by the time you get back for dinner tonight."

Reluctantly, Alex left telling Maryann to call him if she needed anything.

"You know I can get here real fast if you need me. Don't do a thing while I'm gone. I'll take care of everything when I get home."

Maryann smiled faintly, blew him a kiss good-bye, and turned back into the living room. She just needed to sit for a moment to ease the queasiness. She slumped down on the living room sofa and immediately fell into a deep sleep. Soon a harsh voice growled in her ear.

"You thought you could get away from me, didn't you?"

She knew that terrible voice.

"But I've got you and you can't get away from me. You'll never go anywhere without me again," he said, tightening his hold around her neck.

She was terrified, fear coiling in her body. She couldn't move, she was frozen in his grip. She knew she'd never get away from him now. He would kill her. It'd been useless to start this new life with Alex. She could feel Michael's grip around her neck tightening even more.

Just as she felt herself blacking out, Maryann heard glass breaking and suddenly Alex burst into the room. Michael held Maryann pressed up against the wall but Alex pulled him away from her and punched him hard in the stomach. Maryann limped to the front door and as she flung it open to call for help, Dallas dashed in, Jude snarling beside her. Sarah and Carolee followed right behind.

Realizing he was outnumbered, Michael threw Alex off his back and rushed toward the door looking to escape but was met by Maryann's friends wielding some unusual weapons. The shouting and sounds of breaking glass brought them rushing to the front door still carrying Sarah's baking supplies they'd been unloading from Dallas's van.

Sarah raised a large rolling pin over her head ready to strike, as Carolee swung a cookie sheet into the back of Michael's head. As she did, her large purse caught him squarely between his shoulder blades, causing him to stagger toward Dallas who'd been holding a heavy sack of flour. Putting all her considerable strength into it, Dallas whacked him again and again with the sack, until the seams burst open and an enormous cloud of white powder exploded over them all. Jude sank his teeth deep into Michael's ankle, growling furiously.

At the same time, Sarah jabbed him hard in the ribs with the rolling pin, while Carolee repeatedly hit him over the head with the cookie sheet and Jude continued to cling to his ankle. Alex grabbed him by the collar but he broke away and lunged through the door. He staggered down the otherwise quiet tree-lined street bellowing loudly, with Jude still firmly attached to his bloody leg.

Suddenly, Maryann sat up with a start, feeling disoriented. Her heart was pounding. She heard ringing somewhere. It was her doorbell. Relief flooded through her as she realized it was only a bad dream about that dreadful day. Michael, her former husband, couldn't be at the door. He was dead.

That day had actually happened nearly a year ago now, ending with Michael darting across the street trying to escape Alex and her friends and then being crushed beneath the wheels of a city bus. He was killed instantly. Thank goodness Jude had finally let go of his leg when Michael ran across the street or he would have been killed as well. What a smart dog he was!

With the passage of time and Alex's love, Maryann knew she would overcome her irrational fear of the past. At the city morgue she'd seen Michael's dead body with her own eyes. He couldn't have been in Hawaii or anywhere else. But when would these nightmares stop? For now, she could sleep peacefully only when wrapped in Alex's arms. He made her feel so safe. She vowed she wouldn't let Michael dominate her from the grave.

She stumbled her way to the door, hearing a muffled voice.

"It's me, dear. It's Sarah."

Maryann opened the door to greet her good friend and new sister-in-law.

Sarah stood on the porch, smiling from ear to ear. She was in her work clothes, a white chef's coat with the name, *Sarah's Bakery*, embroidered on the pocket. In her arms she held a covered tray piled high with sandwiches and miniature pastries.

"Welcome home. Were you sleeping? Oh, I'm so sorry if I woke you. I just wanted to stop by to say hello and make sure you had something to eat."

Maryann leaned across the tray and hugged Sarah, nearly crying in her arms.

"Sarah, I'm so glad to see you. C'mon in. Have you had lunch? Boy, those sandwiches look yummy, I'm starving."

Maryann was babbling in her relief at seeing her friend. All the bad dreams and nausea were forgotten for the moment.

"Well, these would be great for lunch and I already left you a lasagna casserole in the refrigerator for tonight."

"You truly are this bride's best friend. Let's eat right now, and you can fill me in on all the Lily Court Lane gossip. Tell me about everyone."

"Wait, wait," replied Sarah, smiling, "I want to hear all about your honeymoon first. How was Hawaii?"

"Oh, Sarah, it couldn't have been more perfect. I'll tell you all about it when we all get together to look at our photos. I've missed you all so much and I have gifts for everyone. Now tell me about our friends," she repeated again.

Reaching for a second sandwich—egg salad and pickle relish piled high on a freshly baked croissant—Maryann realized her appetite was back. She just needed to be home. Everything tasted so good now. It must've been a little bug, she reassured herself once again.

"Well, where should I begin? Let's start with your wedding. It truly cast a spell over all of us. You'll never believe what happened after the wedding. Marvin came back to my house and we sat in the kitchen talking all night. Craig and Jane went off to the Gaslamp to celebrate the New Year, and before I knew it, the sun was coming up and Marvin and I were still talking. Then Craig came home and we all ate breakfast together. It was a perfect start to the new year."

"Marvin stayed all night on New Years' Eve?"

Maryann could barely believe it. The same lawyer who had married them? He seemed nice but....

"Yes, and that's not all." Sarah leaned forward smiling as she lowered her voice. "We've been seeing each other ever since."

"On real dates? Do I hear romance in your voice, Sarah? Have you gone and fallen in love?"

Sarah blushed as she made a show of grabbing a cookie. She wasn't ready to announce publically she was in love.

"Everything is going so well, what with my new bakery, and with my health," she said as she knocked three times on the wooden table. "I told him about the cancer and he doesn't care one bit. I even showed him my scars," she said shyly, blushing an even deeper red. "He says I'm smart, and beautiful, and perfect, and he loves me," she finished in a breathless rush. "Can you believe that?"

"Well, of course, he'd fall in love with you, Sarah. You're wonderful, how could he not?" said Maryann, looking fondly at her new sister-in-law.

"Wait, there's still more to tell you. As Marvin was leaving my house that morning, I saw your wedding photographer, Simon, leaving Dallas's house. I've mentioned Simon a few times to her but she refuses to talk about him. It's so maddening."

"I'm not sure Simon is a good choice for Dallas."

Maryann looked serious.

"I met him when he did publicity photos for my friend Kathy's new antique shop in Little Italy. She told me before I hired him that he'd just returned from a traumatic assignment in Afghanistan. He was badly injured and one of his colleagues was killed. Terri said he still has a lot of issues. I couldn't bear to see Dallas hurt again. She's already had so much heartache and disappointment with her ex-husband."

Sarah replied reassuringly, "Dallas is very smart and she's not going to get mixed up in something she's not sure about."

"Sarah, nobody's smart when it comes to love," responded Maryann reaching for another sandwich. They really were delicious.

Nodding in agreement, Sarah said "I suspect she's moved on anyway," and then she told Maryann about Dallas and Carolee's speed dating and online adventures.

Laughing at her description, Maryann questioned, "Really? They're really doing that stuff?"

"Yes, and I think they've met every loser in San Diego."

"Oh, those poor girls," Maryann laughed sympathetically. She was so lucky to have found Alex.

"But our Carolee did find love."

"What? Who is he?" That certainly was news.

"Oh, not a he at all. She adopted the most adorable kitten from the shelter and named her Miss Mittens. She seems happier with the kitten than I've ever seen her. That kitten follows her everywhere, and of course, she's beautifully dressed to match Carolee's outfit. She really dotes on that little ball of fur and you should see the gold charm on her collar engraved with Carolee's name and address."

Maryann leaned back in her chair. It was good to be home.

"I can't wait to see everyone. Has anything else happened?"

Sarah looked down at her lap. "Well, there is one more thing, something I'm very worried about."

When she looked up at her, Maryann could see two lines had formed between Sarah's brows.

"Craig's been spending quite a lot of time with Jane, who by the way, turned out to be an expert mahj player. My son's so taken with her and frankly I'm worried about it. He and Marvin have been working together to locate the true owner of a painting in Craig's gallery—I'll tell you about that later—and now he's even involved Jane in the search. I never thought I'd say this but I'll be glad when he goes back to San Francisco. Jane's not exactly the girl I pictured for my son."

"Why not?" Maryann asked with a puzzled look on her face. "She's smart, has a good career, and she's beautiful. I can understand why he'd be attracted to her."

Sarah clenched her fists in her lap, and muttered, "You can say that because you don't have a son who should be dating someone closer to his own age. She has to be at least six or seven years older than Craig."

Maryann was taken aback. Oops, she thought, she must have said the wrong thing.

Seeing Maryann's reaction, Sarah spoke quickly, "Oh, I'm so sorry, Maryann. I didn't mean to snap at you. I don't know anything about the woman except she's older than my Craig. I've tried to talk to him about it but I got nowhere. I want him to meet someone closer to his age, not a 'cougar' like Jane."

"Oh, no," Maryann gasped. "Did you actually call her a 'cougar?'"

"Well, no," a red-faced Sarah replied, "but I was sure thinking it."

Taking Sarah's hand, Maryann tried to comfort her friend.

"I'm really sorry you're so upset about this. Maybe it'll evaporate when he goes back to San Francisco. Some relationships have a way of fading with a little distance. A few miles away, or the start of a new year, and poof, they're over. Let's hope it's nothing more than a holiday fling."

"Well, I hope you're right." Sarah's voice was subdued.

Wanting to cheer her up, Maryann showed Sarah a video she'd taken on her cell phone of Alex at the luau. They laughed at Alex trying to do the hula.

Maryann gave Sarah all the details of their wonderful honeymoon. The only things she didn't share were the passionate interludes in their stateroom and the frightening incident on Maui. She couldn't have her sister-in-law thinking she was over-sexed as well as crazy.

Sarah looked at her watch, "So what are you doing for the rest of the day."

"I'm going to unpack, put a load of clothes in the washer, then sit down and call Simon about the wedding photos. We want to see them as soon as possible."

"Well, then, I'll leave you to it. I have a few more things to do at the bakery before we close," Sarah said, kissing Maryann on the cheek. "Welcome home, Maryann."

Maryann yawned as she walked Sarah to the door. It was so lovely having a new sister. Feeling sleepy again, Maryann decided to rest before finishing the laundry and making her phone calls.

She couldn't understand why she was so tired. It wasn't like her at all.

25

What's New?

⌒

"Hold on, I'm coming!" called Sarah as she hurried to her front door.

It was Thursday afternoon and she was hosting the mah jongg game today, but it was far too early for the group to be arriving. Annoyed, she ignored the self-defense rule of checking first to see who it was and pulled open the front door.

"Hi, Sarah, I hope you don't mind my coming a little early for our game. If you have a minute, I want to talk to you before the others arrive."

Sarah was surprised to find Jane on her doorstep. Here was the devil at her door, wanting to talk to her privately. Sarah took in the subtle green eye shadow complimenting the beautiful aqua sweater Jane was wearing with sleek black slacks.

"I'd like a few moments alone with you, Sarah, if that's all right," Jane continued. "I need to clear the air between us," Jane said sweetly, with a smile at Sarah. "May I come in?"

Sarah gulped. Here was the opportunity to speak her mind, but suddenly she didn't feel ready. She wanted to be the one to start this conversation. She felt trapped but her good manners won out.

"Of course, Jane, come in," Sarah replied politely, if not kindly. "The others won't be here for a few minutes."

The two women perched on opposite ends of Sarah's flowered chintz sofa.

Leaning toward Sarah, Jane said, "I sense some concern on your part Craig and I may be starting a serious relationship, but I want to reassure you we're just friends," adding silently to herself, 'friends with benefits.'"

"He's a wonderful man, and I really do like him. It's been great fun helping him locate the owner of the painting. But there's nothing more between us than that."

She couldn't reveal to his mother what a great lover Craig had turned out to be and how far things had progressed between them. But that had to stop, she told herself. No more giving in to their impulses and desires. She had to be the responsible one now, even if she hadn't been before. Earlier this morning she'd discovered nature had answered her plea—there'd be no baby this month. Feeling sad yet relieved at the same time, she couldn't stop herself from picturing a child with Craig's eyes and her red hair.

Surprised at Jane's frankness, Sarah paused before responding, thinking she must have been really obvious. She thought she'd hidden her feelings better than that. Had Craig told Jane what she said about her? She felt guilty facing this honest woman whom she'd been thinking of as her adversary.

Jane studied Sarah's face intently. Aha! She was right about Sarah even though Craig never said how his mother felt toward her. Guilt was written all over her face.

Sarah knew Jane expected a response, but for once she was at a loss for words. She just nodded at the younger woman.

Taking this as a sign for her to continue, Jane said, "Meeting you and having you as my new friend means so much to me. I appreciate how you and your friends welcomed me to Lily Court Lane and I feel very much at home here. After my mother died, I was lost and I knew I needed to start a new life for myself. You've all been very kind to include me in so many activities, especially the mahj jongg games."

A tear slowly trickled down Jane's cheek as she thought of having to give up a relationship with Craig; one which might've developed into the something she'd been searching for. She had to be strong now and deny those feelings.

"Oh, my goodness," Sarah gasped, leaning forward and taking Jane's cold hand in her own. "Don't cry," urged Sarah, misinterpreting the reason behind Jane's tears. "I'm glad Craig is such a good friend to you, but you're right, I did worry it was becoming more serious than that. Not that there's anything wrong with you," she hastened to add.

She wanted to say more but she could hear Dallas and Carolee laughing outside on the porch so Sarah stopped talking and released Jane's hand.

Nodding toward the front door, Sarah said, "Let's continue this later." There was much more Sarah wanted to say.

She walked over to open the door while Jane wiped away her tears and rose to greet the others. The moment had passed.

Looking around, Carolee asked, "Sarah, where's Maryann? I'm dying to hear all about the honeymoon."

"I'm sorry to say she's not feeling well today. She's a bit under the weather but I don't think it's anything serious. Alex and I finally persuaded her to see the doctor, just in case."

For several days, Maryann alternated between feeling tired and nauseous and feeling full of energy.

The other women voiced their concern as they settled themselves comfortably around the table and began mixing the tiles. During the game they shared the events of their week.

"You'll never believe this," started Dallas as she blushed furiously. "I ran into Simon. I'm sure you remember him, he was the wedding photographer."

The others nodded, waiting for her to continue.

"I saw him at a conference I went to at the Convention Center of all places."

Unaware Sarah had already learned about Simon's past from Maryann, Dallas shared his story with the other women. Shaking their heads, they all agreed war was beyond terrible. If they ruled the world, there'd be no wars. They were grateful to be sitting in their friend's living room in a peaceful city with delicious cookies and iced tea, very far away from the strife of the Middle East.

They told Jane they were proud to support the troops by acting as hostesses at the USO. Carolee always had to have a new outfit each time they went to a function, saying, "You never know when you might meet Mr. Right, or Sergeant Right. I do love a man in uniform!"

Although Carolee wanted to ask Dallas more about her meeting with Simon, she was bursting to share her own news.

"I took your advice, Jane. I actually had a coffee date with one of the men I met online. I arranged to meet him yesterday at Alex's coffee shop. I told him I'd wear a flower in my hair and he said he'd carry a book with a green cover. When I got there, I kept the flower in my purse so I could have a good look at the guy before he saw me."

Pulling out a wilted gardenia, she held it up.

"It's still in my purse! He must have been at least ninety years old. His online description said he was tall and handsome but he was actually short and fat—and old enough to be my great-grandfather! He didn't look anything like the picture he posted."

The others all laughed asking, "So, what did you do then?"

"I turned around and walked out, pretending I hadn't seen him. I could barely keep myself from running down the street. I went home to my darling Miss Mittens and we curled up on the sofa, me with a container of Rocky Road and Miss Mittens with her catnip mouse. Then we watched an old movie together."

"So you just left him sitting there?"

"Yep, he may still be there for all I know. I did feel sorry for the old guy though, so I called Alex and asked him to go over to the old man with the green book, give him a very soft cookie, and tell him his date wasn't coming. I've learned my lesson. No more computer dating for me. I'll be just like Dallas with a pet as my companion."

Dallas looked away when Carolee said this. She was remembering the sensuous feel of Simon's lips on hers, wondering if she'd ever get the chance to kiss them again.

Turning to Sarah, Carolee asked, "Do you have something you want to tell us?"

Sarah turned bright red.

"Well, yes, I do. I must confess I think I've found an honest-to-goodness beau."

Carolee sang out, "And I know who it is. As a matter of fact, it's someone I know quite well. He's been walking around the office looking distracted and happy, too. What have you done to my boss? He seems spellbound."

Sarah laughed. "Yes, it is Marvin. I've told him about my breast cancer, and he doesn't care one bit. As wonderful as that is, I do have something even more interesting to tell you," and she proceeded to tell them about the mystery of Craig's painting.

"I don't know that much about art, but it looked like something you'd see in a museum. It's really a fascinating portrait of a mother and baby."

"How did the painting come to be in Craig's gallery?" inquired Dallas.

"It was sent there from Germany to be sold but the owner didn't have any information about it. He only knew his grandfather had it for many years. Once Craig studied the painting, he became suspicious so he asked Marvin to help him investigate the provenance of the piece."

"What does that mean?" Dallas wanted to know.

Sarah turned to Jane, "You know a lot more about art than I do. You can answer that better than me."

Jane, flattered to be asked by Sarah, told the women about how paintings had written histories, but this one's history was missing.

"I already saw a photo of the painting at the office," said Carolee. "It's really beautiful."

"I guess I'm the only one who hasn't seen it," interjected Dallas.

Both Sarah and Jane replied together, "I'll ask Craig for a copy to show you."

They looked at each other and smiled. The tension seemed to be easing between them.

Jane continued, "Craig was thrilled when Marvin traced the painting to a woman who lives right here in Point Loma. She reported the painting lost for almost seventy years. Can you imagine that? It'd been stolen from her home in Paris by the Nazis in World War II. It's a tragic story."

When Jane paused, Carolee and Dallas motioned her to continue.

"Craig and I went to her home to meet her. Her name is Emilie Connor and she's a real character, obviously elderly, terribly French, very sharp and witty. We had a delightful visit with her. She gave us some very strong French coffee on antique Sevres china. Very chic.

"The big moment came when she showed us her family photo album and there was the same painting hanging above the fireplace in her family home. We both nearly broke down in tears when we showed her our photocopy of the painting and Emilie said, 'Yes, that's it, that's my painting. After all these years.' The poor old woman was smiling through her tears."

Jane then told them the story of ten-year old Emilie fleeing Paris with her housekeeper and growing up on a farm.

Carolee's face was animated.

"Wow! What a story!"

Sarah agreed with her.

"Yes, and Marvin's advising Craig on what legal steps to take and he'll be discussing it with his partner when he goes back to San Francisco. After their talk, they'll have to contact the man who sent the painting. Craig hopes to bring the painting here so Emilie can identify it as being hers."

"So, we really don't know what the next step will be," Jane added.

The friends sympathized with the elderly lady who had so long ago lost her whole family and they asked many questions about Emilie.

"Did she ever hear anything about her parents again?"

"Nope. After the war ended, she couldn't locate them or any other relatives."

"Where did she go during the war years? How did she get to San Diego?" Carolee wanted to know everything.

"All we know is she stayed on a farm outside Paris with her housekeeper's family," Jane replied. "When she grew up she married an American sailor and he brought her here to a darling house in Point Loma. She's now widowed and lives on her own, although we met her very good friend when we were there."

It had fallen to Jane to answer their questions as best she could. She was the only member of the group who'd actually met Emilie.

"It must have been a very difficult time for such a young girl," murmured Dallas in sympathy. "Can we help her in any way?"

Jane replied, "It's too early to say. Let's see how it goes when the painting's brought to San Diego."

They all agreed this was sensible advice.

The afternoon went well with Jane winning only once, causing Sarah to wonder if she chose not to win on purpose. She had to give her credit, though, coming early to talk with her about her relationship with Craig. It showed good character. Could she be mistaken in her judgment of Jane? Could Jane actually be the right one for her son? Should she put aside her misgivings about their age difference? She still wasn't convinced.

When she shared her concerns with Alex later that night, her brother looked at her long and hard.

"Do you want your son to stay single and alone?"

"No, of course not!"

"Well then, Sarah, you've got to stop interfering in his life."

"I do not interfere! I only suggest."

"Oh, yes, you do, every chance you get. You didn't want him to study art history, or move to San Francisco, or become a partner in the gallery. But he knew his own mind and made his own decisions, even though the two of you had some very heated conversations about it.

"Look at how well everything's turned out," Alex continued. "He's not a child any more. He's all grown up. You have to trust him. If he chooses Jane, then she's right for him."

Such strong words, and from her own brother. Sarah felt like crying. After Alex left, Sarah finally admitted to herself this mother was finding it really hard to let go of her son.

26

Survival

Before meeting Craig and Jane that morning, Pearl had been afraid they were scam artists of some sort, looking to steal from an old lady.

"Emilie," Pearl cautioned her, "You should have a lawyer here to protect you."

Emilie refused, saying it wasn't necessary.

Now, carefully studying the photocopy Craig handed her, Emilie knew in her heart it was her family's missing painting.

"Miss Emilie," said Craig as he accepted a cup of coffee handed him by Pearl, "I think you should come to the gallery to see the painting before we go any further."

"But, *monsieur*, I am too old and frightened to travel on an airplane to San Francisco. I don't think I can do it."

"Well, I'll see what I can do."

Leaning back in her chair, Emilie quickly found herself telling the couple the story of how her family had disappeared and the frightening days that followed.

"Usually the Gestapo raided houses at night so they could round up everybody but that day they came in daylight. I have always felt guilty I survived. If they had come at night, everything would have been so different—but then I would have been with my family."

The only sound heard in the room was the ticking of the grandfather clock in the hallway as Emilie wondered if her family would have been able to forgive her for her easy survival.

"Although Mathilde's family was protective of me, hiding me from the Gestapo when necessary, they all lived in fear of being discovered with a missing child. Keeping me hidden could very well have led to their deaths. There was little to eat during the long years of the German occupation. Rations were meager at best and hiding me meant they had to stretch the little food they got even further. The whole family had to be satisfied with simple farm meals—potatoes grown on their own land and a tough chicken when they were fortunate enough to obtain one. We all grew lean from hunger."

Craig and Jane sat silently, totally absorbed in Emilie's story as she continued in a soft voice.

"Mathilde gave me my school lessons and taught me to sew beautiful dresses. We lacked fine fabric and so we used rags and burlap flour sacks and any material we could find. I thought of my family every day and often cried myself to sleep at night. I hoped with a child's innocent heart that someday I would be reunited with my parents and sister again."

Blotting her tears away, Emilie continued.

"As the dark time crept by, my wish grew that one day I would return to Paris and find them just as I had left them, at home in our house in the 14th arrondissment. Papa would take me up in his arms and I would feel his moustache tickle my face. Mama would feed me marzipan treats and Noemi would want to play dolls with me. This dream sustained me although I think I knew in my heart that day might never come."

Craig and Jane sat transfixed. Even Pearl, who'd heard the story before, eagerly waited for Emilie to continue.

In a soft, trembling voice, Emilie said, "I had so many questions, ones that were never to be answered. Would my family all be the same? They would certainly be older. Would I even recognize little Noemi? Would they in turn recognize me or would I be a stranger to them? As the months passed and I grew taller, I could barely remember the young child I had been at the start of the war."

Emilie paused and asked Pearl to refill the coffee cups. Her mouth was dry and she was getting very tired.

"Several years after the war finally ended, Mathilde returned with me to Paris. I found a position sewing in a small fashion house willing to train a young girl. Mathilde returned to her family's farm because she said life in Paris was no longer for her. She wanted to spend the rest of her days quietly on the farm."

Emilie closed her eyes, remembering their parting scene.

"Mathilde kissed me farewell at the railroad station urging me to visit and write often, or else she would worry about me. I saw her dab away her tears once she was aboard the train. She loved me as if I were her own daughter."

Looking down at her lap, Emilie continued in a sad voice.

"By necessity I was mature for my age. I was just sixteen years old then and would be on my own. I worked hard over the next few years and I discovered I was good at design. The owners encouraged me to develop my talent and soon my designs became popular with fashionable women all over France. But despite my success, I was desperate to find my family. The Red Cross and other international organizations tried to help me. They were very kind but there were thousands of people who had lost their families and everything they owned in the war. It was an impossible task."

"That must've been heart-breaking for you," Jane said quietly.

"Yes, *mademoiselle*, it was, very much. Many times I walked up and down the street where our house still stood, looking for somebody I recognized, but I never found anyone. It took all my courage to finally ring the doorbell one day. Maybe the new owners would know something about my missing family."

Emilie remembered how she'd peered through the front window as she waited for the door to be opened, and saw the space above the fireplace was still empty.

"Finally, a woman opened the door. She was a total stranger. When I asked her if she knew anything about the previous owners, she was very rude, saying '*Non, mademoiselle*. They are gone. Go away or I'll call the police.' When I didn't leave immediately, she shut the door in my face."

Looking directly at Jane who had tears in her eyes, Emilie said, "Oh, *mademoiselle*, I was devastated. I realized then, for the first time since that terrible day, I had to accept the truth. My family was gone. Only I had survived. I was truly alone."

"I know how hard it is to lose your mother so unexpectedly, Miss Emilie," Jane said sympathetically, thinking how difficult it was to accept her own mother's passing after a full and happy life. There was no comparison with the horrors Emilie experienced as a child.

Emilie sat quietly, seeming lost in her memories, when Jane asked, "How did you come to America?

"I'm glad you asked, *mademoiselle*. That is a much happier story. One spring evening several years later, when I was barely twenty, I left work with some friends from the fashion house. They talked me into celebrating my promotion to assistant designer. It was a beautiful starry night and we were at an outdoor table at a little cafe, deep in conversation, when I felt someone staring at me."

Craig and Jane smiled at one another as Emilie's tone changed, and her face lit up.

"Looking up, I met the bluest eyes and the kindest face I had ever seen. They belonged to a young American sailor in uniform. Taking off his cap, he asked me if I spoke English. '*Non, monsieur*,' I replied after my friends translated for me. He gestured with his hands, 'Will you have dinner with me?' He was young and handsome, with an open and honest American face. '*Oui, monsieur,*' I said, leaving my friends to follow my feeling he was someone special. We walked around Paris for a while and found a charming small café serving delicious bouillabaisse. Despite the language barrier we were able to make ourselves understood. That young sailor was Bill and he became my husband."

The rest of that story would remain Emilie's private memory as she recalled how each time their eyes met, the electricity that flowed through them grew stronger.

Later that night, she led him by the hand back to her room and they made love for her very first time. In the morning, she replied, "*Oui, monsieur*" when he asked her to marry him. He had pantomimed the question in the most endearing way by getting down on one knee and taking her hand in his, placing an imaginary ring upon her finger.

"*C'est tres American,*" she thought before she said "*Oui,* yes, yes!"

Many months later, after they had moved back to the United States, she was able to say "*Je t'aime,* I love you," back to him.

Smiling now as she recalled her husband, Emilie told Craig and Jane, "Never for a single moment did I regret my impulsive marriage to this young man. It had been true love at first sight for both of us. My husband was always so loving and supportive of me. When I finally told him the story of that day and my life with Mathilde, he wept with me. He was a beautiful man with a tender heart and he insisted on helping Mathilde."

Emily, almost shyly, said, "Bill told me he owed her a great debt of gratitude, for without Mathilde, I would never have survived and he wouldn't have found me in Paris. Each month when I wrote to Mathilde about my new life in America, Bill would enclose some needed cash to help keep her family's farm running. He continued this until Mathilde died."

Emily then explained she had been quite hesitant at first to list her painting, still frightened of the power evil held over her early years. She knew it was irrational, but she feared the Nazis might come for her.

"You Americans are truly fortunate. You have never experienced such profound evil," Emilie said sadly, shaking her head and sitting up straighter. "Once I overcame my fear and made the decision to list the painting, my hope grew I might find an important piece of my past."

Emilie had held back one vital piece of information, to be revealed once the painting actually sat before her. She knew she possessed irrefutable proof this was her painting.

Craig and Jane saw how tired Emilie looked.

"Miss Emilie, thank you for sharing such personal memories with us. I'll call my partner in San Francisco and arrange for us to bring the painting here to you. Assuming neither he, nor Herr Schmidt, have any objections, we should be able to bring it to San Diego within the next week or two. How would that be, Miss Emilie?"

"*Monsieur*, there are no words to express to you how grateful I am. Your kindness to me touches my heart. I shall never forget it, *vraiment*, truly."

After seeing them to the door, Pearl turned to Emilie saying, "You must be tired, my friend. This has been quite a morning for you. Rest and I'll clean up."

"Thank you, Pearl, for being such a good friend and being here with me today."

"Emilie, you were right. You didn't need a lawyer. They were very nice people and seemed very honest."

Thinking of Bill and their dogs, Emilie smiled as she leaned her head back on the chair cushion, and drifted off for an afternoon nap. The photocopy of the painting fluttered from her lap and landed softly on the carpet next to her chair.

Emilie had been well-loved by an American sailor with whom she had built a wonderful life, and now she had the hope of unlocking a mystery from her past.

27

A Hurried Return

It was midnight when most San Francisco galleries close for the day, and Jack was more than ready to call it a night. He was back at work from his buying trip. The staff had done a fine job operating the gallery after the holiday break, but he was glad to be home.

Craig was still in San Diego with his family and would return to work tomorrow. Jack knew Craig would be pleased with his many purchases of Russian art which always sold well. The painting, "*Mevrouw Van Bruggen Met Emilia*," remained in the safe and the two men would need to decide what to do about its disputed ownership.

Jack had always trusted Craig's good judgment and he didn't doubt him now. Their trust in one another fueled the success of their business. Jack was the experienced buyer, Craig handled the sales. They complemented one another quite well.

Jack enjoyed being in the gallery late at night. His final walk-through took him into the various display rooms. After making sure all the customers had left, he closed the door to his office behind him and set the alarm system.

Saying good-night to Charlie, the security guard, Jack took his umbrella out into the rainy night and made his way to the restaurant down the street. He ordered a late steak and salad before heading back to his apartment. As he rode home on the Muni train, he thought about what a good day it had been. The Bayside Gallery had sold several collages and one small watercolor of a child playing in the park.

He sighed contentedly, shrugging off his fatigue from the long day and his left-over jet lag. Although he loved the travel he got to do, there was no place like San Francisco.

Meanwhile, Craig was shifting uncomfortably in the center seat of the plane where he was crushed on both sides by large, snoring passengers. Trying to relax, he knew he had much to think about. There was the issue of the painting, of course. It looked as if Herr Schmidt would have to find the money elsewhere to build his bed and breakfast. If it were proven it belonged to Emilie, the painting couldn't be sold. It had to be returned to her. Craig found Emilie's story powerful and tragic and he hoped the painting would prove to be hers.

Then, there was Jane. His heart beat faster whenever he thought of her—her lips on his, her body pressed close to him. He liked to see her walking toward him, her red hair glowing in the sunlight and her smile lighting up his whole world.

He hoped he heard a note of regret in her voice when he left for San Francisco. He'd desperately wanted to take her in his arms at the airport, but his stern-faced mother was standing right there with her arms crossed, observing them.

Jane whispered to him, "I hope we can still be friends." What did she mean by that? There wasn't time then to pursue it any further, but he would.

For now, the gallery needed his immediate attention.

Craig arrived on the last flight into San Francisco that rainy Monday night. He rode BART from the airport into the city, and after a brief taxi ride, was back home. He slept fitfully and was ready for his first cup of coffee long before the sun rose.

"Is the painting still in the safe?" was the first thing he asked Jack after they shook hands and greeted one another.

"Yes, don't worry. It's still there and it's fine. I'm anxious to hear what happened when you met Emilie Connor."

"I've quite a story to tell you, and it all started in 1942."

Sitting silently, Jack heard about Craig's meeting with Emilie, her life story and Craig's plan to bring the painting to San Diego.

"That is quite a story. I wondered about the missing provenance but I'm stunned by what you're telling me. I thought we were getting a simple little painting that would turn a good profit for both Herr Schmidt and us. I agree we owe this woman a chance to see if the painting is hers, but we need to call Max right away. What time is it now in Germany?"

In Point Loma, Pearl answered the door at Emilie's house, and was surprised to see a delivery of two dozen magnificent roses.

"Oh, my goodness! Emilie, these came for you." she called out. "Should I read you the card?"

"*Oui*, please, Pearl."

Who in the world would be sending her roses Emilie wondered as she gently touched the soft, delicate petals of the white roses while Pearl read the card.

> "Dear Miss Emilie,
> It was a great pleasure meeting you. I hope to arrange
> a viewing of the painting at your home very soon.
>
> Best Regards,
> Craig Waterman"

Emilie smiled with pleasure as she placed the vase next to a silver framed photo taken by Jim, Pearl's husband, so many years ago.

Young Emilie was standing on the courthouse steps with Bill and Pearl, just moments after she became an American citizen. Emilie sighed as she looked at Bill's dear face. Both he and Jim were gone now.

"That Craig is such a nice young man," Emilie said turning to Pearl, "so handsome, and his friend, Jane, is *tres jolie*, very pretty. What do you think Pearl? Are those two lovers?"

28

The First Time

It was late Thursday afternoon when Maryann swept into the coffee shop having missed mahj that day. Most of the tables and even the comfortable chairs were empty. A few young men clustered at a corner table were focused on their laptops and talking quietly. Ming was busy restocking the stirrers and packets of sugar. Inside the glass cases which were usually filled with sandwiches and pastries, empty spaces spoke of another busy day.

"Hi, Ming, how are you?"

"Welcome back, Mrs. Wolfe," Ming said, blushing as Maryann gave him a little hug.

"Please, call me Maryann. We were so glad you came to our wedding. I hope you had a good time. We'd like to have you over to dinner one night soon, once we get the photos back from the photographer."

"Thanks, I'd really like that."

Ming thought Alex's new wife was pretty but today she looked absolutely radiant.

Looking around, she asked, "Is Alex here?"

"Yes, he's in his office. Go on back."

One day, Ming thought, he would own his own business and if he was lucky he'd have a beautiful bride too. A vision of Cindy floated through his mind for a moment, but he pushed the thought aside. It could never be Cindy.

Maryann was carrying a small square pink box labeled *Sarah's Bakery*. As she entered the office she found Alex pacing behind his desk on his cell phone looking frazzled. His dark hair stood on end. Maryann knew Alex was always tugging at his hair whenever he felt stressed. He must be talking to his coffee brokers, Maryann thought with a smile. It was always challenging for Alex to find the very best coffee beans for his customers at a reasonable price.

Alex broke into a bright smile when he saw her standing in the doorway and motioned her to a chair. As she sat down, he ended the conversation quickly and came around his desk to kiss his new bride.

"You're just what I needed. All day I've been wanting to be at home with you. So tell me, what did the doctor say?"

Maryann handed him the box. "Before I tell you, I've brought you a little treat."

Alex took the box and put it on his desk. Maryann reached over and picked it up and placed it back in his hand.

"No, sweetheart, you have to open it right now. I had Sarah bake this especially for you. After you open it, then I'll tell you what the doctor said."

Alex impatiently opened the box, trying to conceal how worried he'd been about Maryann. He pulled out the cookie.

"Nice cookie," he said.

With a very serious look on her face, Maryann said, "Well, Alex, I have been nauseous in the mornings and you insisted I see the doctor today."

"Maryann, what did he say? You're worrying me."

"Alex, please, first look at the cookie. It's very special."

Cookies, especially fortune cookies, had a very special meaning for them.

Looking down at the boat shaped cookie, he read the little letters out loud, "SS Baby. What does SS Baby mean?"

"Duh, Alex. It's our SS Baby!"

Alex still didn't get it.

"Do you want to go on another cruise so soon? We just got home."

Finally Maryann took pity on Alex, and throwing her arms around him, she laughed with joy.

"No, sweetheart, it's a baby. We're going to have a baby. I probably had some sort of bug while we were on the ship, but I'm not sick at all, now. I'm pregnant!"

Alex fell back and sat down hard on the desktop.

"You're what?" he said, looking stunned.

"I'm pregnant! You're going to be a father."

Slowly a smile spread across his face, and his look of confusion gave way to one of pure elation.

"A baby, our baby? Wow! I can't believe it!"

Maryann said with a little grin, "I was shocked, too, but then the doctor said morning sickness can start as soon as two weeks after conception. It must have happened on our wedding night. It was such a glorious night, second only to the very first time we made love."

Three months had passed since that first night, but the memory hadn't dimmed even a little in Maryann's mind. She recalled opening the door that evening and smelling both Alex's spicy aftershave and the delicious fragrance of hot Chinese food. Fresh from her bath, she was wearing casual pants and a white tee shirt Sarah had given her with the bakery's name on it.

"Special delivery for my favorite girl! Here's the fancy dinner I promised you."

They both laughed as Alex followed Maryann into the kitchen. She was taking two plates from the cupboard when Alex came up behind her and slipping his arms around her waist, he rested his chin on top of her head.

"You smell great," he murmured into her freshly washed hair. He nudged her head to the side so he could kiss her throat and he began trailing sweet soft caresses all the way around her neck and up to her ear. His tongue worked behind and around her ear sending a shiver through her whole body.

"You taste so sweet, so delicious."

He slid his hands up under her tee shirt and cupped her breasts. Maryann gasped as she felt her nipples harden and elongate beneath his thumbs. She felt the length of his body pressed against her back. His erection strained hot and huge against her backside.

"Oh, Alex, that feels so good," she murmured a little shyly.

Alex slid both his hands downward, slipping his thumbs under the waistband of her panties. He caressed her bare behind and eventually found his way around to her flat belly and below, deftly using two fingers to circle her moist center and then gently ease inside her. He sensed exactly how to touch her, arousing her totally as she stood there. Was tonight finally going to be the night?

She felt the ground slipping away as her legs began to tremble. Tension was building, building, building.

"Oh Alex," she moaned as she melted back into him.

Just when she thought she could take no more, Alex gently turned her around and pushed her clothes down into a heap on the floor. She wrapped her arms around his neck and tangled her fingers in his thick dark hair. Pulling back a little, she looked deeply into his eyes. She could see the desire burning there.

"I want you so much," he said hoarsely, tightly holding her even closer to him.

Alex kissed her fiercely—a kiss filled with all the pent-up desire surging inside him. He easily lifted her onto the counter. The granite felt cool to her fevered flesh. His hunger had become so powerful it took every ounce of his self-control to stop himself from moving too fast.

Maryann's fingers traced his hard muscled chest as she parted her thighs and pulled him closer against her, but Alex shook his head.

"Not here, my love. I want to see all of you and touch you and taste every part of your body. I want to see the passion in your eyes. I want to hear you cry out in pleasure."

He'd been so patient all these past months, understanding her reluctance to make love. But he couldn't wait any longer.

She drew back a little, Alex's words making her anxious. He wanted to see her? What would he think? She wasn't a young girl anymore. She wasn't tall and slim. Her body wasn't perfect. Would he still want her after he saw her? Could she go through with this after all?

As if reading her thoughts, Alex reassured her, "You're lovelier than any woman could ever be. You're the woman I've been waiting for."

And straight out of one of the romance novels she loved to read, he swept her up in his arms and carried her up the stairs. She was floating, feeling light as a feather and breathless as Alex slowly walked her backward toward the bed. Carefully setting her down, he bent his head and his lips glided from one breast to the other.

"You are so beautiful," he whispered and circled her nipple with his tongue before pulling it more deeply into his mouth and softly sucking it.

Maryann moaned as she twisted her fingers through his hair, her breath short and shallow.

Trailing kisses down her body, his lips caressed all of her. On his knees, he parted her legs, and teased open the folds of her sex with his tongue, tasting the very essence of her. Grasping his shoulders, Maryann shuddered as she spun out of control in a crescendo of explosions that pushed her right over the edge.

"Oh, Alex," she cried as she exploded with wave after wave of exquisite release. She could no longer remain standing.

Alex rasped, "I can't hold back any more."

All Maryann was able to do was whisper "Oh, please, yes," as Alex lowered her to the bed.

Cupping her face between his hands, he spoke the words she'd longed to hear.

"Maryann, do you know how much I love you? I love you with all my heart, and body, now and forever."

As he kissed her, she could taste herself on his lips.

He quickly tossed his clothes on the floor and lowered himself onto her making sure he didn't crush her with his weight.

Looking deep into her eyes, he said, "I love you and I want to be deep inside you. Right now."

Maryann was finally ready to say the words Alex longed to hear.

"Alex, I love you, too. I want you. Yes, now."

He gasped as he entered her for the very first time.

"This is where I was meant to be," he said, looking intently into her eyes. "You're so tight. I don't want to hurt you."

"Alex, you'll never hurt me."

Hearing this, he began to move, at first so slowly over and over, and yet again, stretching her to accommodate him. Finally he thrust deeply into her and she came apart beneath him. Hearts pounding, they gloried in the aftershocks of their lovemaking.

Alex smiled at Maryann's glowing face.

"Darling, I have a brilliant idea. Stay right here. We're going to have us a little picnic in bed. You don't think I'd let you get away so fast, did you?"

He laughed as he bounded naked out of bed, and pulling on his boxers, he went downstairs to retrieve the Chinese food cartons from the kitchen.

For a moment Maryann stretched luxuriously basking in the afterglow, feeling totally fulfilled as she never had before. Getting up, she found a long tee shirt and shorts in her closet. She returned to the bed just as Alex entered the room carrying food containers and chopsticks.

"That's not fair," Alex said as he came back. "You got dressed. I prefer you naked!"

Maryann giggled as she helped Alex set the food out right on the bed. Placing large white napkins in their laps, they sat cross-legged opposite each other with their knees touching. They took turns feeding each other bites of food directly from the containers. Alex was an expert with chopsticks and he showed her how to use them.

"Alex, this is delicious. I didn't realize how hungry I was until I started eating."

"A good workout will do that to you."

They both laughed.

After a valiant struggle, Maryann put down her chopsticks in exasperation and used her fingers to eat the rest of her food.

She popped a large fantail shrimp into Alex's mouth and then she did the same for herself.

"If I had to rely on chopsticks every day I'd go hungry," she chuckled.

"I'd never let that happen," Alex said, as he dipped a crispy wonton into the sweet and sour sauce. Holding his hand under it so it wouldn't drip, he fed it to Maryann.

After they'd eaten their fill, Alex opened the plastic bag of fortune cookies.

"Dessert time," he announced. "Let's not forget these."

"Oh, Alex, please, I'm just so full. Maybe I'll try one later."

"No, these fortune cookies are very special. It'll be fun to read our fortunes together," Alex said, looking at her expectantly.

Maryann took the cookie Alex held out to her and snapped it open. She nibbled on the crunchy sweetness, until Alex urged impatiently, "Well, what does it say?"

"What?"

"Your fortune! What does it say?"

"But Alex, they never say much of anything".

With that, Maryann pulled out the strip of paper and read the message. There, in large block letters, was printed, "Maryann, I love you. Will you marry me?"

Maryann looked up at Alex, her eyes shining with surprise and unshed tears of joy.

"Alex! This is amazing! How did you do this?"

"Simple. I had all the cookies made with the same question. Well, what's your answer?"

She looked at him sitting across from her and without pausing for even a second she answered, "Yes, Alex. Yes!"

"Please be sure. You know I might not be able to give you a child."

Maryann placed her finger across his lips. "Hush, Alex, we've talked about that before. You're all I want."

"You've made me the happiest man in the world," Alex exclaimed as he leaped from the bed, almost upsetting the nearly empty food containers.

Maryann laughed watching his quick save before the soy sauce spilled. He leaned over and kissed her so tenderly Maryann felt she was the most cherished woman of all time.

Their next kiss grew into a passionate interlude, and there amidst all the napkins and chopsticks they made love again. This time it was slow and lingering but no less exhilarating as they explored each other's bodies.

All Maryann could do was gasp, "Oh, Alex, more," as stars exploded behind her eyelids.

Now, here she was, carrying Alex's child, giving him the most cherished gift a woman can give the man she loves.

Alex grabbed Maryann and spun her around, saying, "You copy cat! You used my cookie trick again! I love it! Thank you, my darling wife. A life with you and a family of our own are what I want most."

"Are you sure you're okay with this, Alex? I know we didn't plan on having a baby."

"Okay with this? A baby, our baby? This is the best news you could've given me. Do we have enough room for a nursery or should we start looking for a bigger house?"

"No, darling, our house is perfect for a baby. We have plenty of room. We're not ready to leave Lily Court Lane just yet." And not for a very long time she thought to herself.

Barely containing himself, Alex pulled her outside his office and into the coffee shop, shouting "Hey everyone, we have a big announcement to make. We're having a baby!"

At this news, the staff burst into applause, and even the men playing chess at the corner table looked up and clapped. One look at the happy couple and everyone could see how much in love they were.

"Coffee's on the house," Alex announced.

29

It's My Choice

Ming watched Alex and Maryann as they floated around the coffee shop. He was envious. Would he ever have someone in his life he loved so much?

He thought of his parents. He'd never seen them kiss or show any affection toward one another, at least not in public. For many years, he'd wondered if they even liked one another. Theirs was a typical arranged Asian marriage, a match made by their parents, a young couple who'd work hard and have a family.

Love? He thought if he asked either parent about it, they would probably scoff at the very notion. For them, marriage meant business, not love.

When the family had determined it was the right time for Ming's father to marry, Lloyd had followed his father's command and was promised to Dorothy Choi, the daughter of his father's business partner. Lloyd's only other alternative was to return to the family's village in China where a matchmaker would've shown him photos of the young women she deemed suitable candidates for him. He would then select a photo he liked and the couple would meet briefly under the watchful eyes of their parents.

But what Ming didn't know was his father had already met Dorothy at family gatherings and, secretly, he liked what he saw. She was petite and smiled shyly at him, so it was easy to agree with his father's plan. Marriage to Dorothy would cement relations between the Choi and Sun families. Dorothy's horoscope was auspicious and her dowry sufficient to please his family. Lloyd was more than satisfied with his parents' choice of a bride for him.

Ming wanted to marry for love just like Alex and Maryann and his marriage to be far different from his parents'. He thought of Cindy again. He was so attracted to her, but more than chemistry, she was so much fun and had goals for her life he admired. But the simple truth was she wasn't Chinese and that would be a huge obstacle for his family. Not for him. He knew what he wanted.

Later that afternoon, Ming and Cindy walked along the Martin Luther King Jr. Promenade toward the fountains where in the summertime laughing children would run through the spray. It was a typical San Diego scene just before dinnertime in mid-February. On restaurant patios, heat lamps glowed orange warming the sweater-clad patrons who were enjoying their wine and appetizers.

When Ming told Cindy about Maryann and Alex's big announcement, Cindy's reply surprised him.

"Yes, I already knew. As a matter of fact, Sarah was the first to know but we were all sworn to secrecy until Maryann told Alex."

Then Cindy told him about the cookie. At first, Ming didn't understand why it was a joke. Having a baby was serious business in his world. Then he shook his head and smiled.

"Ming, I'm getting hungry. How about sushi?"

Ming didn't care what they ate, he was so happy just being with her. The blue streaks in her black hair shone in the dusky light, and she was dressed in her usual black leather jacket and jeans. She was the most beautiful girl he'd ever seen.

So what if she wasn't Chinese. Cindy had captured his heart and he hoped she felt the same. No, he would not have an arranged marriage despite all his mother's schemes.

Impulsively, Ming turned to Cindy and lowering his lips to hers, met hers for the first time. She opened her soft lips beneath his and he deepened the kiss, sending tingles through her.

She pulled back for a moment a little surprsied, and looked up into his face.

"Well, it's about time, Ming!"

Then throwing her arms around his neck, she planted a fierce kiss on his lips unlike any he'd ever known, one he hoped to repeat again—and soon.

Even though they were in public, they stood locked in each other's arms for a few long moments. Dog walkers and tourists smiled and parted to walk around them.

A young bike rider called out as he rode by, "Hey, guys, get a room!"

With that comment, the couple broke apart laughing, and resumed their walk. But this time they were holding hands. Ming was in heaven, and Cindy beamed as they walked along.

The night was young and so were they.

30

A Nightmare Shared

Simon sat with Maryann and Alex while they ordered almost every picture he'd taken of their wedding. When they told him about the coming baby, Simon, of course, congratulated them but privately, he was envious they could have so much trust in a future he strongly doubted. Even though time had passed since his return from Afghanistan, every day still remained a challenge for him.

After leaving them, he sat in his van for a few minutes and then surprised himself by phoning Dallas. He did it not knowing what kind of reaction she'd have.

"Hi, Dallas, It's Simon. I promised to show you the wedding pictures. I'm still on Lily Court Lane so if you have some time, would you like to see them now?"

"Oh, hello, Simon," Dallas answered, surpised. "Well, I guess so," she said hesitantly; her curiosity winning over her caution.

"I'll be right there."

Dallas went to her window and saw Simon getting out of his van. Her heart thumped. Was this a mistake?

Now, here he was sitting comfortably on her sofa showing her the photographs. Sitting next to her made him feel relaxed and at peace, and reaching down, he patted Jude lying at his feet. He was still feeling guilty about the New Year's Eve they shared and his callous exit the following morning. He had chastised himself repeatedly wishing she would forgive him. He'd apologized for his rudeness when he took her to lunch, but still wished he'd called her the very next day. Every time he wanted to, something held him back.

He seemed to be wallowing in guilt and self-pity. He told himself he had to pull himself out of this hole. This wasn't the way he wanted to live his life.

As he glanced at Dallas with her long legs curled under her, dressed simply in a UCSD sweatshirt and jeans, he was aware of the special woman she was. He was drawn to her and suspected that many men would want her. She certainly deserved better than a broken down photographer still suffering from the trauma of his war experience.

Interrupting his dismal thoughts, Dallas said, "Simon, these are wonderful photos," as she closely studied the images on his lap top.

"I'm glad you like them."

"But Simon, there are far too many of me."

"Forgive me, Dallas, I couldn't help myself. I shot what I saw, a beautiful woman."

When she said "thank you" and looked into his eyes, Simon felt a sinking sensation. Would he flee from her this time? He hoped not.

Later that night, Dallas awoke with a start. Darkness still shrouded the houses on Lily Court Lane. As her eyes adjusted to the darkened room, she realized Simon was no longer beside her. Yes, they'd ended up in her bed again, making electrifying love this time, and then they'd fallen asleep in each other's arms, Simon holding her naked body tightly against his own.

But now she found him standing at the open window across the room. His handsome nude body was silhouetted in the moonlight. She went to stand next to him and as she gently touched his arm, he turned toward her.

"Go back to bed, Dallas," he sighed. "It's the same old thing for me. I have such a hard time sleeping and I have the same nightmare again and again. I keep replaying that roadside explosion. No matter how much counseling I get, that day keeps haunting me."

Dallas spoke in a low, soothing voice, "Everything's going to be okay, Simon, you'll see," and she took him in her arms.

As he leaned his head against her shoulder, Simon ground out, "Nothing's okay. Nothing will ever be the same again."

Dallas knew she had to break the spell of his nightmare. In this state, neither of them would have a peaceful sleep. Only one thing had eased her emotional pain in the days following her divorce allowing her to unwind.

"Simon, I have an idea. This may sound strange but it works for me. Maybe it'll work for you, too. Let's go for a run."

"Run? Right now? What time is it?" He looked at the bedside clock, answering his own question. "Three a.m."

"It doesn't matter. Let's just go."

He looked at her like she was crazy, but then said okay. They dressed quickly and ran out into the night, with Jude happily following along. They headed toward Seaport Village where they could run along the water's edge. Dallas made sure not to outpace Simon, staying at his side and encouraging him on. It was a brightly lit route which she frequently ran, challenging enough without exhausting them completely.

When they came back to Lily Court Lane almost an hour later, the sky was still inky black, flecked with an array of winter stars. Dawn was a couple of hours away and San Diego still slept. They passed no other runners and only a few people who appeared to be headed to a very early morning at work.

"How are you feeling now?"

"Much better, thank you." Then Simon added with a little grin, "I'll remember the 'Dallas cure' the next time I have a nightmare."

Returning upstairs and switching on the light, they found Jude was already sprawled across the bed.

"Let's shower and then I'll make us some coffee," Dallas said.

Peeling off her damp clothes in front of him felt so natural to her. She turned to Simon, pulling off his hoodie and yanking down his sweat pants. Wordlessly, she led him into the bathroom.

They'd made love earlier so this would be just a cleansing shower to cool them down from their run, she told herself. How wrong she was.

Seeing each other naked immediately rekindled the fire within them. Once they started soaping each other in the warm, steamy air, the innocent shower quickly turned into something quite different. Dallas found Simon's body masculine and sexy with his broad shoulders and smooth chest, a line of dark hair leading her eye to his growing erection, now engorged and ready.

Lathering her hands, she began to wash Simon slowly and carefully—his back, his chest, his arms. He made a guttural, yearning sound deep in his throat.

"That feels great, please don't stop. I love your hands on me," he said in a voice that was halfway between a pant and a whisper.

Dallas continued her soapy exploration, but when she was about to take him into her hands, he stopped her, placing his hands over hers.

"Not yet, Dallas. My turn."

Simon took the soap from her hands and slowly lathered her shoulders. Then his hands drifted to her breasts. He fondled them, encircling her nipples, and as the water ran over them washing away the suds, he drew one at a time deep into his mouth, sending sparks through Dallas from her chest to her groin. She'd never realized how sensitive her breasts could be.

She moaned as heat charged through her body. His hands continued to caress her, sliding over her ribs, her belly, and then finally her waiting center. He circled it over and over, then gently pushed a finger inside her. Just as she thought how good this felt, he pressed a second finger into her, and moved faster and faster.

Kneeling in front of her, he stroked her with his tongue, as the warm water rained down on them.

The feeling intensified.

"Let it build, Dallas, let it build."

Dallas's only reply was a moan of pleasure.

Seconds later she exploded around his tongue and fingers. After a moment or two, she returned to earth and as the water continued to rinse them, Simon rose and leaned back against the wall.

"Now it's my turn," Dallas said and slid down his body, engulfing him between her lips. Running her tongue along the length of his shaft caused Simon to groan aloud, and Dallas could feel his legs wobble.

Continuing the relentless back and forth with her lips and tongue, Dallas realized she'd never dared to do anything like this before. Simon was making her realize how powerful a woman could be and her desire to please him made her respond without restraint.

Simon gently held her head as she pleasured him until he could stand no more. He was a man on fire. Before he burst, he pulled Dallas up, the slick friction of their wet bodies rubbing against one another made him gasp.

Sucking on her moist bottom lip, he lifted her body astride him, impaling her with his throbbing shaft. Pressing her back against the wet wall of the shower, he pushed deeply inside her, holding her there as she bit back a moan.

Dallas felt his fullness pulsating inside her. Simon pulled his head back to look into her eyes, watching a look of almost unbearable excitement grow on her face. He was tightly inside her and lowering his hand, he stroked her as they moved together. Her hips rose to meet his thrusting fingers.

She clung to him as she climbed the mountain peak toward another shattering explosion causing her to cry out as her body jerked against his hand.

"Oh, Simon, don't stop!" as if he would or could.

Simon reveled in her pleasure and was no more able to stop himself than he could stop time. Moments later, he spiraled out of control, reaching his own climax. He was surprised and overwhelmed by the force of his release.

They slid to the shower floor weakened by the hot water and the force of their passion. They sat side by side, soaked and spent. They looked at each other and began to laugh with abandon.

Taking a few moments to recover, Simon rose effortlessly from the floor, turned off the water, and reached for a towel. He helped Dallas stand and wrapped her in its fluffy folds. He lifted her effortlessly in his arms and carried her into the bedroom.

"Hey, Jude, time to move over, buddy."

Jude opened one eye, snuffled, and moved over to his own dog bed. Dallas couldn't help but laugh.

Simon smiled down at Dallas as she lay on the bed. "I'll be right back."

Returning with more dry towels, Simon carefully wrapped Dallas's dripping black hair. He tended to her beautiful body, gently drying every part of her, causing her to giggle as he even dried behind her ears and between her toes, a broad grin turning up the corners of his mouth.

Putting aside the towel, he looked at her.

"You are magnificent. What you do to me—your taste, your scent."

This time, he entered her slowly, with long deliberate strokes, teasing her, taunting her, until she could take no more.

"I can't," she sighed and then she did.

31

The Morning After

Dallas was humming as she made breakfast burritos filled with scrambled eggs and cheese, tomatoes and green peppers. The coffee was hot and strong with a hint of cinnamon and Mexican chocolate. Simon devoured every bite and refilled his coffee cup several times. They sat together at her kitchen table chatting about the day ahead.

She enjoyed having Simon there; her ex-husband Rey never lingered over breakfast. He was always in a hurry to be somewhere else, anywhere away from her, and he never made love to her the way Simon had last night.

As she made a fresh pot of coffee, Dallas recalled the final day of her married life with Rey, the day she learned he was gay. The months following were filled with pain and Dallas avoided the dating scene until Carolee persuaded her to try online dating. But that hadn't turned out so well. She thought she'd never recover from Rey's betrayal, but these hours spent with Simon beat anything she'd ever experienced in the past.

While it was true each of them brought their own ghosts to the relationship, his war memories and her broken marriage, they'd made a good start on kicking those ghosts out of their lives.

Simon's voice brought her back to the present.

"Dallas," he spoke quietly, "last night was terrific for me. I'd like to see you again, soon." Then with a wicked smile, he continued, "Lady, you have amazing powers to heal the wounded—and I don't mean at your gym."

They both laughed.

Leaning forward and playfully kissing him on the tip of his nose, Dallas assured him, "Last night was super for me, too. You're pretty amazing yourself," she said pointedly looking at his hands causing them both to laugh again.

He rose from the table and took her in his arms.

"When can I see you again?"

"Tonight? Dinner?"

"Tonight at six and I hope you like Thai food."

"Love it," she said, ready for dinner and whatever else might follow.

Patting Jude and whistling as he stepped off the porch, Simon walked toward his van feeling like his old self, like he'd felt before going to Afghanistan.

At that very same moment, Marvin was saying goodbye to Sarah at the house next door.

The two women waved to one another and smiled. Will you look at that, Dallas thought. Sarah had an overnight visitor, too. We'll have to talk about that. And Sarah thought, so he's back. Good for you, Dallas.

Simon remembered Marvin from the wedding. They shook hands and exchanged greetings.

Marvin said, with a sheepish look on his face, "Beautiful day isn't it?" and blushed bright red.

Simon noted the red face and the all too apparent embarrassment and found it humorous. An old-fashioned man in this day and age. Who'd have thought it?

As the two men parted, going their separate ways, Marvin thought to himself, he couldn't do this much longer. Simon must have thought he'd spent the night at Sarah's when he just stopped by for breakfast. He'd come over to cheer her up a little. Since Craig returned to San Francisco, she'd been feeling a little down.

He'd always considered himself to be a patient man, but even a patient man has his limits. He wanted the whole world to know how he felt about Sarah. He was ready to shout it up and down Lily Court Lane. It was time for them to go public with their relationship.

As he walked toward his office, Marvin tried to remember the name of the diamond dealer whose shop was nearby. Together they'd create a beautiful engagement ring for Sarah, a perfect reflection of his love. He would ask her to marry him as soon as the ring was ready. He hoped she would say yes.

He was quite sure of his feelings for her. Sarah brought out all the tenderness in him that had been suppressed for so long. This fabulous woman made him feel younger and more vital than he'd felt in years. How his life would change if she said yes.

In Dallas's kitchen a short while later, Sarah explained Marvin had been there just for breakfast, nothing more. He was trying to lift her spirits, she said.

"But I'm relieved Craig had to go back to San Francisco. He and Jane were getting a bit too friendly over this painting business. You know, Dallas, she isn't exactly the girl I hoped he would like."

Dallas frowned in surprise, "Why not? I think Jane's just great."

Sarah brushed her words aside. "You too? Well, I just think she's way too old for him. But when I tried to talk to him about it, he just about bit my head off."

Noticing Sarah's distress, Dallas gently disagreed with her friend, "Jane's not old. She's just a few years older than me, and she certainly doesn't look or act old. Age is no big deal these days."

"No one understands. She's not what I wanted for my boy."

"Your boy? Sarah, listen to yourself. Your 'boy' is no longer a boy; he's a man now and has been for some time. It's not up to you to make his choices. It's not important what you want, it's what he wants. How would you feel if Craig told you to stop seeing Marvin? The age difference between you and Marvin is a lot greater than between Craig and Jane, but I don't hear Craig saying, 'He's too old for you, Mom.'"

"Oh, he wouldn't do that" was her quick reply. "He cares about me too much."

"Exactly! See what I mean?"

Sarah felt a little beaten up and close to tears. No one understood, not Alex, not Maryann, and now not Dallas. Well, they were all wrong. She refused to believe she could be one of those controlling mothers who wanted to keep her son to herself.

Sarah would always remember the sight of Craig in his preemie incubator, with tubes coming out everywhere from his tiny body. His eyes were covered against the glare of the warming lamps, and tiny mittens covered his hands as they waved weakly in the air. She vowed then she'd never let anything or anyone harm him. It was so hard to accept he was no longer a little baby needing her protection.

Sarah changed the subject. "I didn't know you were seeing Simon?"

"He came by to show me the wedding pictures."

Laughing now, Sarah added, "Looks like there were a lot of them. Did it take all night?"

Dallas said with a straight face but a wicked tone, "Sometimes these projects take all the time and energy you can give them."

Just then Jude barked at someone passing on the street. It was Carolee dressed in the bright red plumage she so favored, with shoes and handbag to match.

"Hi, girls," she called out with a cheery wave as they came to the door.

"Hi, Carolee, you're bright and cheerful today."

They chatted for a few minutes about Miss Mittens' latest trick, their new self-defense class soon to start at the gym and Craig's departure for San Francisco. The group parted as Sarah left for her bakery, Carolee for her office and Dallas for her gym.

Leaving her house just then, Jane waved to the three friends as they hurried off. She had a lot to think about this morning and hoped a brisk walk in the fresh air would help clear her mind. She'd just had an upsetting phone conversation with Craig.

When he called from the gallery, Jane reminded him again they could only be friends.

"Why do you say that?" he asked with a hint of anger in his voice. "Don't you feel what's happening between us?"

"I do, but ...."

"There are no 'buts' here, Jane," he interrupted. "What does a few years difference in age matter anyway?"

"Well, that's not how some other people see it on Lily Court Lane."

"Exactly who do you mean?"

Jane was silent.

"If you are referring to my mother, I'll talk to her when I'm back in San Diego. You and I aren't done, Jane, we're just beginning."

Jane remained silent, unsure how to respond. She'd promised Sarah they were only friends.

"I'll call you again tomorrow. Oh, by the way, Jack and I are making arrangements to bring the painting to San Diego. I'll tell you more about it tomorrow."

"No, Craig, please don't call me," Jane replied, but she heard only a click as the phone went dead.

"Thank you for meeting me," Sarah said. "I need to talk to you. I know you'll understand, you're a mother, too."

Carolee nodded for Sarah to continue. The two were having afternoon coffee together. After greeting Ming, they'd taken their coffees to a window table and made themselves comfortable.

"Sarah, you look so upset. What's bothering you?"

"Oh, Carolee, I just don't know where to start. I'm so upset with Craig."

At Carolee's encouraging look, Sarah unburdened herself. Jane just wasn't the right choice for her son.

"Do you think I'm wrong? I want him to be happy."

Carolee sighed. She was sad to see her good friend so upset.

"Sarah, you can't predict which relationship will work. Even those matches that check off all the "right" boxes—age, religion, education—often end badly. The only advice I can give you is be careful what you say to Craig. You don't want to damage the relationship you have with your son.

Sarah had tears in her eyes.

"I just don't know what to do. Am I wrong about Jane? Everyone seems to like her so much."

"The only important thing is how Craig feels."

"Well, that's no secret."

"Then that's the answer. Maybe you just need some time to come to terms with it."

Carolee hugged Sarah feeling sorry for the pain she was feeling. There was really nothing she could say or do to help her. Sarah, herself, would have to work through her feelings for Jane. Carolee could only hope she'd be able to do so.

But for now, Carolee had to rush home and make dinner for Cindy.

32

A Mother's Love

Cindy had called Carolee saying she had something important she wanted to discuss and inviting herself to dinner. Now, she was romping on the living room floor with Miss Mittens who'd become the new ruler of the household. Carolee had fixed Cindy's favorite meal—meat loaf, mashed potatoes and glazed carrots—planning for them to watch an old movie after dinner.

"How much longer 'til dinner, Mom? Can we talk before we eat? I'm meeting a friend later."

Carolee hid her disappointment. No movie tonight. Instead she asked lightly, "Oh, who?"

"Ming from the coffee shop, you remember him."

Carolee was surprised. She cautioned herself not to overreact the way Sarah had with her son.

"Oh, I just saw him today at the coffee shop. I didn't realize you knew him that well."

Carolee studied her daughter's flushed and happy face as Cindy talked about their plans for the evening ahead and then it hit her why Cindy looked so different tonight.

She blurted out, "You're not wearing your nose stud or your eyebrow ring!"

Shrugging dismissively, Cindy replied "Oh, I'm so over them."

Well, well, that's interesting, Carolee thought with a smile as she turned back to check the oven. Did Ming have anything to do with the missing face jewelry, she wondered.

She believed Cindy's piercings resulted from her rebellion when she learned Carolee hid her adoption and her birth mother's letter from her. Cindy accidentally came across the letter and learned the sad truth. Her birth mother loved her, but she had to give her up.

Carolee tried to explain why she kept the letter secret for so long, but her excuses sounded hollow even to herself. The truth was she wanted to shield her little girl from any pain, but keeping the truth from her had been unfair and badly hurt their relationship.

Marvin handled the private adoption and over the years, he'd urged Carolee repeatedly to tell Cindy about her adoption. But he never said "I told you so," when Cindy left the house in anger refusing to speak to her.

The days following had been excruciating ones for Carolee. She was lonely and missed her daughter. Marvin had been a tower of strength then, becoming a go-between. The counseling sessions he arranged helped them discuss their issues and begin to rebuild trust between them.

"You said you wanted to talk before dinner. Well, I'm all ears," Carolee now reminded Cindy.

"Come, sit over here," Cindy said in a very grownup voice, patting the sofa next to her, "and bring Miss Mittens with you."

The two sat side-by-side, one so blond and the other so dark, with Miss Mittens purring on Cindy's lap, as Carolee waited expectantly for Cindy to begin.

"Mom, I think I'm ready to look for my birth mother now, but I wanted to talk to you first. I don't want to upset you, so I need to know how you really feel about it. I'm not sure how I feel about it myself. I'm afraid to actually meet her. What if I do find her and she doesn't want to meet me or have a relationship with me? I'd be heart-broken."

"Oh, honey, remember I did meet her the day she brought you to Marvin's office. I saw the sadness in her eyes when she explained she couldn't keep you. She wanted the best for you and I think she'd be happy to know you've grown up to be a beautiful young woman. She'd be very proud of you, just like I am."

Cindy smiled at this, although there were tears in her eyes.

Giving Cindy a hug, Carolee continued, "I don't feel upset about this. I've been waiting for you to make this decision, and I understand, I really do. I think many adopted children worry about the same things. I knew this day would come and all along I was afraid I'd lose you, but in my heart I know now that can never happen."

"Oh, Mom, you're absolutely right, it will never happen. You're my mom forever." Cindy leaned over and kissed Carolee on the cheek. "Ming told me about some of the newer web searches that might help. An adoptee and the birth mother can be reunited only if they're both looking to find each other. I can't do this by myself though, I need your support. Will you help me? I need you so much, Mom."

"You've got me, and I'll do anything I can to help you," responded Carolee fiercely, bringing a smile and a tear to Cindy's face.

Tears hovered at the corners of Carolee's eyes as well. It felt so good having Cindy sitting next to her, still needing her.

"No time like the present," she suggested and when Cindy agreed, they headed for Carolee's computer.

Cindy sat down at the desk with Carolee beside her. Looking at the framed baby picture of Cindy prominently displayed, Carolee could clearly recall the morning that changed her life forever, the moment when she first met baby Cindy.

Carolee arrived early at work one bright spring morning twenty-two years ago, planning to finish some legal documents left from the previous day. A frail young girl stood waiting outside the law firm's doors carefully holding a sleeping infant in her arms. The baby was wrapped in a shabby but clean pink blanket. Carolee saw how frightened the girl looked, with dark circles under her eyes.

Surprised to find her there so early in the morning, Carolee politely asked her, "How can I help you?"

"I want to see the *abagado*, the lawyer, *por favor*," the girl responded in a timid voice. Carolee unlocked the office door and beckoned the girl and the baby into Marvin's inner office. As Carolee seated them, the baby looked up at her. Her large black eyes seemed to glow in her round face. Then the baby began to suck vigorously on her thumb, so much so Carolee was thankful the infant had no teeth. Carolee couldn't help herself. She reached down and gently stroked the baby's soft cheek.

"How old is she?"

"Three months. Would you like to hold her?" the girl asked, holding the baby out toward Carolee.

Carolee opened her arms and took Cindy, holding her next to her heart. The baby solemnly looked up at Carolee and then broke into a wide toothless grin. Carolee felt her heart lurch and she wished the moment could last forever. Instantly she fell in love with the baby in her arms. At that moment she couldn't guess this child would grow to become her greatest love.

Now, she sat next to her grown daughter, helping her find the young unfortunate girl who had given her baby up for adoption. Cindy's hand trembled as she bravely pressed the "send" key and her information was hurled into the vast internet universe.

Turning to Carolee she hugged her hard and said, "Thanks Mom, I couldn't have done that without you. Ming was right; this is the way to go. Now let's eat. I'm starved!"

The computer was closed and the two went off to the kitchen to have their dinner.

Handing Cindy a dinner plate, Carolee asked, "What's Ming studying? Did I hear he's taking evening classes?"

That was all the encouragement Cindy needed to start talking nonstop about Ming. How smart he is, and how focused, working full-time while studying for his master's degree in business administration at night.

"Doing all that and he's so much fun to be with," a beaming Cindy said.

As Carolee listened, she realized this was sounding more serious than she thought at first.

"Is he a casual friend, or is he becoming someone special?"

"I don't know yet, but I hope he is."

"Isn't he Chinese?" Carolee now asked Cindy.

"Yes, how cool is that?"

How did his parents feel about their son dating a girl who wasn't Chinese? Carolee began to worry. Her Cindy was special, and she didn't want her to get hurt.

So as she cleared the table, Carolee asked in a casual voice, "Have you met Ming's family yet?"

"No, not yet, but we've talked about it. It's still too soon."

Then she told Carolee how his parents' marriage had been arranged by their fathers. It became obvious Cindy knew a lot about Ming's family even though she hadn't met them.

"Ming can trace his family back generations, and he has some interesting stories about uncles escaping from China and even swimming to Hong Kong in the dead of night."

"Is that where he's from, Hong Kong?"

"No, he was born here, in the U.S. In Massachusetts, actually."

Cindy was slicing the apple pie she'd baked while Carolee filled their cups with decaf coffee.

"You know, Mom, Ming and I discussed my plans to open a restaurant and he said it sounded realistic to him. He has experience in the restaurant business because his family owns a fancy Chinese restaurant in Rancho Bernardo. He thinks now that I'm finishing my culinary training, I'm ready to take the next step, and we should start looking at possible locations for my bistro."

Carolee caught the use of "we." She wondered why Ming was working at the coffee shop instead of the family restaurant, but decided to postpone that question for another time.

Instead she said, "It's nice that Ming wants to help you but you really should talk to Uncle Marvin and formalize a business plan before you go much further. He did wonders for Sarah when she wanted to start her bakery."

"Oh, sure, Mom, I will," she replied, thinking of stodgy Uncle Marvin. "Now enough about me, Mom. What have you been up to lately?"

The conversation lightened as the two women laughed at Carolee's misadventures with online dating. Cindy couldn't stop giggling when Carolee described the dreadful speed-dating scene leading to her decision to give up men and adopt Miss Mittens instead. At this very moment the kitten was curled up in a kitchen chair looking impossibly comfortable and cute.

With a twinkle in her eye, Cindy asked, "And have you told Miss Mittens she's adopted?"

Carolee turned back from the dishwasher with a sinking heart, until she saw the playful smile on Cindy's face. She started to laugh feeling relieved the past was finally behind them and apparently forgiven.

33

Mothers and Sons

_____

While Cindy was having her second slice of heavenly apple pie with her mother on Lily Court Lane, Ming sat at his family's dining room table in Rancho Bernardo. He nodded at his mother in appreciation as she placed another tasty item on his plate. As usual, Dorothy had outdone herself in preparing this special meal. He was content to be here in the company of his family, but at the same time he felt awkward seated next to the guests. Here sat yet another of his mother's obvious attempts to fix him up with an acceptable girl.

He felt his heart had already been taken by Cindy. He'd have tell his mother about her, but he wasn't looking forward to that conversation. Not one bit.

Dorothy looked around the large round table set with chopsticks and platters of steaming hot food waiting to be eaten. She sighed with contentment, feeling complete with her family gathered around her. To her left sat Dwight, her eldest son, with his pregnant bride, then came Dorothy's daughter Mei and her fiancé, next her husband Lloyd, and their guests with their lovely daughter. On Dorothy's right sat her favorite son, Ming. Her oh-so-stubborn son, as she often thought to herself. Look at him sitting there barely making conversation.

Dorothy was dauntless in her attempts to find Ming a suitable wife. She often staged dinners like this one inviting the eligible daughters of her friends, her mah jongg cronies, and Lloyd's business associates. Ming was expected to spend time with the lucky contender for his heart, exchange some pleasant conversation, and then ask to see her again. Dorothy was determined one of these dinners would surely lead to talk of marriage.

That conversation had yet to take place. Ming carried out his mother's agenda in every way except the most important one. He'd never shown the slightest interest in any of the girls Dorothy insisted he meet.

Tonight's choice was an accomplished pianist, a college graduate, from a good family in Hong Kong and very pretty with her long black hair and nice manners. As far as Dorothy could see, this girl was perfect for her son. She and Lloyd planned to confront Ming later and insist it was time for him to make a decision. He was old enough at twenty-five and finishing his graduate degree. It was time for him to marry.

Ming, sipping his fragrant chrysanthemum tea, caught the look his mother cast his way. Knowing what was on her mind, he groaned to himself. His thoughts strayed as he imagined himself dancing with his arms around Cindy, pressing her body close to his.

Seeing her son's face light up, Dorothy smiled, jumping to the conclusion he was pleased with her latest attempt. Ah, yes, this was finally the one, she just knew it. She looked at Lloyd across the table and he nodded. He, too, had misread the look on Ming's face.

They both would have been shocked to know Ming was silently rehearsing a very important speech, one they were sure to dislike. He planned to tell them he appreciated their efforts to find him a good wife. He knew they were trying to look out for him, but he was a grown man, able to make up his own mind. He was extremely proud of his Chinese heritage, but he'd grown up in a different world where men and women made their own choices when it came to marriage partners. And he intended to do just that.

In fact, he would say to them, "Someone important has entered my life, a beautiful girl who's educated, ambitious and comes from a good family. I admire and respect her and hope you will grow to love her. But, Mom and Dad, there's something else I need to tell you. She's not Chinese."

Every time he went over the speech in his head, he just couldn't get past those three words. She's. Not. Chinese. Oh, boy….

He'd be firm with them, he told himself. All their fix-ups were over. He was sorry to disappoint them, but he needed to live his life the way he chose.

With that resolve in mind, Ming rose from the table, thanked everyone for coming and then was gone. Dorothy was furious and she felt her face grow hot with both anger and shame at her son's rude behavior.

Ming quickly forgot the awkward dinner and his hasty departure as soon as he walked into the club and saw Cindy waiting for him. He immediately noticed the missing face jewelry.

"Cindy, you're not wearing your nose stud or eyebrow ring. What happened?"

"Oh, it was just a fad. I guess I grew out of it," was all Cindy said.

When they danced, Ming was reluctant to let her go and Cindy felt like she belonged in his arms. He breathed in her sweet fragrance, and his lips brushed her hair. Closing his eyes, he knew, this was the girl he wanted sitting next to him at his family's dinner table.

Later, they walked back to Carolee's house and he pulled her close as they said goodnight on the porch. After one tender kiss Ming slowly released her. Cindy walked through the door of her mother's house with Ming's kiss lingering on her lips like raindrops on a lily pad. She knew he would warm her dreams all night.

The next morning, Ming debated when to start the dreaded conversation with his mother. He was even tempted to write it down as if it were a school speech. He needed to be prepared. But his thoughts were interrupted when his cell phone rang. He knew who it was without looking at his phone.

"I couldn't wait any longer, son," she said, putting aside her displeasure at his behavior the night before.

Ming's heart sank, "Hi, Mom."

"Wasn't she lovely? She told her mother she thought you were so nice, and so handsome."

"Mom," Ming broke in. "Don't start making wedding plans."

"Why not? Your father and I think she's the one. She's perfect. We couldn't find anything wrong with her."

"No, Mom, she isn't perfect for me."

Her voice rose, "Yes, son she is. We saw your face when you turned red, it was a sign you liked her, too."

"Mom, it wasn't that. I told you, you've got to stop doing this. I'll choose my own wife when I'm ready."

"You keep saying that, but you never bring anyone home for us to meet. Time is passing, son. You say you are dating but we don't know anything about these girls. We won't be around forever to help you make the right choice. We want to see you settled with a good girl," Dorothy said with a slight catch in her voice.

Ming groaned in frustration. Here was the guilt trip he'd been expecting. His mother was an expert at it. Tears were a weapon for her.

Finally Ming blurted out, "Okay, Mom, I'll bring a date to dinner, but at the restaurant, not at home."

"Why? Isn't our house nice enough for her?"

Uh-oh, not a good start, Ming thought as he rushed to smooth his mother's ruffled feathers.

"No, it's not that, it's too much work for you. Let's have dinner at the restaurant so we can all relax and enjoy it."

And so they could make a quick escape when Cindy had had enough of their questions, assuming she would even agree to go. Besides, the restaurant would be a much more neutral place so his mother would have to control herself in front of their staff and the other diners.

Ah, his mother thought, so he has someone after all.

"Tell me all about this girl," she demanded.

"No, Mom, I want you to meet her first."

They set a time for the following week, and the conversation finally came to a close leaving Ming feeling somewhat cowardly. He'd avoided revealing his date was not Chinese, usually dressed entirely in black, and had the most beautiful expressive eyes he'd ever seen. He hoped his mother could overlook some of her more exotic features and see into Cindy's beautiful soul.

Now he had a new worry. Would Cindy even want to meet his family?

It was going to be a long, long week.

Thirty or so miles south of Rancho Bernardo, another mother fretted over her son's romantic interests. While Craig wanted to hurry back to Jane, Sarah worried about her son's return. She missed him, she did, but maybe it would be better if he stayed in San Francisco.

Ah, mothers and their sons. There was no culture in the world where a mother didn't worry about her son and how he'd fare in the world without her to care for him.

34

The Banquet

The din of loud voices speaking several different languages spilled out from the restaurant. Clattering dishware and clinking glasses were usually welcoming restaurant sounds, but tonight the normal clamor was almost more than Cindy could handle. She knew Ming's parents were waiting to meet her and she wanted to get this dinner eaten and over with as quickly as good manners would allow. She was scared to death.

Ming refused to think about the catastrophe that was about to happen. He realized he had little control over his mother's reaction to just about anything, but this might rival the loudest New Year's Eve fireworks ever seen.

He knew his mother was expecting a Chinese girl. He should've prepared her. Yet if he had, she probably would've cancelled the dinner.

Cindy consulted her own mother on what to wear for this important occasion.

Carolee suggested tactfully, "Perhaps a soft color would be nice, rather than the usual black you like. Something feminine, yet serious looking."

Ming merely shrugged when asked the same question.

"It doesn't really matter," he said.

In his eyes she would look perfect, but he knew in his mother's eyes, no matter what Cindy wore, she'd be all wrong.

After worrying all day, Cindy finally chose a navy blue dress with her usual black tights. Tonight, no nose stud or eyebrow ring. She would do everything she could to make his family like her, but she would still be herself. She threw back her shoulders and tried to feel brave. She was determined to put her best foot forward.

Ming murmured words of encouragement and, placing his hand on the small of her back, gently propelled Cindy forward. The large restaurant, with its bright lights, shiny red walls, golden light fixtures and red and black patterned carpet, was crowded to capacity.

Following the hostess, they had to weave their way between the closely packed tables to where Ming's family sat waiting, looking stiff, quiet and obviously uncomfortable. So many people were seated at the table. Cindy had expected only his mother and father, not the whole family.

Ming was pleased to see his brother and sister had come tonight. He hoped this would make the dinner easier for Cindy. He really should have told them and gotten their help with his mother, but he hadn't thought of it and now it was too late. He could only hope for the best.

The family was seated at a round table in the rear of the main dining room, the only group not smiling or talking. Cindy's first instinct was to turn and run. As she neared the table, she saw Ming's mother was again wearing a *cheong sam*, like in Ming's family photo. This one complete with a gold dragon embroidered on the front.

Cindy gasped inwardly, "Oh my God, she's the dragon lady! I hope she doesn't breathe fire in my direction." Cindy could feel hostility directed toward her and thought this dinner was going to be even worse than she'd imagined.

Ming's family all looked shocked as they stared at the couple approaching the table. A white girl was the last person they expected to see with Ming.

Maintaining his composure, Ming's father, Lloyd, politely rose to greet them formally. He offered Cindy the seat next to him directly across from Ming's mother. She glared at Cindy and only nodded, offering no welcoming word or smile.

As Cindy sat down, feeling awkward and uncomfortable, it dawned on her no one in the family had been prepared to see Ming with a girl who wasn't Chinese.

Ming introduced Cindy to everyone. With an expression just this side of a scowl, Dorothy nodded but remained stiff with her arms folded tightly across her chest. Her daughter-in-law seated on one side of her and her own daughter on the other formed a wall of total silence. The awkwardness was all the more obvious in contrast to the loud laughter coming from the happy tables all around them.

Ming tried to ease the tension by asking if everyone else had already ordered.

"No, son, we were waiting for you," his mother replied, finally speaking but with an undercurrent of anger in her voice. "But we did order the Peking duck and the soup ahead of time so the kitchen would be prepared. For the rest, we decided to wait and see what you wanted," she repeated, her voice cold with unspoken fury.

"Yes," his father interjected politely trying to defuse the unbearable tension. "We wanted to meet you, Cindy, and see what you would like. I do think you'll enjoy the appetizer."

Seeing how obviously upset his wife was, Lloyd was doing his best to smooth over the unpleasant moment.

The appetizer, salt and pepper crispy calamari, quickly appeared and was set on the lazy Susan at the center of the table. Using the serving chopsticks, Lloyd courteously placed several pieces on Cindy's plate.

She smiled her thanks at him and tentatively picked up her fork. She placed one of the smaller pieces in her mouth. It was delicious. Maybe dinner wouldn't turn out so bad after all, at least the food was promising. Cindy realized she was hungry and became a little more at ease.

Finally, the family began to speak to each other in Chinese as they debated the merits of the various dishes to order. With Ming translating for her, Cindy didn't feel excluded.

How different this family dinner was from the one Ming shared with her own little family last night. For one thing, there were only the three of them at the table and it'd been a simple home-cooked meal in her mother's quiet kitchen, a Caesar salad, herb-roasted chicken, baked potato and asparagus.

Cindy had baked a delicious cherry cobbler for dessert and when Ming asked what he could contribute, he was told to bring vanilla ice cream to top off the hot cobbler. A very American meal, unlike the one taking place tonight.

Last night the conversation flowed easily, and her mother beamed to see how happy Cindy looked with Ming. It was a meal all about family and acceptance.

Now seated at this table in *The Golden Dragon Restaurant*, Cindy realized she was the only one who'd been brought a fork in addition to her chopsticks. This won't do, she thought. Firmly putting down her fork, she picked up the chopsticks attempting to lift a bite of the calamari to her mouth. Oops! It fell into her lap.

She quickly folded the piece into her napkin and looked around. No one appeared to have noticed her faux pas. Good thing she'd chosen to wear a dark color. Although Cindy was adept at using chopsticks, tonight she was all thumbs. Ming's ever-watchful mother had in fact seen Cindy drop the calamari on her lap and thought how clumsy this girl was.

"Cindy, do you have a favorite dish you'd like to suggest?" asked Ming's sister, Mei.

She would behave politely, even if her mother didn't. Cindy seemed very nice, and she wondered what it would be like to have her as a sister. Ming should have prepared them, she thought, even if he didn't want to tell their mother. But Mei could understand and even sympathize with him. She remembered how harshly her mother had treated Douglas when she brought him home for the first time. She'd been too afraid to tell Dorothy they were already engaged.

"Well, I do like seafood," Cindy said, grateful Mei was being so pleasant, "and I do enjoy trying new foods from around the world. But I think you all would know best what to order," was Cindy's diplomatic reply.

"Do you like Chinese food?" was the first question his mother directed to Cindy.

"Oh, yes, Ming's been teaching me how to cook Chinese food. I've already learned to make moo shu pork, and I think it's your recipe."

She turned to smile at Ming. When Cindy turned back, she saw his mother's scowl had deepened further. Uh-oh, had she said the wrong thing?

That was her son's favorite dish, Dorothy thought. This girl wants to steal him away from us. It was all but impossible for Dorothy to think rationally about her son.

At last the menu was decided and the order given to their waiter in Chinese. Now it seemed everyone at the table had a question to ask Cindy. Ming's brother, Dwight, started by asking, "What do you do for a living?" Followed by his wife, Jennifer, who smiled as she asked, "Where did you go to school?" Then Mei wanted to know, "Where did you meet Ming?" Looking at Dorothy who had yet to ask a question, Lloyd asked Cindy about her parents.

Cindy felt as though she was being grilled, but she replied directly and honestly to each and every question. She had nothing to hide. She was proud of her mother and she was grateful for having been adopted by her. She was straightforward when she replied she knew nothing about her birth parents. Her breath caught as she realized she'd just revealed her most personal secret to Ming's family.

Ming's mother was taken aback. Adopted? If so, this girl was no one. She didn't know her family or her past. How could she understand tradition and how to honor one's ancestors? Yet, while Cindy had no roots, she spoke lovingly about her mother which made Dorothy's heart soften slightly toward this unsuitable girl her son had suddenly brought into their midst. While she seemed to be a nice girl, she was still the wrong girl for Ming. Obviously.

Cindy was grateful when the walnut shrimp appeared, and the questions stopped for the time being. Her nervousness had subsided a little and she was easily able to lift a shrimp to her mouth, but she eyed the glazed walnuts doubtfully.

Ming noticed and taking her hand he helped her guide a walnut to her lips. They gazed into each other's eyes as Cindy crunched down on the crispy walnut. When they looked away, they saw the others watching them. Their faces betrayed them.

Thankfully, the dishes began to arrive in quick succession. A trolley was wheeled to the table and their server carved the Peking duck, enfolding the crispy skin into fluffy pancakes with green onions and hoisin sauce. Cindy was surprised when the waiter wheeled the rest of the bird away. Where was he going?

But then, she gave a startled gasp as a steamed whole fish was placed on the table directly in front of her, its open eye staring up at her.

Ming explained, "You are the guest at the table so it is our tradition to place the fish head before you."

Cindy smiled weakly in appreciation murmuring, "Thank you so much," hoping all the while she wasn't expected to eat it.

The dead fish continued to stare at her from its platter.

Careful to avoid the bones, Ming lifted a section of the fish and placed it on Cindy's plate. She gingerly took a mouthful, but found she didn't care for it. Too fishy, she thought. Leaning down she deposited the mouthful in a tissue and placed it in her handbag.

As she straightened up, she whispered to Ming, "I really don't like the fish," and he discreetly removed the rest of it from her plate.

Cindy breathed a sigh of relief when the next dish appeared.

"You'll like this," Ming reassured her.

It was the duck meat, now diced and mixed with vegetables and served in lettuce cups. Lovely, she thought, finishing every bite. This was followed by a delicate savory soup. A large oval platter appeared next with two red lobsters chopped into large chunks and then reassembled to give the appearance of a whole lobster. Using the special fork provided to each person at the table, she expertly lifted out the succulent flesh from the shell.

At this point Cindy leaned closer to Ming. "I'm getting awfully full," she whispered.

"It's necessary," he replied, "for you to at least taste each dish. But you must finish all the rice when it's served at the end of the meal."

Cindy was puzzled. "The rice comes at the end of the meal?"

"Yes, its traditional, we always have eight dishes at a banquet, with the rice served last. It's considered unlucky to leave even a grain of rice behind in your bowl."

Ming explained that in Chinese the word for the number eight means prosperity. It then became clear to Cindy that this was not an ordinary family dinner but a banquet meant to welcome her--except his mother didn't seem very welcoming.

As the eighth dish was set down, Ming's father turned to Cindy. "We ordered this especially for you because you said you liked seafood."

It was an edible basket woven from a vegetable Lloyd said was taro, holding a mixture of seafood including scallops, shrimp, and brightly colored fresh vegetables. Cindy enjoyed a single scallop, which was all she had room for, while Ming moved the shrimp to his plate.

Cindy breathed a sigh of relief when their waiter brought the large platter of steaming house special fried rice, indicating that the dinner was finally coming to a close. The waiter ladled the rice into small individual bowls.

There was friendly laughter around the table as Cindy maneuvered her chopsticks and lifted some rice to her mouth. She had persisted until she finally succeeded.

A watchful Dorothy noted Cindy's determination, thinking to herself, this girl won't give up easily. While she still didn't like the girl, Dorothy respected how hard she was trying to fit in with Ming's family.

When the platter of sliced oranges and small bowls of steaming hot, sweet, red bean drink were placed on the table, Cindy felt Ming's leg pressing against hers in their pre-arranged signal. She nodded and smiled at him as he turned to his mother.

"Mom, Cindy and I have to leave now. We're catching a movie downtown and it'll take us at least a half hour to drive there."

As the young couple rose from the table, Ming's father stood and awkwardly patted Cindy on the shoulder, an unexpected sign of acceptance and approval from this very reserved man.

Cindy was touched and gave him a bright smile, and then, impulsively, she walked around the table and leaning down, she gave Dorothy a little hug. Ming's mother shrugged off Cindy's hand and turned her head away. As the other two women rose, Cindy kissed each on the cheek. They smiled, but only Ming's sister kissed her back, saying, "I'm so happy to meet you. I hope to see you again, soon."

"Thank you so much for this wonderful dinner. It was lovely meeting you all," Cindy said as she smiled at everyone in turn.

Feeling relieved dinner was over, she and Ming made their escape.

When they were safely seated in Ming's car in the parking lot, Ming exploded with laughter.

"The look on my mother's face when you hugged her was priceless. What made you do it?"

In a traditional Chinese family, such a show of spontaneous affection from a new acquaintance was unusual.

"Oh, I don't know. She's your mother and I want her to like me."

"Thank you for overlooking her rudeness. My father liked you very much and Mei did, too. Dwight always sticks up for me, so he'll be on our side. But as for my mom, only time will tell," Ming replied seriously but then he couldn't keep a straight face and he laughed again.

Cindy didn't see the humor.

"Ming, I really should be angry with you. You hadn't prepared your mother for me. She expected me to be Chinese."

"I'm sorry but I wanted so badly for my family to meet you. If I'd told her you're not Chinese, I wasn't sure she'd agree to come."

"Well, I'm annoyed with you but I'm relieved it's over with. Don't leave me in the dark like that again," she said sternly. "That was a little bit different from the dinner we had with my mother," Cindy said sarcastically as she only half playfully poked him in the arm. "She knew all about you before I brought you home."

"Cindy, we needed to meet each other's families. No matter what. I want my family to realize how important you are to me, and now they know."

Cindy grew silent as she pondered Ming's statement.

"I can just imagine the conversation they're all having now that we're gone."

35

Under the Same Moon

After Ming and Cindy left the table, everyone felt Dorothy's displeasure with her son. Mei finally spoke up, "Mother, I really liked her a lot. She seems very nice."

Dwight started to say something but stopped when Jennifer poked him in the ribs. He'd wait until his mother calmed down.

Saying a quiet goodnight, the group dispersed. They wanted to escape Dorothy's angry mood.

"I will not lose our son because of your stubbornness," Lloyd insisted, as he pulled their car out of the parking lot.

Dorothy sat next to him silently fuming. Lloyd knew by her expression she was not pleased with him or with Ming, although she offered no response to Lloyd's comment. The two deepening furrows creasing her forehead spoke volumes.

"Dorothy, you have done everything you can to help him find your idea of the perfect wife. Please try to understand he has his own plan. We must trust our American son to make his own decision."

Lloyd wanted to take her hand and comfort her but he knew she wouldn't welcome the gesture. Dorothy wasn't a demonstrative person, choosing to express her love for Lloyd through little everyday gestures. She cooked his favorite foods; fluffed up his pillows, stood over him to make sure he took his blood pressure pills and at night reached out for him in the darkness of their bedroom.

He was still surprised and pleased at how passionate she could be when no one was watching. To the world she presented an expressionless face, but he knew her better and now he could feel her seething beside him.

Finally she sighed, "Ming must have a good Chinese wife. I'm afraid he'll forget who he is and what it means to be Chinese. I have nothing against that girl, but from what I see, American girls are not dutiful to their husbands. The old ways have always been good enough for us. Our marriage was arranged and we're still together."

"But, Dorothy, when I first saw you, I knew you were the girl for me and I fell in love with you. You looked like a lotus flower in your pink dress and then you smiled at me when your mother wasn't looking. Do you remember that moment?"

She turned toward him in the car, the slightest hint of a smile forming on her face.

"Yes, I do. You were taller than the other boys and you smiled so much. I thought you were very handsome. I knew right away you were the perfect match for me, too. But I didn't tell my parents because they never asked."

Dorothy sniffed and Lloyd wondered if there were tears in her eyes.

After a long moment of silence, she asked, "So, you think we should welcome this girl, even though she is not Chinese?"

Thoughtfully, Lloyd replied, "It may be the only way we can keep our son in our lives. And she does seem to be a nice girl. That's the important thing. He could have chosen a Chinese girl we disapproved of, so let's give this girl a chance. After all, he's not asking her to marry him. He's just following American ways. He'll see her for a while and get to know her and her family before he seriously considers marriage. We shouldn't overreact."

"But what if it does happen? What about our grandchildren? They won't be Chinese."

"Oh yes, they will. They will be part of us and they will be both Chinese and American. They are our future. And, don't forget Dorothy, we are like the living willow—flexible and steadfast, not like a dead oak. We are *juk ka* but our American-born son is *juk sing*."

Dorothy smiled to hear Lloyd use these words from their childhood.

"We are flexible bamboo bending in the wind and then springing back," he continued. "That's why we're *juk ka*, we can compromise and we survive. *Juk sing* cannot bend in the wind. They can be stiff and stubborn and break under the strain. So it is up to us to find a compromise, and to change with the times. We need to be smart right now."

They finished the drive home in silence. As they pulled into the driveway, Dorothy sighed once more.

She said in a quiet voice, "Okay, I will invite this girl and her mother to dinner next week."

Lloyd smiled. "You are my very smart wife."

"Pah," she said under her breath, feeling she'd lost the battle for the moment. But she wasn't ready to admit defeat yet.

Lloyd affectionately held her arm as they entered their tidy house. Like Dorothy, he too had never been publically demonstrative, despite his deep feelings. Ming would have been surprised at the tenderness in his father's loving gesture. There were many things about his parents' marriage he didn't know.

Driving downtown on I-15 from Rancho Bernardo, Ming continued trying to explain his mother's rude behavior and was only making matters worse. Cindy realized it wasn't just her imagination, even Ming noticed his mother had been rude to her.

"Ming, your mother hates me."

"No, that's not true. That's just her way. She doesn't hate you. If anything, she dislikes that you're not Chinese. I remember she acted the same way when Dwight brought home Jennifer. She's Chinese but her family is from Taiwan, not Hong Kong, so it took a while for my mother to accept her. Now, she treats her like her own daughter."

That didn't make Cindy feel any better.

"I wanted to like her. She's your mother after all, so how could I not like her? But she's making it very hard." Now Cindy was seeing Dorothy as the domineering, nasty, cold dragon she'd first thought her to be.

"She wants to arrange my life because she thinks she knows what's best for me. Most Chinese marriages are still set up by their families. My mother isn't comfortable with the American custom of finding your own marriage partner. She says marriage is a business, and marrying for love is foolish. She was disappointed when neither Dwight nor Mei let her pick their partners, so now she's determined to choose the perfect one for me."

Cindy was starting to believe this new relationship was doomed. With every mile they drove, she became more convinced it would be easier for both of them if she broke it off before things went any further.

As if he were reading her mind, Ming said, "Please don't give up on me, Cindy. Give my mother some time. She'll come around. I just know it."

"Ming, let's not talk about it anymore tonight," Cindy said, feeling depressed. "Do you mind if we skip the movie? I have a headache and I just want to go home."

Actually she needed to be alone to think things through.

A heavy silence filled the car. Ming's heart sank. Had his mother ruined everything for him? He drove Cindy to Carolee's house, where she planned to spend the night. As they pulled up, Cindy didn't wait for Ming to get out instead she quickly jumped out by herself.

"Goodnight Ming. I'll talk to you soon," she called to him and then she was gone.

Ming wanted to stop her so they could talk some more, but then he thought better of it. What more could he say? He would give her time to calm down, but he wouldn't give up. Cindy meant way too much to him to lose her because of his mother.

Meanwhile, in San Francisco, Jack and Craig were closing the gallery for the night. It'd been a very satisfying week for them. Business had been excellent. Their conversation soon turned to a discussion of the painting which Craig had already started calling "Emilie's painting."

"I think Max took it all pretty well when we called him the other day," Jack said. "I'm glad we checked the time difference. If we'd have woken him up he might not have been quite as agreeable."

"Yeah, I was surprised at his response, too. I got the feeling Max was worried about how his grandfather had gotten the painting in the first place. He may be starting to think the painting's not his after all, given that Emilie Connor has such a compelling story. By the way, Emilie sounded very excited when I called to tell her we'd be bringing the painting to her house."

Jack nodded. "I wish I could be there with you, but one of us has to stay here when the next shipment arrives from Russia. It's good the lawyer will be there with you in case something unexpected comes up."

"Yes, Marvin felt it was in our best interests he be present at the viewing. I'm glad we hired a security firm to go with us when we take the painting to San Diego. We don't want to take any risks in case it turns out to be much more valuable than we thought."

The painting was at this moment casually propped against the wall next to Jack's desk. They'd removed it from the safe to study it, realizing it might never be theirs to sell. Both men were struck anew by its brilliance. After their talk, they returned it to the safe and locked the gallery for the night.

During his ride home on the streetcar, Craig thought about the coming weeks. He was excited about bringing the painting to Emilie in San Diego, but thoughts of a certain redhead intruded. He'd call Jane in the morning. On this trip he planned to spend an entire night with her. He longed to feel her lips and hands on his body and wake up beside her, inhaling the soft fragrance of her hair and skin. If his mother knew how he felt about Jane, he could just imagine her face turning the same shade of purple as Jane's front door.

He laughed at the thought and then decided he really should call his Uncle Alex to ask for advice. Alex always seemed to know the best way to handle Sarah. Craig had no doubt she'd be upset once she learned how serious he was about Jane.

Most of Emilie's waking hours after Craig's phone call had been spent thinking about the painting's arrival. What if the painting wasn't hers or was a clumsy copy? Could she handle such a disappointment at her age?

Not for the first time, she wished her husband, Bill, was still alive. He'd stand beside her and give her strength. She'd told him the story of the painting many times during their marriage. Would this be a satisfying ending to her story? At her age each day felt like a gift and she was determined to live long enough to see the painting come home to her.

That same evening the women of Lily Court Lane were meeting at Sarah's house. She called the group and even Jane to come over and sample some of the new cookies she was planning to make for Valentine's Day. Sarah was feeling a little down lately and she hoped seeing her friends would cheer her up.

She hadn't heard from Marvin for nearly a week since the morning he stopped by for coffee, a few days after she'd told him about the breast cancer. Where was he? Why hadn't he called? Had he changed his mind about her scars? She put those anxious thoughts aside as she greeted her friends.

Sarah placed plates of cookies and cupcakes on the table for everyone to taste. This would be an early Valentine's Day party for the women. Dallas arrived wearing her usual sleek athletic outfit, Carolee was sparkling in a bejeweled tee shirt and fashionably ripped blue jeans, while Jane was looking elegant as always in a cobalt blue dress.

Sarah, on the other hand, seemed unusually disheveled with her hair sticking up at odd angles and a streak of flour on her cheek as she greeted Maryann when she arrived breathless and late, wearing a new striped top over black slacks.

"I've just bought my first maternity clothes, Sarah. I can hardly wait to wear them. But if I keep eating like this, I'll need a bigger size," Maryann joked, giving Sarah a hug.

"You're eating for two now, honey, so just enjoy it," Sarah replied.

The women greeted one another with hugs and remarked how glowing Maryann looked. Then they settled down to sample Sarah's beautiful baked goods. Between bites of cookies, they started talking about the mysterious painting.

"It's coming to San Diego," Sarah confided. "Craig is bringing the painting here in two weeks. The German owner is coming, too. He's even hired a security guard to accompany them. Can you imagine that?"

Jane added, "With the supposed owner. We're not really sure who owns the painting. Marvin says we have to wait and see. There are legal considerations even if the painting is proven to be Emilie's."

Sarah's head jerked up as she heard Marvin's name mentioned. Where had Jane seen him? That damned Jane was everywhere, the very bane of Sarah's existence.

With a playful sparkle in her eye, Carolee asked, "Is this German guy single?" causing them all to laugh. But no one knew the answer to that question.

While the others were talking, Dallas's thoughts drifted pleasantly to Simon. They were now seeing each other almost every night and he often stayed the entire night. Even though the nightmares had abated somewhat, they still continued to jog most nights. It helped to calm him and he was able to relax and sleep more soundly.

Dallas's body tingled at the very thought of him and she could hardly wait to see him tonight. She'd asked herself more than once whether this was love or just a wonderful affair. She couldn't tell and truly, she didn't care one bit, it felt so good. Deep inside, she longed for true love, yet she feared marriage. The memory of Rey made her feel reluctant to give herself completely to any man.

Sarah tried to call the women to order as she handed out slips of paper.

"Now, ladies, please let's talk about the cookies. Rate them on a scale from 1 to 4 with 4 being the most delicious."

"Sarah, that's going to be really hard because your cookies are always a ten," Carolee exclaimed.

The colorful cookies were all different kinds. There were crème-filled cookies, chocolate bar cookies, lemon drops, heart-shaped ones with red sprinkles and even a platter of sugar-free cookies Dallas was certain to approve.

Carolee continued, "We can't vote, Sarah. We like every single thing you bake and these look so gorgeous, just perfect for Valentine's Day!"

"C'mon girls, you gotta help me out with this," Sarah insisted, looking a little flustered. "This is serious business. I'm counting on your help to decide which ones to make and how many of each."

The women were taken aback at her outburst realizing something else must be bothering her. It couldn't be the cookies.

Carolee had a suspicion and so she casually asked, "How's Marvin, Sarah?"

It was all Sarah could do to keep her composure.

"He's fine, I guess. I haven't heard from him for a whole week."

The others froze when Carolee asked the question, fearing Sarah was on the verge of tears and this would push her over the edge.

Ah ha! She'd hit it, Carolee thought, and immediately changed the subject. She wouldn't reveal Marvin's secret even though she ached seeing how upset Sarah was. So Carolee leaned forward and selected her first cookie to sample, uttering a very satisfied "yum."

Picking at the cookie crumbs in her lap, Maryann wondered how many cookies she'd eaten. Too many, she thought, feeling guilty as she took yet another one. After all, Alex had insisted she was too thin. The nausea had finally eased and she was beginning to enjoy being pregnant. She didn't even mind when her feet hurt or her back ached. She was going to be a mother.

When their delicious task was finished, and all the latest gossip exchanged, the women kissed each other farewell, and waved goodnight as they went back to their homes and closed their doors.

As she swept up the few remaining crumbs, Sarah wondered where on earth Marvin was. He always liked her cookies. Well, too bad, she thought.

36

An Unanswered Question

⌒

Several days after the cookie marathon, Sarah awoke feeling even more listless. It was a bright February morning, but the cheery sunlight failed to raise her spirits.

Her bakery had been open for hours. She called in to check with her staff and then fell back into bed. They were efficient and could manage without her for a morning. Cindy reported they'd started baking the new Valentine cookies.

When she woke up several hours later she could barely pull herself out of bed. Today marked the second day she'd called in sick. Sick, she thought, more like sick at heart. She was usually dressed by five a.m. and happily rushing out the door at full speed, ready to open the bakery by six.

She'd always been a morning person, ready to tackle the day ahead. But these last few mornings had been difficult for her. The listlessness lasted well into the day and she'd even forced herself to join the Thursday mah jongg game.

She knew she should be looking forward to Craig's visit next week, but she still had to deal with the Jane "thing." Marvin had been strangely absent all week. Had he changed his mind about her? Had her history of breast cancer scared him off after all? She didn't know what it was, but something was wrong.

Should she call him and find out? No, she just wasn't up to it today. But she knew that was just an excuse. In reality, she feared being rejected.

She wasn't lonely exactly. Dallas stopped by with more of her mother's mouth-watering tamales and talk of her blossoming romance with Simon. Carolee phoned and regaled her non-stop with tales of her latest failure in making a love connection.

"I'm through with men," Carolee had vowed yet again to Sarah.

Let's see how long that resolution lasts, thought Sarah. The two friends made plans to go to the gym later in the day, but Sarah wasn't sure if she'd be up to it. Oh well, she thought, she could always cancel.

Putting on her oldest bathrobe and dragging herself downstairs, Sarah turned on the TV, sat down and stared at the screen. She made no move to get ready for the day. She fell into a light sleep, interrupted by the ringing cell phone.

Oh no, she thought, looking at the screen. It was Jane. What could she want? Hadn't she done enough damage already?

She tried to sound cheery as she said, "Good morning, Jane."

"Hi, Sarah. I was just by the bakery and Cindy said you weren't feeling well. Is there anything I can do for you? Do you need me to get a prescription filled or would you like me to bring you lunch?"

Sarah felt like saying, my health is none of your business.

Instead she responded politely, "No, I'm fine, thank you. I don't need a thing."

"Are you sure I can't help you?"

"Really, I'm fine, just fine," Sarah repeated impatiently, wanting to end the phone call.

"Okay," Jane responded, "I'm glad to hear it."

She paused for a moment and then plunged forward.

"Sarah, could we have dinner together tonight?"

This was the last thing Sarah expected her to say. She had no desire to spend even one more minute than necessary with her, but she was curious to know why Jane wanted to see her. She paused for a moment before answering. Maybe this would give her a chance to speak her mind to Jane once and for all. She hadn't had a chance to do so when their talk was interrupted before the mah jongg game.

She answered reluctantly, "Yes, all right."

"Have you tried the new Italian bistro on Fifth Avenue? Is six okay with you?"

"I guess so," Sarah replied, trying to sound enthusiastic.

Dinner would be a short affair, she promised herself. She'd just say what she wanted to say, eat and be home for an early night. After the call, Sarah tried to reason with herself. Enough. Enough of this self-pity. It was a beautiful day and she needed to get dressed.

There was a knock on the front door. Now what? Standing on her tiptoes, she could see the top of Marvin's bald head through the decorative glass in the door. What was he doing here? Why hadn't he called before coming? And her in her bathrobe!

She patted her hair in a futile attempt to look presentable and opened the door a crack, "Hello, Marvin."

"Can I come in, Sarah?" he asked as he leaned forward to kiss her.

She moved her head away from his puckered lips. She wasn't going to let him kiss her today after such a long unexplained absence, but she did notice the fresh spring flowers he carried.

"Are you ill, Sarah? I went by the bakery and they said you weren't coming in and I got worried."

Hearing real concern in his voice, Sarah opened the door a bit wider.

"As you can see, Marvin, I'm not exactly dressed for visitors."

Her voice was a little cool compared to her usually warm self.

"These are for you," he said, holding out the bunch of pink and white tulips.

It was a beautiful bouquet and Sarah immediately loved it, but she kept her hands close to her side.

"Why the flowers? It's not a special day."

"I thought they'd cheer you up if you weren't feeling well."

The flowers were very tempting and she adored tulips. After some hesitation, the flowers won her over and she opened the door wider as she took the bouquet.

"Thank you. Please come in."

"Sarah, my dear, I can't stop thinking about you," Marvin said, looking flustered and very nervous.

"But Marvin, I haven't heard from you for a whole week. A very long week, I might add. Where were you? Did I do something to upset you? I've missed you so much." She knew she was babbling and she was starting to feel teary-eyed.

Amused at Sarah's outburst of anxiety, Marvin walked toward the living room.

Turning to face her fully, he answered, "No, my dear, just the opposite. I wanted to show you in the best way possible my intentions are honorable. But I had a few things to do first."

Honorable? What kind of things?

"Whatever are you talking about?" Sarah asked with some annoyance as she found a vase for the flowers.

When she turned around, Marvin was stiffly settled on one knee, having placed his hand on the arm of the sofa to balance himself.

"Oh, Marvin, are you all right? Did you fall?"

"I'm fine. I just want to do this the traditional way," he said as he reached into his pocket and pulled out a small black velvet box. "After I left you here last week, I couldn't stop thinking about us."

"Oh, Marvin, that's so sweet."

Still holding the unopened box, Marvin continued, "I am an old-fashioned man. Sarah, I want to spend all my nights with you and wake up every morning with you in my arms. I want to give you all my love, every minute of every day. Please make me the happiest man in the world and say you'll be my wife."

"Oh, Marvin...." Her voice trailed off.

She didn't know what to say. She was overwhelmed by his declaration of love.

"Make no mistake about it, dearest Sarah. I am totally, completely, madly in love with you."

"I love you too, Marvin. But this is so sudden," Sarah responded with a tremor of doubt in her voice. Marvin beamed jubilantly when Sarah said she loved him. Half the battle was won!

"Why wait? Marry me now, darling Sarah!"

Opening the box, Marvin revealed a sparkling large diamond set in an art deco platinum setting surrounded by glittering pave diamonds.

It was a gorgeous ring and Sarah gasped, "Oh, Marvin, it's so beautiful."

Marvin, still on one knee, proudly told her how he had designed the ring with the help of his jeweler friend.

"It's a little like you," he explained. "It's a sparkling gem set in a traditional setting surrounded by people who love you. Me, especially."

"Marvin, I love you and this beautiful ring," but then she paused.

She didn't know why, but she suddenly felt hesitant.

"Do you really think it could work, us being married? We're a little old and set in our ways."

"I know what I want. I want you and I want our life together and I want it to start as soon as possible. We can stay here on Lily Court Lane if you want to, or we can go and live wherever you like. I'll do whatever you want. I just want to be with you, to love you, to laugh with you and enjoy our life together, my dearest Sarah, and I hope you feel the same about me."

Marvin groaned as he rose from his bended knee and taking the ring out of the box, he reached for Sarah's hand and placed the ring on her finger. It fit perfectly. Sarah looked down at the ring and then back at Marvin. She was so moved she felt the need to lighten the moment or she'd surely start to cry.

"I really must get a manicure before I can show this beautiful ring to all my friends."

Marvin laughed, "Is that a yes? Please make me a happy man and say you'll marry me."

Sarah wanted to say "yes", but something inside her was holding her back. She felt thrilled yet frightened. She needed time. Her life had been moving so quickly this year she felt almost breathless.

Hesitantly, Sarah finally answered, "I need a little time to consider your wonderful proposal. I do love you with all my heart but I just have to take some time to think about this."

She looked at him with a more serious expression, not the joy Marvin had hoped to see on her face. Sliding the ring off her finger, she pressed it into his hand.

"You keep this safe for me and let me think about everything. I'll have an answer for you very soon. I promise you, my love, I won't keep you waiting too long."

Replacing the ring in the box, Marvin reluctantly shoved it into his suit pocket. He was disappointed, but she hadn't said no and she clearly did love him, so he knew the odds were in his favor. Lawyers do have a way of being persuasive, but he was afraid if he pressed her too hard now, she might turn him down.

"Can we have dinner tonight?" he asked instead.

"I would love to," Sarah replied, "but I can't. I've already made dinner plans."

His heart sank. Was there someone else?

Seeing the look of concern on his face, Sarah rushed to calm his fears.

"Oh, no, Marvin, don't be worried. I'm meeting Jane for dinner."

He was relieved.

"Jane? Well, that's a surprise and a nice one, too. I'm sorry we can't have dinner but I am glad that you're finally giving her a chance.

She seems like a really nice woman and I could see Craig is very taken with her."

Sarah held her tongue. Not Marvin, too, she thought, not wanting to discuss Jane with him. Sliding her hand under his arm, Sarah walked Marvin to the door. He was disappointed. The morning had not ended the way he had hoped.

Trying to reassure him, Sarah repeated, "Don't worry, Marvin dear. I won't keep you waiting very long."

She was reluctant to give Marvin an immediate answer because her history of breast cancer always hung over her, making every important decision a difficult one. After Marvin left her with a peck on the cheek, Sarah suddenly felt much more energized and hurried to get dressed. All at once she felt happy and bursting with excitement. Looking in the mirror as she applied her lipstick, she said to her reflection, "He loves me! He really loves me."

She no longer felt angry. The hurt she'd felt had turned to anger and finally to sadness. Now she understood why she'd fallen into such a state. She really loved this man, she was sure of it, but did she want to marry him?

Just a short while later, she opened the door to her bakery, calling, "Do we have enough cupcakes?"

37

Decision Time

As the day passed, Sarah's every thought led her back to Marvin's proposal. On the treadmill next to Carolee at the gym, she thought of taking long walks by the bay with Marvin. On the rowing machine, she wondered if Marvin was a good swimmer, and on the stationary bike she planned a picnic lunch she would pack for them when they went to Balboa Park. Would he collect seashells with her as they strolled along the beach in Del Mar?

Sarah barely listened as Carolee told her about Cindy's strained relationship with Ming after the uncomfortable dinner with his family. Then, laughing, Carolee told her she had learned a new word yesterday.

"Ming told Cindy he picked up the term 'spaving' in one of his business classes. Have you ever heard that word? It means spending to save and I do enjoy getting a good bargain on sale. I 'spave' a lot."

Carolee realized how distracted Sarah must be when she didn't immediately laugh at the joke or tease Carolee about her clothing purchases as she usually did. What was she worrying about? Craig, Marvin, something else? Whatever it was, Sarah didn't seem eager to talk about it, despite Carolee's urging.

At six o'clock that evening Jane knocked on Sarah's door. She wore fitted jeans, a midnight blue leather jacket and a beautiful gold cashmere scarf that framed her lovely face. Sarah felt her breath catch as she greeted her dinner companion. It was no wonder Craig was so attracted to her. She had to admit the woman was beautiful.

Sarah was pleased she'd taken a little extra time getting herself ready for dinner. She wanted to be at her best and certainly didn't want to be Craig's frumpy old mother standing next to this glamorous woman. She had chosen her best olive green wool slacks and a buttery soft, rust suede jacket. She needed all her "armor" tonight.

Not speaking much at first, the two women walked the few blocks to the Italian restaurant in the Gaslamp. The evening had turned cool and they decided to sit indoors at a window table where they could watch the passing crowd. Candlelight, crystal wine glasses and crisp white linen tablecloths all combined to create a warm and inviting atmosphere. The daisies on each table added a touch of spring. The air was filled with the delicious fragrance of garlic and herbs and the sounds of lively conversation and muted laughter.

As they studied their menus and chatted about what to order, the two women discovered they both liked the same dishes. When the waiter brought a basket of fragrant garlic bread and a dish of olive oil, they agreed it was a good thing there was no one to kiss tonight.

"Let's order some wine," Jane suggested.

"That would be fine. Why don't you choose?"

"Do you like Chianti? It would be perfect with our meal."

Sarah agreed. She idly wondered if Jane was trying to impress her, but she refused to be won over. Despite her misgivings, the evening seemed to be going well. Both women ordered Caprese salads with thick slices of juicy heirloom tomatoes, mozzarella cheese, and fresh basil drizzled with olive oil. They clinked their glasses filled with the ruby red wine, and wished each other good health. There's a safe toast, they both thought to themselves.

Jane hoped when Sarah got to know her better, they could become friends. Sarah was surprised to realize she was having a good time and wanting the evening to be a pleasant one, she decided to rethink her main purpose for having dinner with Jane, and not tell her she was all wrong for Craig.

The wine broke some of the tension between them and conversation began to flow, haltingly at first, but then more freely.

"Have you heard anything more about the painting?" Sarah inquired. "As far as I know, the plan is still the same. Craig is bringing the painting to San Diego to show it to the lady in Pt. Loma."

Jane nodded, "Yes, and I can't wait to see the real thing, rather than just a computer image."

"Me, too. We've all heard so much about it."

Hmmm, was it the painting or Craig Jane couldn't wait to see?

Jane didn't mention the dismal phone conversation she'd had with Craig, but Sarah could see Jane's mood had suddenly changed. Had Craig broken off his relationship with her? Sarah certainly hoped so. The thought lightened Sarah's mood ever so slightly. So maybe she wouldn't need to have that talk with Jane after all.

"It makes me so sad when I think about what Emilie went through as a little girl." Jane sighed, saying "Emilie suffered such a loss. Can you imagine, coming home from school one day and finding your whole family gone? She's such a remarkable person, so full of life despite what she had to endure at the age of ten. Never to know, never to be able to bury your loved one. How sad that must be. So unfinished."

Seeing Sarah's interested, Jane continued, "After hearing her story, I knew I had to finish saying goodbye to my own mother. Emilie gave me the emotional nudge I needed to finally make the trip to Florida last week and scatter my mother's ashes in the Gulf of Mexico. It was on that very beach where she and my father first met and fell in love."

Sarah felt unexpectedly touched by Jane's confiding in her. She spoke with so much feeling about her mother, she must have been close to her. How nice it would have been, Sarah thought wistfully, to have a daughter of her own.

As Jane busied herself unwrapping the linen cloth on the bread-basket, Sarah couldn't contain herself any longer. She blurted out, "Marvin asked me to marry him!"

She felt herself blush when she realized how impetuous her outburst had been. Jane was by no means the person she envisioned being the first to know, but it was too late now to take back her words.

She had kept the proposal bottled up inside her all day. When she saw Carolee at the gym, waved to Dallas from her doorway, and even saw Maryann, her dear sister-in-law, out for her "pregnant lady" afternoon stroll, Sarah had held herself back. Why on earth would she reveal her secret to Jane, her archenemy, the cougar who might take her son from her?

"I am so happy for you both. Congratulations!"

Sarah held her hand up, "No, wait! I haven't said yes, yet."

"Sarah, really?" The surprise in Jane's voice was evident. "May I ask, why not? I know it's none of my business but he seems like such a nice man, and you look so happy every time I see the two of you together."

"I keep worrying what people will think about our marrying so soon after my husband's death. I ask myself if I am being disloyal to Harry, and, then, what will Craig think?"

Her brain-to-mouth filter just didn't seem to be working at the moment.

Weighing her words carefully, Jane replied, "I know Craig wants you to be happy. Your happiness means everything to him."

"Really? Well, I'm just not sure."

"There's only one important question, Sarah. Do you love Marvin?"

Sarah paused for a moment before responding.

"It's the only thing I am certain of. I love him very much. When I didn't see him last week I missed him so much and I acted like a crazy woman."

"Well, then, Sarah, it seems to me your answer is clear. You should marry him."

Sarah responded with a question, "Have you ever wanted to get married."

Jane looked sad as she simply replied, "I never met anyone I wanted to be with forever," silently adding to herself, "until now".

Wrapped up in her own concerns, Sarah didn't pursue Jane's answer any further.

Instead she said, "There's another more serious reason for my hesitation," and then she told Jane about her breast cancer.

"You know as I talk about it, it strikes me what I'm really afraid of is my cancer will come back. Is it fair bringing someone into my life when I could get sick again or even die?"

Sarah's voice shook as the words tumbled from her lips. This was her most secret fear. This conversation shouldn't be happening, Sarah thought. Why was she baring her soul to Jane of all people when all she'd planned to say to her was, "Stay away from my son?"

"Sarah," Jane said, leaning toward her, "We'll all die one day. None of us know how much time we have left. Finding true love in whatever shape it comes, whenever it comes, is a true blessing. No one should be alone unless they choose to be. Do you realize how lucky you are? We all worry about loss and death, that's the bitter-sweet quality of life. But loving and being loved in return, that's all that counts, that's what makes it all worth living."

As she spoke these heartfelt words, Jane reconsidered her situation with Craig. She came to the realization she couldn't allow anyone, not even his mother, to influence their relationship. Only she and Craig should decide their future, if there was to be one. As much as she wanted Sarah to like her and be her friend, she knew it would be Sarah's choice to make. For herself, she couldn't give Craig up.

Sarah softened as she listened to Jane's words. She realized Jane could be talking about herself as well. In a flash, she realized suddenly if Jane really did love her son, their age difference shouldn't be an issue. Deep inside, Sarah could feel a tiny sliver of her heart begin to thaw and her mistrust weaken.

"I'll think about what you said, I really will," was Sarah's only reply.

Then her face lit up as she smiled at Jane for the first time, a warm welcoming smile inviting more conversation.

Maybe it wouldn't be so bad to have grandchildren with red hair. Suddenly she knew what her answer would be and she could hardly wait to call Marvin.

But it was a call which needed the privacy of her own home.

After finishing their eggplant parmesan, they ordered tiramisu to share along with their decaf cappuccinos. Sarah spoke of her session at the gym with Carolee, and Jane shared news about a new hotel in Tahiti she was planning to recommend to clients. Conversation flowed effortlessly as though they'd been friends for a long time.

The two women enjoyed the crisp evening air as they strolled back to Lily Court Lane. Saying goodnight they both agreed how much they looked forward to Craig's return with the painting next week. Sarah leaned forward and kissed a surprised and pleased Jane on the cheek.

Sarah could hardly wait to get inside her house to call Marvin. Then she would call Craig as well, to tell him of Marvin's proposal and about the lovely evening she'd just shared with Jane.

The minute she heard Marvin's voice at the other end of the line, Sarah could only say, "Yes, yes, my love, yes! Bring that ring back to me right this minute."

Smiling with a great sense of happiness and with some relief, Marvin couldn't resist teasing Sarah a bit and so he asked, "Who is this?"

"It's me! Your bride-to-be!"

And they both laughed with joy.

"I'll be right over."

38

Say Hello for Me

Dorothy started right in, no hello, no how are you this morning?

"I know Mom," Ming replied, trying to remain polite, "but not this time. This is too important ...."

Dorothy cut in impatiently, "We're Chinese. You must listen to your father and me."

"But, Mom," he interrupted her. "That's not good enough. I want more. Don't make me choose between my family and Cindy. I really like her and I want all of you in my life. I was born here. I'm an American and I want to follow American customs."

He hadn't planned to be so blunt, but he couldn't stop himself. Ming heard a gasp and then there was silence on the other end.

Dorothy covered the phone as Lloyd entered the room. He took one look at her face and knew instantly what she was up to.

"Dorothy, you promised."

Dorothy, with angry tears in her eyes, handed the phone to Lloyd.

"Here, you talk some sense to him. He's being impossible."

Taking the phone, Lloyd said, "Ming, your mother is upset. She's crying."

Sure, thought Ming, she always cries when she wants to get her way.

"Dad, she's the one who's being impossible. You know how she can be. Make her understand. I will make my own choices. I won't argue with her, but I can't give in to her on this. I told Mom I care about Cindy and this is my life we're talking about, not hers."

Lloyd thought to himself, oh, the drama of being young and in love, but he spoke in a calm voice.

"You know your mother only wants what's best for you."

Dorothy standing next to Lloyd, straining to hear the conversation, nodded her head in agreement.

"I do know, Dad, but it's her version of what's best for me."

Lloyd now surprised his son by telling him, "I liked Cindy. She's a very nice girl and the whole family liked her. We were impressed by her honesty and her plans for the future. Her obvious devotion to her mother was pleasing. Not many young girls care that much about their mothers. Perhaps if you give her time your mother may come around."

All this time, Dorothy had stood glowering and waving her arms, her moist eyes black with rage. Several times she stamped her foot, but Lloyd waved her away as he continued.

"No matter how much your mother protests, I could tell she was charmed by Cindy. Remember, in your mother's mind, no one is good enough for you."

Dorothy nodded at this.

"Just give her some time, son."

At that, Dorothy stomped off into the other room. She'd had enough of these two men in her life.

The conversation ended without resolution. Seated on the sofa in his living room, feeling disappointed with himself, Ming knew he hadn't handled things very well. He should have prepared his mother for meeting Cindy, but he'd dreaded her reaction. At the very least, he should have confided in Dwight and Mei. He felt like such a coward and he was frustrated by his mother's stubbornness. Yet he was hopeful because of the surprising encouragement offered by his father. There was no doubt in his mind—he cared about Cindy and now he just had to convince Cindy of it.

⁓

At the bakery Cindy was taking a tray of French baguettes out of the oven. She'd decided she wasn't going to see Ming ever again. She loved her own mother too much to come between Ming and his mother.

When Carolee heard Cindy's decision, she was upset for her daughter, but she respected her feelings. When asked, the best advice she could give Cindy was, "Follow your heart, but be careful," although it was not in Carolee's nature to be cautious about anything.

Cindy wailed, "But, Mom, my heart is broken in two. One half says be with Ming no matter what. The other half says run as fast as you can away from his domineering mother."

Carolee could only nod in sympathy, but she wisely remained silent. She knew she couldn't make decisions for Cindy anymore. Her child had blossomed into a grown woman. Affairs of the heart needed no intervention, especially from a well-meaning mother, be it Ming's or Cindy's, or even Craig's.

For the next couple of days, Cindy had trouble deciding which side of her heart would win out—the rational or the romantic. She needed time to think it through.

Cindy made sure she was always too busy for the nightly phone calls and texts from Ming. It was clear he missed her as much as she missed him. Nevertheless, she deleted his messages.

⁓

A few days later, Ming decided he had given Cindy enough time to cool down. He sat in his car parked outside the bakery resolutely waiting for her to appear at the end of her workday.

Cindy had made no plans for the evening and took her time closing the bakery unaware Ming was patiently waiting outside. She missed Ming so much she felt a hollow place in her stomach. Lost in thought, she carefully locked the bakery door and turning to walk away, she bumped into Ming's broad chest.

His arms came around her, steadying her as he drew her to him. He kissed her, gently at first, an experimental tasting of her lips, then cupping her face, he kissed each eyelid, her forehead, and then the tip of her nose.

Pleased and laughing in spite of herself, she tried to push him away, but he held her tight.

"Stop kissing me," she ordered in a stern voice. "What're you doing here, Ming?"

He thought it was a good sign she didn't move from his arms.

"I'll never stop kissing you, I love you and I want to keep kissing you for a very long time."

As the words came tumbling out, Cindy's mouth fell open, and Ming, too, was surprised he'd uttered the words aloud.

"We can't talk here," she replied, trying to pull away.

"What's to talk about? Do you love me, Cindy?" he asked, his voice husky with emotion.

Pushing Ming into the doorway of the bakery, Cindy replied in a very serious voice, "Yes, I do, but, you know that's not the issue."

"Then what is the issue?"

"Your mother! You know how I feel about family, especially mothers."

Ming started to laugh and Cindy became cross.

"I don't see what's so funny," she said.

"What's so funny is you are just like my mother, so fierce and determined," and with that he swept her up in his arms again. Lifting her off the sidewalk, he spun her around as he repeated over and over, "I love you, I love you."

"Put me down this minute," she ordered, kicking her feet in the air.

He had a disconcerting way of sweeping her off her feet, emotionally as well as physically.

Doing as she asked, he lowered her gently to the sidewalk, saying in his most serious voice, "I do love you, you know, no matter what you say. I love you today and I'll love you tomorrow and for all our tomorrows together."

Stopping her words with a kiss, Ming then told Cindy of the surprisingly positive conversation he had with his father.

"Your father liked me? Your family did, too?"

A single tear began to roll down Cindy's cheek.

Oh, no, another crying woman, Ming thought. What's a man to do?

"Don't cry, Cindy. This is good news. It'll be fine, you'll see."

Cindy gulped between sobs, "It's just I'm so glad to see you again." Throwing her arms around his neck, she whispered "I do love you, I really do!"

Then ignoring all the passersby, she kissed him fiercely, sending a sizzle crackling through him.

Days later his father proved right. The next time his mother called Ming at work, she said reluctantly just as she was ending the conversation, "Oh by the way, say hello to Cindy for me."

Ming knew this didn't mean his mother was reconciled to his choice of a partner or that life with his family would go smoothly for them in the future, but it should be enough to convince Cindy there was at least a chance for them.

39

The Will

In Düsseldorf, Germany, Max Schmidt was packing his carry-on bag. He regarded himself in the bedroom mirror and flicked a piece of imaginary lint off his impeccable pinstriped suit. He liked his life to be uncomplicated. His business relationships were simple, and ever since his divorce, he'd kept his relationships with women loose and casual. He'd learned he wasn't the marrying kind.

What an unpleasant shock the phone call had been, taking him completely by surprise. The news was not at all what he'd expected to hear. Not only had the painting not been sold as quickly as he'd hoped, but tomorrow he was flying to San Francisco to meet Craig and together they would travel to San Diego.

Max didn't like surprises, especially one like this where there was a good chance he would lose part of his grandfather's legacy, the painting of the mother and child. The painting itself didn't interest him, except for what monetary value it might have. That's what was important to him.

He'd been delighted to find himself the sole heir of the huge rundown castle. The few remaining servants were pensioned off and Max began to plan his conversion of the castle into a bed and breakfast lodging, with perhaps a charming restaurant facing the front courtyard. He had an eye for good business deals, and he hoped his dull days spent as an accountant would be left behind for a livelier and more social career. He wanted to meet some attractive women and enjoy life.

The Baron had left him only enough actual cash to get started with his plans and as he himself was not wealthy, he'd need to liquidate much of the art and the other valuables remaining in the castle. At the reading of the will, the attorney informed him his grandfather had called him to write a codicil to the will. The attorney read it aloud.

"To My Grandson Max,

My castle is now yours. It served our family well and survived the war years, but now it has become a cold and empty place. After your grandmother died, and your father left, there was no reason to continue maintaining all the rooms. These days my bones ache from the constant drafts and perpetual dampness.

Use the money I am leaving you to restore the main rooms. The castle must remain in our family or it is to be offered to the German government and placed in a national trust. It must be preserved.

You may dispose of any items inside the castle, however, I caution you about the small painting of the mother and child which is very special to me. Only my eyes have seen it for more than sixty years. Although, unfortunately, you have had no art education, make no mistake, this is a treasure, but one that must be kept private. It is against your best interests to sell it or make it public...."

Here the codicil stopped and the attorney explained the old man had been stricken by what proved to be a fatal stroke. The codicil remained unsigned.

Max had been relieved that the lack of signature allowed him to do what he wished with the silly little painting. He never liked his cold and distant grandfather anyway and he didn't understand why he wanted him to keep the painting private. So he would sell it as quickly and quietly as possible. He then decided not to have it appraised by an art expert in Germany. Instead he sent it to his American acquaintance, Jack Hillson, in San Francisco. That should be far enough away to bring a rich American buyer and little publicity. In his mind's eye, Max could see the castle restored to its former glory. He had grand plans.

As he checked his passport, Max thought of his grandfather again. A tricky old fellow, he concluded, a man with many secrets but little warmth. He wondered what secrets the old fellow took to his grave. He thought it unfortunate they hadn't spent much time together, but his father forbade it, for reasons he never revealed. He always said, "You are better off away from him, Max."

But now there was an old lady in San Diego claiming the painting was hers, stolen from her childhood home in Paris. How could she possibly prove such a thing after so many years had passed? If her story were true, how had the painting come into his grandfather's possession? Max realized that Germany's past held many untold shameful stories, especially about the Nazi years when his grandfather was a young man and an officer in Hitler's army. But he refused to worry. This painting couldn't possibly be hers.

Max wished again his grandfather was still alive to explain how he had obtained the painting. It would save him this bothersome trip to America. What had happened on the day his grandfather had died? Why had he felt it necessary to add a codicil to his will? What had he left unsaid? Too many unanswered questions.

Max knew only what his grandfather's attorney had been able to tell him. He'd received an urgent call from the old man, and had arrived at the castle in the late afternoon. He came alone as instructed, and began writing as the Baron dictated. All at once, there was silence. The attorney looked up to find the Baron slumped over his desk.

Max would have been astonished if he'd seen his grandfather's activities earlier that same day. The Baron, frail and barely alive, had raised a shaking right arm in salute to his dead Fuhrer. He attempted to click his heels together but the effort proved too much, nearly toppling him to the floor. Steadying himself, he lifted his eyes to the wall in front of him.

There, in the cellar's dim light, hung the painting of a young woman holding in her arms a smiling infant with golden curls. Such perfection, he marveled. *Mevrouw Van Bruggen Met Emilia.* A Flemish masterpiece? He still thought so. Light caressed the cornflower blue folds of the mother's gown and shone on the child's upturned face. The Baron was moved. No one had ever loved him the way this mother loved her child.

After so many years of silence, the old man knew the time was near when the painting might come to light. His days were ending, his lifeblood weakened by illness and old age. Just yesterday, the doctor had given him a grim report.

"Not much time left, Baron, I'm afraid," he'd said when he listened to the irregular thumping in the old man's chest.

The Baron took great joy that he'd fooled them all, escaping after the war had ended and living out a long life. No tribunals for him, no prison or suicide pills. He lived his life in privacy with the considerable wealth he'd amassed during the war by stealing money and selling possessions from those he had helped oppress and murder. He never felt regret for the loss of so many lives. He was only following orders he told himself.

As he leaned heavily on his cane, he felt proud. He'd won, he cackled now. He still had his masterpiece and he had survived all the searches for him. One last glimpse, just one more, he had promised himself this morning when he shakily rose from his bed.

When he died, his grandson, the last of the family line, would claim this legacy. He hoped his grandson would have enough sense to know what to do with something so beautiful and valuable. It would be a sin for it to be tossed into a back room or set aside in ignorance. He decided to call his attorney immediately and add a codicil to his will. The Baron hated the thought of dying. This final loss of control maddened him.

Slowly and painfully he climbed the stairs out of the climate-controlled cellar, as he recalled the afternoon when he'd entered the devastated house in Paris and saw the painting for the first time. The family had been taken away earlier that day and he was responsible for their subsequent deaths. He relished strutting into the empty houses to collect the valuables he found there. He already possessed a secret stash that would adorn his castle when he returned home one day as a war hero. Overcome with greed, he ignored a noise from the floor above him, and seized the painting.

He hadn't thought of that sound for years. Could anyone have seen him? No, no one could have survived, he reassured himself yet again.

40

The Letter

Outwardly calm but trembling inside, Emilie sat on her living room sofa waiting, her ankles crossed, her hands folded in her lap. A petite woman, Parisian to the core, she wore her best dress, a simple Lanvin grey dress with long sleeves, the hemline reaching just below the knee. Her headband held back her perfectly coifed grey bob with pearl earrings her only jewelry this morning. Her bright fuchsia lipstick and nail polish matched perfectly, and she wore the perfume of her youth, Guerlain's *L'Heure Bleu*, the Blue Hour. The soft scent reminded her of her husband.

The young man from the gallery was bringing the painting from San Francisco, along with its self-proclaimed owner who had traveled all the way from Germany. There would be others present as well, including a lawyer representing Craig, and a security guard to protect the painting.

With their arrival expected at any minute, Emilie's friend Pearl helped set out the flaky croissants still warm from the oven. Emilie had asked her to stay for the meeting. Pearl had shared so many other important moments with her, helping her through the sad time after Bill's sudden death.

At last the doorbell rang and everyone arrived together. When Pearl opened the door, Craig, anticipating Emilie's apprehension, crossed the room quickly. He held both her outstretched hands and greeted her warmly.

"Please don't stand up," he said as she attempted to rise. "I know this must be very difficult for you, Miss Emilie."

Her cold hands trembled in his. "I am so glad to see you again, *Monsieur*."

She had insisted Craig call her by her first name. She liked this very polite and charming young man. Then she greeted Jane, the beautiful woman who was obviously in love with Craig.

"The day has finally arrived. I've waited a very long time for this moment. Seventy years," she said, shaking her head before turning to a very blond man.

He stepped forward and introduced himself as Max Schmidt.

"I am very pleased to meet you, Madame and very anxious to clear up this matter," he said as he bowed formally and took her hand. "I would like to add I am sorry for the loss of your family."

Emilie nodded, acknowledging his comment.

Craig and his partner, Jack, had explained to Max the story of Emilie's tragic childhood and the disappearance of the painting. The story both saddened and worried Max. Did his grandfather have a secret past? Could he have been a thief or worse? There was so much he didn't know about Germany and his family back then. No one ever spoke about those days.

"Thank you for your willingness to come here today," Emilie quietly replied to Max. "You may have much to lose."

"We will see," was his cryptic reply as he stepped back, his brow creased with worry.

Next, Craig introduced Emilie to Marvin who gently took her hand. Then he introduced Carolee who was present as Marvin's paralegal. Carolee greeted Emilie and sat down in a chair opening her notebook, ready to take notes, a small tape recorder at her side.

"Miss Emilie, do I have your permission to record the conversation today so we'll have an accurate record?"

Emilie replied, "Of course, *Monsieur* Miller."

At the back of the room a uniformed security guard stood holding a black leather portfolio case. Craig motioned him to come forward and he carefully placed the case on the cleared coffee table. Emilie gestured to Pearl to wait before setting out the coffee and croissants. Putting on white gloves, the security guard took the key from Craig and unlocked the chain holding the case to his wrist and stepped back.

The moment had arrived and everyone in the living room grew silent and expectant.

Craig asked everyone to be seated as he took the chair closest to Emilie. Opening his laptop, he explained to Emilie that he was making the necessary connection to bring Jack Hillson into the room by video conference from the Bayside Gallery.

Turning the screen so that Jack could see everyone in the room, Craig introduced him to Emilie.

"Good morning, everyone. Hello, Miss Emilie, it's a pleasure to meet you. I'm sorry I couldn't be in San Diego with you today."

Carolee switched on the tape recorder and started taking notes as Craig proceeded to speak in a formal manner.

"We are here today to resolve the provenance of a painting. It is entitled '*Mevrouw Van Bruggen Met Emilia*' which is possibly a missing painting also known as '*Madame DuPont Avec Emilie.*' Jack Hillson, my partner at the Bayside Gallery in San Francisco, agreed to our transporting the piece here to San Diego.

"The painting was received on consignment from Herr Max Schmidt who has also joined us today. Mrs. Connor claims that the painting in question belonged to her family. Until recently, the painting was kept in a castle in Germany. It came to Herr Schmidt as a legacy from his grandfather's estate. No record could be found of its ever having been sold.

"Since there was no provenance available," Craig continued, looking over at Marvin, "I decided, with the help of attorney Marvin Miller, to investigate the history of this artwork and that investigation led us to Emilie Connor."

Herr Schmidt remained standing, a restless look on his face.

As she looked at him, Emilie decided he seemed like a pleasant and handsome young man, tall, blond and blue-eyed. He reminded her of the German soldiers she had seen in the Paris of her youth. Today he seemed to be just an ordinary young man standing nervously in her living room. She knew he would pace the room if he could.

In turn, Herr Schmidt looked at Emilie, thinking this meeting would be a total waste of his time. What proof could she possibly have? The painting was his. Yet it was best to clear things up as quickly as possible so he could return to his project at home.

Craig asked the guard to lift the lid of the case and remove the painting.

"For the record," he said, "we are now opening the case to reveal the painting."

Emilie rose from her chair and intently watched the guard as he lifted the small painting from the case. Craig donned white gloves, and taking the painting from the guard he turned it so Emilie could see it from where she was standing by her chair. She gasped, and with a shaking hand took a lace-trimmed handkerchief Pearl handed her. She dabbed at her eyes as she sank back into her chair.

"*Mon Dieu!*" she exclaimed, looking up at everyone. It was all there, the blue gown, the mother tenderly holding the baby. In a trembling voice she said, "*C'est ma peinture!* It is my painting!"

All eyes were focused on the overwhelmed elderly woman, until Craig turned the painting so the others in the room could view it.

Herr Schmidt, frowning but still in control of himself, spoke in a firm voice, "Madame, I appreciate your agony over the loss of your family, and your wish for this painting to be the one taken from your family, but it cannot be. This painting was in my grandfather's collection for many decades. A whole lifetime. You can imagine my surprise when he died and left it to me. Most of his collection went to the Düsseldorf Art Museum so this painting must have been very dear to his heart. I regret to have to say this, but I need to see proof this is your painting."

Clasping her hands tightly, Emilie spoke in a quavering voice, "I have your proof for you, *Monsieur.* When I came home from school that awful day, my family was missing and our house had been ransacked, but the painting still hung above the mantel in the front room. I was a child of ten, and so terrified by what I saw I hid myself upstairs in my closet. I must have fallen asleep and when I awoke, I could hear boots walking across the living room floor. Papa never wore boots. I heard a man's voice mumbling some words I did not understand. I was very afraid. I stayed in my hiding place until our housekeeper, Mathilde, found me many hours later. The last thing I saw as I left the house that evening was the empty space above the fireplace. Whoever was in my house that afternoon took the painting."

"That is all very well and good, Madame," Max said impatiently, "but it is still not proof."

Just as he thought, it was all the nonsense of a senile old lady.

"Wait, *Monsieur,*" Emilie raised her hand to stop him, "I do have your proof." Turning to Craig she requested, "Would you please turn the painting over?"

Craig did so, and found himself looking at the peeling, aged, brown paper backing on which was written in a faded spidery handwriting, the name *"Mevrouw van Bruggen Met Emilia."*

Emilie continued, "Craig, please peel back the lower right hand corner, and you will find all the proof you need, proof as to the ownership of the picture. I saw my father leave a message for me there. I had returned home that morning to get my schoolbooks. It was my tenth birthday and in my excitement I had forgotten them.

When I entered the house, I saw Papa placing something into the back of the painting. I knew it had to be part of my birthday surprise and I quietly crept away so as not to spoil his secret. My father and I always played games hiding things around the house. "

Craig looked to Marvin, who in turn asked Max, "Do we have your permission to lift the backing paper of the painting, Herr Schmidt? We'll be very careful not to harm it."

Emilie interrupted, saying "Just peel it back a bit on the lower right-hand corner, and you will easily find what is hidden there. But before we do that, let me show you our family portrait taken the year before the painting disappeared."

Stepping forward, Pearl solemnly handed Emilie the family album open to the photo she had seen so many times.

"Here, this is the photograph," Emilie said as she removed the yellowed photo from the album and handed it to Herr Schmidt.

Max saw a family portrait taken in front of a Parisian fireplace. Shocked, he saw something above the mantel clearly resembling his painting. His heart sank. He wondered again if somehow his grandfather had been instrumental in the terrible events of that day. Even as he denied this ominous thought to himself, he felt shame rising in his throat. Had his grandfather been a Nazi thief? Max didn't know. This was never discussed in his home, nor did his grandfather ever mention those years on the rare times Max was allowed to visit him.

The photo was passed around the living room for everyone to see while a white linen cloth was placed on the coffee table. Craig gently placed the painting face down on it, and using a small pocketknife, he carefully peeled back a bit of the brown paper. Carefully reaching inside, he felt nothing. He feared for Emilie, there would be no proof.

But then, his fingertips caught the edge of something and he was able to slowly work it to the corner and gently slide it out. It was as Emilie promised, an old envelope, yellowed and very fragile, papery thin to the touch. Everyone in the room seemed to be holding their breath.

"I believe this is yours, Miss Emilie," Craig said as he handed her the unsealed envelope.

On the outside of the envelope, in elegant copperplate handwriting, were written the words *Ma Chere Emilie, Juin 1942*.

Max Schmidt looked pale and uncomfortable. Carolee, glancing up from her note pad, felt sorry for the handsome man who it seemed was about to learn an unpleasant truth about his grandfather. She was sure Max was innocent of any wrongdoing. His shock when he saw the envelope convinced her he couldn't have known how the painting had reached his grandfather.

Emilie returned the envelope to Craig. "Please, help me open this, *Monsieur*. My hands are shaking too much."

Craig carefully opened the envelope and removed a single translucent sheet of paper. Still wearing white gloves, he handed it back to Emilie where she sat in her chair looking delicate and frail. She carefully unfolded the letter.

The room was tense and expectant as she read it silently to herself. Then she handed it back to Craig and in an emotion-filled voice asked him to read it aloud and translate it so everyone could understand it.

Craig carefully took the letter from her, saying "It's a good thing I studied French, Miss Emilie. I hope I can remember enough to give you an accurate translation."

Jane smiled at his modesty, knowing he was fluent in French.

He began to read.

"My Dearest Daughter Emilie,

I am writing this letter to you on your special tenth birthday. I know I have teased you many times the little girl in the painting above the fireplace looks like you. We both know that while you resemble her, this is a baby from a long time before you were born. Mama and I want this to be your painting in celebration of your tenth birthday today. We hope in time you will show it to your own little girl.

Before the German invasion, we had the painting appraised. This old family heirloom has proven to be very valuable, a work by a Flemish master. Although you know it as "Madame Du Pont Avec Emilie," its correct title is "Mevrouw Van Bruggen Met Emilia." Always remember the painting came to us by helping a young man in need.

Today is a very happy occasion for us but now I must tell you something very serious. These are dark days for all of us who love France. Your mother and I are in constant danger. If something should happen to us, and I pray it does not, keep the painting safe. If for any reason Mama and I are not with you, and it must be sold to help you, speak first to Monsieur Duval at the Louvre.

Please take care of your little sister. Watching you and Noemi together brings us great joy as parents. Whatever happens, know that your Mama and Papa will always be with you. We love you so very much. Trust only Mathilde to keep you safe and do as she says.

Mama and I will continue to work for the day France will be free.

Happy birthday, dear child! Keep these words close to your heart, but do not save this letter.

Vive la France!

Your loving,

Mama and Papa"

These valiant words written by a frightened and loving father touched everyone in the room. Emilie wept as though her heart might break. She could see her father seated at his ornate rosewood desk in his study with his fountain pen in hand. Only many years later did Emilie realize her father was very worried although he presented a calm face to his family. His words in the letter vividly brought him into this room in San Diego.

Max moved to her side and knelt before her. He took her fragile, white, blue-veined hand in his own young strong hand and looking up into her tear-stained face, he smiled sadly.

"Dear Madame, forgive me and my family. The painting is truly yours."

Everyone in the room felt tears of joy and sadness and glancing at the monitor, Craig saw Jack was also clearly moved.

Turning to Jane, Craig said in a low voice, "It means so much to me to have you here with me today." He leaned forward and gently kissed her on the cheek. Then he quietly added, "We'll talk before I go back to San Francisco."

Jane guessed he would be saying goodbye again. Yet another goodbye, she sighed to herself as she replied, "Thank you for inviting me. It's been wonderful to be part of this. It meant more to me than you know."

After the emotion in the room subsided, conversation resumed as everyone wanted to get a closer look at the painting and read the letter even though it was written in French. Each person saw something extraordinary in the painting relating to their own lives. Carolee recalled meeting her adopted daughter for the first time, and felt sadness for a child's lost family. Jane looked at the mother with envy, thinking how much she wanted to have a child, and how she missed her own mother. Craig felt great pride in restoring this incredible work of art to its true owner, and reversing a great wrong. Pearl was thrilled for her friend, whose heart she knew was lightened at last.

Standing to one side of the painting, Marvin, ever practical, wondered what Emilie would do with the painting. If she planned to keep it in her home, would it be safe? Max saw the plans for his bed and breakfast fading, yet he was happy because in some small way he had restored his family's honor. He wished to believe his grandfather was innocent in the disappearance of Emilie's family, but he knew in his heart that wasn't so. He would return to Germany empty-handed, but with the knowledge he had done the right thing.

Carolee switched off the tape recorder, closed her notebook, and placed both in her large designer handbag which today was chartreuse. She approached Max as he stood by himself sipping coffee, looking a little sad.

"I am so sorry, Herr Schmidt. You have lost your painting, but you did such a courageous thing."

Max wished his father was still alive so he could call and tell him this incredible story. But he was alone in the world.

"Thank you, Madame," he said formally. "It is much better the painting has been returned to its rightful owner. It can never replace her family but maybe it will bring her a measure of peace."

Carolee found Max very handsome in a Teutonic sort of way and was reluctant to let him go. She'd taken one look at him when the introductions were being made, and pronounced him the closest thing to a movie star she'd ever seen. Here was her Daniel Craig in person!

"Are you planning to return to Germany right away?" she asked, smiling and looking up into his bright blue eyes.

For the first time Max really saw Carolee and noticed her lovely eyes and concerned expression. Carolee, this lovely blond dressed in her bright clothes with such a serious look on her face, caught him off guard.

"Please, call me Max," he paused and gave her a slight smile. "I think I will be staying a few more days before I return to Germany."

"I would love to hear about your plans for your bed and breakfast, Max. Don't you just love castles?"

"Well, if you are really interested, can we discuss them over lunch?"

"That would be very nice, Max."

41

A Home Run

As Craig stood on the sidewalk in front of Emilie's house, Max walked by, and with a smile announced that he was taking Carolee to lunch.

"Max, you are certainly a good sport. I can't imagine giving up something so beautiful."

"Ah," Max replied, getting into the limo next to Carolee, "but as you can see, all is not lost. There are many kinds of beauty."

Craig laughed. He liked Max and hoped he would find a way to build his bed and breakfast. Finding himself without transportation gave Craig just the excuse he needed.

"Hey lady, how about a ride?" he called out to Jane. "It looks like Max has found himself a prettier lunch partner and I really want to talk to you."

"I'll drop you off on my way to Petco Park. I'm picking up season tickets to have for client entertainment."

The moment they got into Jane's car, Craig leaned across and gently kissed her.

"Hello, my love. It's been too long."

Her cheeks flushed with emotion, but she said, "Oh, Craig, please stop!"

"Why? Even with all this business about the painting, I never for a moment stopped thinking about you. You, Jane. You can't deny what's happening between us. I know you feel it just as much as I do."

"It can't work. You must see that."

"Why must I see that? I don't see that. We can make it work," Craig urged as he gently cupped her face with his long fingers. "We belong together. You know it, too."

Shivering at his touch, as desire spiraled through her, Jane forced herself to be practical.

"Craig," she said resolutely, "I want to be with you, too, but we live so far apart, you in San Francisco and me here in San Diego. A long distance relationship almost never works out and I'm not looking for a sometime lover."

"I don't want any distance between us, Jane." He paused and looked deeply into her concerned eyes. "Marry me, Jane, and come live with me in San Francisco."

It wasn't the most romantic of proposals, but Craig couldn't wait a moment longer to make this wonderful woman his.

Jane was stunned. "Craig, do you know what you're saying?"

"We can get married right away. Let's call Mom and Marvin right now and tell them. So, please say you'll marry me, darling. I love you very much and want to be with you always."

She felt unable to breathe as all the objections ran through her mind. What about the differences in their ages? What would Sarah think? What about her business? What about her new house? She just didn't know! She didn't know what to think or how to answer him.

"It's such a big step, Craig—and so soon. We really haven't known each other very long. What if we find out we're not compatible when we really do get to know each other? I didn't expect this. Oh, but I do love you. You're everything I've always hoped for."

"Well, then?" Craig said with an expectant smile. "Haven't we learned anything from Emilie? She'd known Bill less than 24 hours when she said 'yes'. Sometimes you just have to go with your instincts and follow your heart. Don't overthink it. You have to have faith and trust in yourself and in me. I love you, Jane, with all my heart and I want us to be together, always."

Tossing all reason aside, she impetuously answered, "Yes! Yes, I will." She had learned that lesson from Emilie, she thought. Accept love when it's offered. Don't squander the chance for a passionate and true love.

Over a late lunch, Marvin and Sarah toasted the happy couple who could hardly wait to get away from them and disappear behind the purple door at Number Seven Lily Court Lane.

Craig and Jane never made it to the ballpark that afternoon. They were locked in each other's arms talking, planning, and exploring every inch of each other. Skimming his teeth along her jaw, he nibbled his way around to her ear, where he whispered how much he loved her. They proved again and again that love is ageless and that mothers can learn to accept their sons' choices.

One couple did make it to the ballpark that day. Cindy and Ming were seated on the grass unpacking their picnic basket. Ming brought *char shu bow*--golden brown buns stuffed with roast pork, and *dan tat*--crispy pastry cups filled with a creamy egg custard. Cindy baked a fragrant loaf of rosemary bread to accompany her homemade hummus. She was pouring her favorite drink for a warm afternoon--a combination of fresh lemonade mixed with iced tea, when Ming's cell phone rang.

"Where are you, son? Why is there so much noise? I can hardly hear you," his mother shouted into the phone.

"Mom, I'm at the ballpark with Cindy, and the Padres just scored a home run."

His mother had no interest in the silly game so she came directly to the point.

"Son, bring Cindy and her mother to dinner on Thursday this week."

Ming was shocked and nearly dropped the phone. He looked down at the screen on his cell phone. Was this really his mother or some elaborate joke? What he couldn't see was Lloyd standing at Dorothy's elbow with a very fierce and determined look on his face.

"Cindy's right here, Mom. You can ask her yourself."

Ming, shaking his head in disbelief, handed his cell phone to Cindy. She took it reluctantly with a look of surprise mixed with apprehension.

"Hello," Cindy said cautiously, uncertain how to address Ming's mother. Should she call her Dorothy or Mrs. Sun? She opted to call her nothing at all and play it safe.

"Cindy, you and your mother must come and have dinner with us this Thursday."

Cindy turned to Ming, her mouth falling open in surprise and caught him smiling back at her.

Poking him in the shoulder, she responded to his mother, "That's so very kind of you. I'm sure my mother would love to meet you. I'll call her and see if she can come. May I call you back in a few minutes?"

As the call ended, Lloyd nodded at Dorothy in approval.

"See, that was not very painful after all. It is a first step, and you have made your son very happy."

Dorothy sighed with regret.

"I guess we live in different times. In my day, a child had to make his parents happy, not the other way around."

Hearing about the dinner invitation, Carolee whooped in amazement.

"The old dragon actually called you? I wouldn't miss dinner for anything. Please tell her I accept with pleasure. We'll have to go shopping for new outfits. This is an important event and we need to look our very best," the always-fashionable Carolee added. "Got to go, darling, call you back later," she said, smiling at Max who sat across from her at the table refilling her wine glass. Sadly, Max would be gone by then.

Later that night, in her cozy home in Point Loma, Emilie said her prayers. Exhausted from the day's excitement, she fell asleep looking at the painting now propped up on her dresser across the room. She would need to decide what to do with it, and soon. But first she would go to the cemetery and visit Bill. He had been right in urging her to register her lost painting, and she wished he could know she had her family back in a small way. He would be so very happy for her. What a dear man he had been.

Papa's letter meant even more to her than the painting. The precious envelope was carefully tucked beneath her pillow. The letter inside it was like having Mama, Papa, and little Noemi back with her. Suddenly, she smiled as it came to her. She knew exactly what Papa would want her to do with the painting.

42

Autumn Leaves

The days of spring and summer drifted by and the golden shades of autumn fell on Lily Court Lane. The liquidambar trees, brilliant in their deep crimson and yellow foliage, were beginning to shed their leaves. They swirled in the afternoon breeze and crunched underfoot on sidewalks crowded with the usual shoppers, tourists and workers. The weather was quite warm, a hallmark of fall in San Diego.

Six women gathered at Maryann's house this afternoon. Four of them were seated at the table intently studying the tiles in front of them while Jude and Miss Mittens napped contentedly under the table. Jane and Emilie were sitting nearby watching the others play. Hopefully someone would win soon.

They were meeting at Maryann's house so she'd be more comfortable. Her swollen feet and large belly made every movement an effort. Her due date was just around the corner.

Dallas called out "five dot" as she discarded a tile.

"I'll take that," Sarah said and placed it on her rack with three other "five dot" tiles she exposed. She discarded a joker.

As she picked her tile from the "wall" in the center of the table, Carolee asked "Are you trying for a joker-free hand, Sarah? We'll all have to pay if you succeed!"

Sarah smiled to herself. Carolee had guessed right. It was a difficult hand and she needed only one more tile to call out "mahj" to win the game and the money.

Maryann, attempting to concentrate on her tiles, tried to take her mind off the nagging ache in her lower back. She shifted in her seat once again, trying to find a more comfortable position, but nothing seemed to be working.

Jane, noticing her discomfort, asked "Maryann, can I get you anything?"

"No, I'm fine, I guess," Maryann replied. "But thanks for asking."

Glancing over at Jane, Sarah thought how wrong she'd been about this woman who'd come into her life and would soon be marrying her son. Her friends had been so pleased when Sarah told them of her change of heart toward Jane. But as good friends, they'd wisely refrained from adding, "we told you so."

Sarah remembered what a good time they all had when Craig flew down from San Francisco to spend a long Labor Day weekend with his fiancée and the newlyweds, Sarah and Marvin.

"Something smells good," was the first thing Marvin said when he and Sarah arrived at Jane's house. He was carrying a bottle of chianti and Sarah had brought freshly baked apple tarts from her bakery.

"Why, thank you," Jane replied as she hugged them both. "I made eggplant parmesan, with pasta and garlic bread."

"And," added Craig, "I helped toss the salad."

As they sipped their chianti, Jane and Sarah smiled at each other remembering the special dinner they'd shared some months before. Sarah beamed at Jane, as the younger woman bustled around her kitchen preparing the dinner.

An autumn wedding! Sarah could barely contain herself. She loved weddings, and had already created the design for the vanilla wedding cake and the special chocolate groom's cake she would make at her bakery. As happy as she was, she was sad Jane would be moving to San Francisco after the wedding and no longer be a part of the daily life on Lily Court Lane. It seemed Jane was just unpacking her boxes and now she'd be leaving. The two women would just have to find ways to remain close to one another.

Jane still couldn't believe her good luck. She'd always dreamed of finding true love and making close friends, and now here she was, surrounded by good friends and marrying her dream man with his mother's blessing. She'd miss their weekly mah jongg games but she and Craig planned to keep her house on Lily Court Lane and return for frequent visits. When they told her, Sarah's heart lifted at the news.

Emilie sat contentedly on the sofa watching her new friends at mah jongg. They'd sensed how lonely she was, and made her a part of their life on Lily Court Lane. Although Pearl was a loyal friend, she was often out of town visiting her children and grandchildren. As they got to know Emilie better, she delighted them with her outrageous tales of selling designer clothes to the rich, eccentric women of San Diego.

"Oh, yes, Madame Evanston would order several designer outfits at one time with all the accessories to go with them. She would not be happy until she spent more than fifty thousand dollars at one time."

"Now that's my kind of clothing budget!" Carolee exclaimed, making everyone laugh.

Soon after the painting was returned to Emilie, Carolee had introduced her to Sarah, Maryann and Dallas over lunch one afternoon. After she got to know them a little better, Emilie confided in them the hardships she and Mathilde's family had suffered during the years of the Occupation. She told them about the lack of food, the bone-chilling winters, and the utter turmoil the Germans inflicted on France. Then her face lit up as she spoke of meeting her husband, Bill, and how she had immediately fallen in love with him.

The women were touched by the romance of the story. Carolee leaned over and gently squeezed Emilie's hand wishing something like that would happen to her. When she admired Emilie's antique pink gold wedding band studded with rubies, Emilie smiled in remembrance.

"This is not the original ring Bill gave me. Oh, no, Paris at that time was not a place to buy jewelry. Instead he gave me his class ring," and she laughed, adding "I had to wrap it with tape to keep it from falling from my finger. When we finally arrived in the United States, Bill gave me this ring. It belonged to his mother."

At this, a sad look passed across Emilie's face. She did not have a child of her own to pass the ring on to.

When questioned about her plans for the painting, she told them all very little.

"With the help of Craig and Marvin, I have made a good plan for my painting. I will tell you soon, but until then, it will remain my secret."

From her tone, they knew they should stop questioning her until she was ready to tell them more.

Sarah won the game and as she collected her winnings, she couldn't help but glance down at her left hand which held an eternity band with dazzling diamonds alongside her matching engagement ring. Even though she protested about the expense, Marvin insisted she enjoy it. He wanted the world to see how much he loved and valued her. Secretly, she was thrilled with his extravagance.

Their wedding took place in Sarah's garden in late July. It was a small, quiet gathering attended by friends and family amidst the fragrant roses Sarah loved to grow. Nearly two months had passed since that beautiful wedding afternoon. She still felt like the princess who had kissed a frog and discovered her prince.

Sarah rapped on the table three times for good luck as she thought how every day brought laughter and joy into her life. Then she thought, would there be grandchildren? She certainly hoped so and thinking of babies, she noticed Maryann shifting in her chair again, still unable to find a comfortable position for herself.

Dallas, sitting out as the next game was underway, got up, took a pillow from the sofa and placed it behind Maryann's back.

"Here, maybe this will help."

Dallas was eager to have the afternoon come to an end. She'd agreed to meet Simon for an early dinner. He sounded excited when he told her he had something important to discuss with her. As she turned her attention back to the game, Simon was nervously pacing in his apartment, rehearsing his words.

His career had blossomed. He'd found new satisfaction in taking beautiful candid portraits of people, developed a large following in the bridal photography business and free-lanced for a local television station as well as for a newspaper. He had more than enough work to keep him busy and had no plans to return to the battlefield. His nightmares were less frequent now and he believed he was healing.

When Dallas told her friends she'd taken Simon to Mexico to meet her family, they hoped there would be yet another wedding on Lily Court Lane. Dallas's parents greeted Simon like a long lost son immediately making him feel like part of the family.

"He's very nice, Dallas. I like him a lot," her mother told her in a whisper. "He's a big, strong man and he eats good." She beamed as Simon ate huge amounts of her Mexican cooking. "I can see he's a good man, too. You should marry him."

Her father nodded in agreement, while her brothers hung on Simon's every word as he told stories about his travels and photography.

Dallas frowned at her mother's words knowing she had no intent to marry again. She cared for Simon more than she wanted to, but she was bound and determined never to be vulnerable again. As for Simon, it hit him like a ton of bricks when he saw her with her family. He must have been in love with this fantastic woman since the first moment he saw her coming down the stairs at Maryann's wedding.

Dallas sat next to Emilie on the sofa so they could look through the photo album Carolee had brought today. Many of the photos showed Max standing proudly in front of his new bed and breakfast looking very handsome. Carolee had just returned from a trip to Germany for the grand opening.

It was there she learned Emilie had given Max a substantial reward for the safe return of her painting. It was more than enough money to help him open his new business. Max told Carolee he called Emilie often to let her know the progress of the renovations. He said the business was doing so well he was already beginning to repay her. What Emilie saw as a gift, Max saw as a loan.

Carolee blushed with pleasure when Max said, "The painting brought a beautiful blond woman into my life who both delights and intrigues me."

Carolee told her friends Max invited Emilie to visit him and stay at the renovated castle, but they all knew she would never go to Germany.

Several photos showed Carolee standing at the bow of a cruise ship, her face glowing in the late summer sun. Max had taken her on a sightseeing cruise on the Rhine River he loved so much. They watched the castles go by and held hands as they enjoyed their time together. Max seemed charmed by her exuberant spirit, and was very tender in his attentions to her. She was pleased, but, Carolee cautioned herself, with men you never know.

When the time came for Carolee to return to San Diego, Max begged her to stay longer.

"Please stay with me. There is so much more for us to see and do together. I am not ready yet to let you go."

His kisses and lovemaking became a powerful encouragement to remain, but San Diego and Lily Court Lane called to her. How would Marvin get along without her to run the office? Most important, she'd never been away from her daughter for more than a week.

On the long plane ride home, she thought about Cindy and Ming and the amazing dinner that had taken place when the two families finally met. Carolee could tell Dorothy still wished Cindy was Chinese, but she had grudgingly admitted Cindy was a nice girl.

Carolee had charmed Dorothy with her open friendliness and genuine warmth. Her friends on Lily Court Lane were not surprised to learn that in the short time they'd known each other, Carolee and Dorothy had lunched several times and checked out the nearby fashion malls. The two women discovered a common passion for shopping, enjoyed watching the same television shows and playing mah jongg with their friends. Carolee and Dorothy could almost be mistaken for sisters.

One night after dinner, Ming and Carolee had a private moment while Cindy was out of the room.

"I want you to know I'll always be there for Cindy, and I'll always take good care of her," Ming earnestly assured Carolee.

Carolee smiled and patted his hand.

"I appreciate that very much, Ming. What more could any mother want?"

Carolee's life felt comfortable and secure now. She was certain she wouldn't change a thing. She loved her life just as it was, with her friends, her work, her daughter and her cat. Yet, away from Max her bed felt empty and cold.

Shortly after Carolee returned from Germany, she had an important conversation with Cindy.

"Mom, Ming asked me to move in with him. I thought about it and it feels right. We want to be together. What do you think?"

Although Carolee worried it might be a bit too soon, she wisely kept her opinion to herself.

"Honey, promise me you'll take your time making any big decisions, though."

"We will, Mom. We're not going to run off and get married or anything," Cindy laughed. "And Ming's mother still isn't all that happy about Ming dating a non-Chinese girl. She'll need time to get used to us living together. By the way, thanks for spending time with her the past couple of months. I think it's helping her to accept me."

Carolee was sure this move would be a topic for discussion when she had lunch with Dorothy the following week.

"Oh, I've enjoyed being with her. She's quite a character and really funny." Then changing the subject somewhat, Carolee asked, "Now that you'll be living at Ming's, what do you think about my renting our house in Del Mar? I have the name of a guy who's been looking for a place there. He's an artist and wants to be near the beach so he can paint seascapes," Carolee said in her best nonchalant tone.

She didn't let on she'd already met him and that she liked what she saw, especially his long, lanky frame and sunbaked skin.

"Oh, sure, Mom. Go for it."

Carolee hadn't revealed to Cindy a gift she planned to give her when she found the right location for her bistro. She'd been saving all the rent Cindy paid her to live in the Del Mar house and now she could add even more to Cindy's account.

Unconsciously touching her lips now, Carolee glanced across the mah jongg table at Maryann as she thought of Max and the passionate kiss he'd given her as they parted at the airport. She had to admit she did miss him, much more than she thought she would. Her reverie was interrupted as Maryann, squirming again in her chair at the mah jongg table, bumped against Carolee's leg.

"Sorry," Maryann murmured, as she gently rubbed her stomach. It was really aching badly.

43

An Unexpected Arrival

Maryann felt a stab of real pain dart across her huge belly. She began to gently massage the area where her daughter was kicking fiercely. Calm down, little girl, Maryann spoke silently to her unborn child. Ever since the baby started kicking, she began having silent conversations with her. She and Alex even put her sonogram picture on their refrigerator and Maryann would gently touch it each time she walked by.

She wasn't feeling hungry today, not even a little. She hadn't eaten any of the delicious lunch she'd prepared for the others. She was feeling too queasy to eat and the day was moving way too slowly for her. She woke up early that morning to see Alex off on a one-day business trip to meet with his coffee brokers in Tecate, Mexico. Then she was overcome by a furious drive to clean the entire house, changing all the sheets and towels, and doing every bit of laundry she could find. She was determined to get her house in order. Right that minute.

The furniture was all in place in the all-pink nursery which was well stocked with diapers, lotions, and baby powder. The room just needed a few finishing touches to make it perfect for her baby girl whose name was still being kept secret. Sarah finished sewing a pink baby quilt for the cooler nights to come, and matching pink gingham curtains with a cushion for the rocking chair which Emilie helped to select.

"I can hardly wait to rock in it and hold your dear baby," Emilie told Maryann.

Emilie had drawn especially close to Maryann and Alex. She was reminded of her own Bill, as both men had been career Navy and they were delighted to adopt her as an honorary grandmother.

Carolee stenciled a mural of baby animals on the wall above the crib, and Dallas picked out a baby gym to hang over the crib. As an honorary aunt, she just knew her niece would love to exercise and be doing pull-ups in no time.

Looking around the table at the faces of the women as they studied their mah jongg tiles, Maryann felt grateful to have found such good friends.

Ouch! There it was again, that feeling. Only this time it was much stronger. Suddenly Maryann wished Alex would hurry back from Mexico. Their conversation this morning was still fresh in her mind.

"But Alex, Tecate is so far away."

"No, honey, it's really not. Tecate is just across the border. I promise I'll be back by late afternoon, and probably before your mah jongg game is over. And besides, if you need me, just call and I'll be back in a flash. I wouldn't go if it wasn't so important, but you know how hard it is to get these guys to come all the way from Chiapas. They're really doing me a favor to meet in Tecate."

"Promise?"

"Yes, with all my heart."

He wasn't worried. Everyone knew that first babies took a long time to arrive.

Even as he was walking out the door, she started feeling stronger twinges and wished he'd come back.

Feeling a jolt of real pain now, Maryann didn't know if she could continue to play much longer. Perhaps she should ask to sit out even though it wasn't her turn to do so. Feeling pressure in her stomach, Maryann pushed herself back from the table, and stood up with some effort.

"Girls, I think I need to take a bathroom break."

No sooner had the words left her mouth than a stream of fluid gushed down her legs. Stopping in her tracks, she looked down in shocked dismay.

"Oh, shit!" she declared, in a most un-ladylike manner.

Sarah, the only one there with any actual birth experience, rose quickly and went to her.

"Maryann, it seems like no one is going to win this game. If I'm right, your water just broke and 'our' baby is on her way!"

Maryann felt another strong spasm of pain.

"Oh, my God! No, that can't be, it's too early! I'm not ready!" she said in panic. With that, Maryann sank back down on the chair and groaned, "I want Alex! He should be home by now."

Putting her arm around her sister-in-law, Sarah reassured her, "Don't worry, honey. He'll be back long before the baby arrives. We'll take good care of you," she promised, "and you've got us, all of us. Everything will be fine, just fine. You'll see."

Sarah now directed everyone as was her wont.

"Maryann, sit right here. Dallas, get the minivan and bring it around front. Carolee, take the pets home and meet us at the hospital. Jane, get Maryann's bag from her closet. I helped her pack it just yesterday. Emilie, get a couple of towels from the closet in the hall."

"Maryann, what is the telephone number for the doctor? We need to call her right now."

"The doctor said she'd meet us at the hospital. I left a note for Alex on the kitchen table." And hopefully he'll get to the hospital in time to see his daughter born, Sarah said under her breath. This was no false alarm.

The women all rushed to do Sarah's bidding, and Maryann was gently and quickly shuffled into the van with everyone piling in behind her. While Dallas drove, Maryann sat doubled over, moaning, Jane's arm around her as Sarah began timing the intervals between contractions, reminding her sister-in-law to breathe deeply. The contractions grew alarmingly close together. It wouldn't be a long labor. This baby girl was very much in a hurry!

Dallas brought the van to a squealing stop at the emergency entrance to the hospital, and Maryann was whisked away in a wheel chair with Sarah following closely behind. Carolee and Jane were impatiently pacing in the waiting room while Emilie sat in a chair nervously twisting her fine lace handkerchief between her fingers when Dallas came rushing in from the parking garage.

"What's happening? Did I miss anything?"

Just then, the nurse came in handing out clean gowns.

"Let's get you changed into your scrubs."

They scrambled into them as quickly as they could.

"Are you ready ladies? Let's go."

And following the nurse, they all walked together down the long corridor toward the birthing room to share one of life's most profound moments with their good friend.

Despite the group's presence and the comfort of having them around her, Maryann's eyes kept going to the door in search of Alex.

"Where is that man? I need him. I want Alex," she panted, her face red with effort, adding a few expletives each time she had a strong contraction.

"Don't worry Maryann, I'm sure he's on his way," comforted Emilie as she spooned several ice chips between Maryann's dry lips.

Sarah kept trying to reach Alex. Still no answer. Carolee kept fluffing the pillows at Maryann's back, and Jane took over the timing of the contractions. Dallas sat at the side of the bed, holding Maryann's hand, allowing her to squeeze as hard as she needed to when the contractions became unbearable.

The nurses, of course, were efficient and friendly, but not terribly sympathetic. They'd seen it all before. Maryann's true comfort came from her Lily Court Lane friends.

Things moved quickly now as Maryann entered the transition stage of labor, the time right before the baby would be born. She was totally consumed by a fierce desire to push the baby out as quickly as she could. She became unaware of her friends gripping her hands, one on each side of the bed, and the doctor standing expectantly at the foot of the bed waiting to catch the baby.

Taped on the wall facing Maryann was a photograph of the Hawaiian beach where Alex had taken her on their honeymoon. Maryann chose to use it for her concentration point to help her focus on her breathing and help get her through the labor pains. Staring at it now, she breathed in and out, panting as she had been taught. Damn it, where was he? He was supposed to be here and share this with her.

She felt totally overwhelmed with the need to push, but the doctor shook her head. "Not yet, Maryann. Hold on just a little longer."

"You hold on, doctor, I can't wait," she yelled as she was gripped by a tremendous contraction so fierce she felt like her belly was being squeezed through a drinking straw. "I changed my mind. Give me something."

"No, it's too late for that now."

But then the doctor finally directed, "Go ahead. Push, Maryann! Push as hard as you can."

Just as the top of the baby's head crowned, the door flew open and Alex came rushing into the birthing room, flustered and pulling on scrubs, his hair standing on end. The friends backed away from the bed so he could reach Maryann's side.

"I'm so so sorry, my love, it took me a very long time to cross the border. And I forgot that my cell phone wouldn't work in Tecate. Then, when I finally did cross back into California, the phone battery died, and when I got home I found your note...."

Alex trailed off, looking desperate. Would Maryann ever forgive him?

Maryann didn't hear anything her husband said as she clutched his hand so tightly he thought his fingers would turn blue. With his other hand, Alex leaned over and tenderly smoothed the hair back off her damp forehead. Caught in the middle of a huge push, Maryann had no words for him. A primal cry erupted from her as she gave one final huge push and the baby popped into the doctor's waiting hands.

The very welcome sound of a baby's lusty cry filled the room.

"You have a healthy daughter," the doctor announced after examining the infant.

"And she's beautiful, just like her mother," added Alex, although Maryann was sure she didn't look beautiful at this moment.

The exhausted new mother smiled in triumph through her tears. A girl! Our very own baby!

Proudly Alex thanked the doctor, and turned to the others, saying, "Thank you ladies for being here with us when we needed you."

"Can we tell them now, Alex?"

Maryann looked up at him as he nodded. They'd carefully chosen their daughter's name, ready to welcome her into the world. But they'd told no one yet.

"Emilie Rose, meet your new aunts and your grandmother!" Maryann hoarsely whispered, her mouth feeling as dry as dust.

Emilie gasped when she heard her own first name and realized this new life was being named for her. Tears ran down her cheeks. No one had ever before done such a kind thing for her.

The nurses had been busy weighing and measuring Emilie Rose who was now wrapped in a pink blanket and placed across Maryann's slightly flatter tummy. Tears shone in Alex's eyes as he looked down at his wife and new daughter. Feeling a little weak in the knees, he sank down on the side of the bed to kiss his wife and the pretty pink bundle on her stomach.

Blissfully smiling up at him, Maryann gently held her baby in her arms cooing to her.

"Emilie Rose, my little baby girl, meet your daddy," and she handed her to Alex.

He accepted the precious baby, and proudly holding his daughter for the very first time, he beamed at everyone crowded around the bedside. They were all laughing and crying at the same at seeing the red-faced, beautiful infant who was so loved by everyone present and who at that moment was wailing at the top of her lungs.

44

Halloween

Carved pumpkin faces glowed in the early evening light in front of houses decorated with straw scarecrows and steaming witches' cauldrons. Jane had lined up a row of grinning pumpkin heads along the porch and a dancing skeleton hung on their purple front door.

Inside, Craig stood surrounded by cartons and bubble wrap. Having returned from their honeymoon in Tahiti, they were preparing for their move to San Francisco when their doorbell chimed once again.

"Trick or treat!" little voices cried from the porch.

"Your turn, honey," Craig called out to Jane.

All up and down the street you could hear the happy cries of children calling out "Trick or Treat!"

Jane grabbed the bowl of wrapped candy bars and opened the door to find three little goblins thrusting forward pillowcases already heavily laden with candy. Ghosts, skeletons, tiny soldiers, and princesses had taken over Lily Court Lane this evening.

"Here you go," Jane said with a smile, as she dropped handfuls of candy into each of their pillowcases.

"Thank you! Thank you!" the little voices sang out in chorus before they scampered away to the next house. Parents stood on the sidewalk waiting patiently for their costumed offspring, hoping it was time to go home.

Looking up from his packing for a moment, Craig admired his new bride in her Halloween costume. While he wore jeans and a torn T-shirt like a rugged James Dean, Jane had joined the other ladies of Lily Court Lane dressing up as witches for Carolee's party. It would start later after all the young ghosts and goblins had ended their evening and were safely back home with their goodies.

Jane, with her long red hair, deep burgundy velvet witch's cape, and tall black pointed hat, made for a fetching sorceress. Craig was undeniably under her spell and looking forward to some romantic witchcraft of their own later that night.

She caught his "come hither" look and lit up. She knew what he was thinking and her heart fluttered with anticipation.

"I hope that's the last of the trick or treaters. We're nearly out of candy and I'm dying to look at the photos Simon sent us today. I promised myself I wouldn't look at them until we were together. Do you think it's too early to turn off the porch light?"

They were interrupted yet again by the doorbell. This time when they answered, they were met by three familiar faces. Maryann, dressed in a sparkly black witch's costume, held baby Emilie Rose, not quite two months old, dressed as a fuzzy round orange pumpkin. Her apple cheeks were rosy red in the cool night air and she was fast asleep in her mother's arms. Alex, standing behind his wife and daughter, was dressed as a swaggering pirate. He gave a huge smile showing off his fake gold tooth and an eye patch.

"Trick or treat! Welcome back from Tahiti!" Maryann called out. "We just wanted to stop by and say hello before the party."

Maryann leaned forward to kiss Jane on the cheek, being careful not to disturb the baby, while the men exchanged hearty handshakes.

"We're on our way to pick up Emilie. Pearl's visiting her grandson in New York, but Emilie decided to come to the party after all. We'll see you later at Carolee's."

As they walked down the path away from the house, Maryann called back with a laugh, "I just can't wait to see how Carolee's decorated her house."

Once the porch light was turned off, Craig joined Jane, ready to look at Simon's photos, which brought back happy memories of their special day.

San Diego in early October, the beach on Coronado, the blue of the ocean waves, the setting sun painting the sky behind them during their vows. Simon's photography, as always, captured the beauty of it all, and the candid unpredictable moments which always happen when friends are celebrating together.

One photo caught the men at the beach tossing a Frisbee to one another moments before the ceremony. Ming was leaping off the ground, reaching to catch the Frisbee tossed by Alex. Simon had included some wonderful silhouette shots of Ming and Cindy walking on the beach, holding hands. He'd also captured Sarah and Marvin sharing a kiss when they thought no one was looking. There were pictures of Maryann and Alex as a new family, loving each other and holding their baby girl.

Then there were the photos capturing the tenderness developing between Carolee and Max who was visiting from Germany. The women guessed a romance had blossomed between the two since Carolee's visit to Germany, and now Max had flown in especially to be with them for the wedding. They thought they were being discreet, but everyone saw they could barely keep their hands off each other. Everyone hoped Carolee had found love at last.

One photo showed Emilie looking happy to sit on the sidelines watching as everyone enjoyed their time at the beach in front of the historic Hotel Del Coronado. She was sipping yet another cocktail topped with an orange slice, a cherry and an umbrella, and it wouldn't be her last.

Earlier that morning, Simon took candid shots of the women at the beauty salon where they were having their hair done and their toenails painted frosted blue. Jane explained to Emilie the tradition of something old, something new, something borrowed, and something blue. Emilie found it quaint and not French at all.

"Every fashionable Lily Court lady," Jane earnestly told her, "will have blue toe nails for the wedding. That will be our something blue."

Now that Emilie was an honorary Lily Court Lane member, she agreed to forgo her shocking fuchsia polish in favor of ice blue. Just this one time.

Later, back at the hotel where the wedding party was staying, Simon's camera captured Jane as she stood before the mirror in her wedding gown. She had chosen a pale peach dress baring her lovely neck and shoulders and molded to her beautiful figure setting off her exotic beauty. Around her wrist she wore a gold bracelet that had been her mother's. Two creamy gardenias were pinned in her long red hair, and her lips were painted a brilliant coral. Her bouquet was composed of peach colored roses and white gardenias whose fragrance enveloped her wherever she went.

Craig could almost smell their fragrance as he looked at the pictures with the same awe he'd felt that day marrying Jane, his own true love. He'd never been so happy. He had everything now, a wonderful wife to share his life with, a happy mother, and a thriving business. After all the favorable publicity the gallery had gotten from the recovery of the painting, it was busier than ever and Craig and Jack were planning to open a branch in San Diego. This would allow Jane and Craig to live here for at least half the year.

In keeping with a happy Lily Court Lane tradition, Sarah's pearls were worn once again. That particular photo showing Sarah fastening the pearls around Jane's neck brought a sentimental tear to Jane's eyes as she recalled Sarah's words.

"Jane, you're my daughter now. I'd like you to wear the pearls my mother wore at her wedding and I hope someday your daughter will wear them at hers."

"Are these the same pearls Maryann wore for her wedding?"

"Yes, and I wore them when I married Marvin." Holding both of Jane's hands in her own, she lovingly said, "I wish for you and Craig all the happiness in the world."

"Thank you so much, Sarah. I know my own mother is watching over us on this special day and she's pleased you will be in my life."

Simon's photos had indeed captured every important moment and now having seen them all, Jane and Craig looked at one another with love and lust.

"I love you!" they said in unison and laughed as they climbed the stairs.

When they arrived a little late at the Halloween party, they found Carolee's house ablaze with candles, flying bats and cobwebs everywhere. As guests arrived at the front door, they were greeted by spooky, eerie sounds as if entering a haunted mansion. This would be the most memorable Halloween bash ever thrown on Lily Court Lane. The guests drank Bloody Marys, danced to the Monster Mash, and even bobbed for apples.

Carolee's witch's costume was, of course, over the top perfect, with its layers of black tulle, a satin bodice, and tiny fake black spiders attached to the veil floating from her velvet witch's hat. A tall, tanned, handsome man dressed as a starving artist in torn jeans and paint splattered shirt stood attentively at Carolee's side when Sarah and Marvin arrived.

"This is John," Carolee said introducing him. "He's renting my house in Del Mar."

Hmmm, competition for Max, Sarah wondered?

Dorothy and Lloyd could stay only a short while as Saturday night was a busy time at *The Golden Dragon*, their restaurant in Rancho Bernardo. Dorothy, wearing an elegant black *cheong sam* embroidered with a red and gold dragon, and carrying a large hand painted fan, was accompanied by Lloyd dressed in a plain, dark business suit.

When questioned, he claimed to be Clark Kent, causing an incredulous Ming to laugh outloud.

How times change, Cindy thought as she hugged Dorothy hello and kissed her on the cheek. She turned to smile at Ming who had dressed as Prince Charming to accompany her—his own Cinderella. She could hardly wait for the party to end so she could introduce Ming to the thrills of the "Haunted Hotel" in the Gaslamp. Like her mother, Cindy loved the excitement of Halloween.

It was a close competition, but Marvin won the prize for the best male costume, a day on the water donated by Alex's rowing club. His green frog outfit was perfect for his stocky figure. Before they left for the party Sarah lovingly placed a crown on his head to show everyone he was truly her prince.

Emilie, looking like Audrey Hepburn in "Breakfast at Tiffany's," was wearing a long black evening gown, elbow length white satin gloves and wielding a long onyx cigarette holder. She tilted her tiara rakishly to one side as she accepted the prize of a spa day for the best female costume.

"*Merci beaucoup*," she said. French and glamorous even on an American Halloween.

Late that night the party was finally winding down and most of the guests departed for home having devoured deviled eggs, chicken fingers, spare ribs, and pumpkin mousse. Under Cindy's supervision, Max and Ming were taking down the remains of the pumpkin shaped piñata.

"Hurry up, Ming," an impatient Cindy directed eager to get to the "Haunted Hotel."

A little bossy, Max thought, hoping she didn't get that trait from Carolee.

Receiving a message on his cell phone, Marvin had to excuse himself as one of his clients needed to speak to him urgently.

"No holiday for lawyers or frogs," he said.

Simon was still taking pictures as Alex handed Emilie Rose to a beaming Emilie who was seated on the sofa. Craig and Jane had stolen out to the porch for a lingering kiss.

The original four women friends, witches in costume only, reunited in Carolee's kitchen for a final toast of the evening. To Maryann, Sarah, Dallas, and Carolee, Lily Court Lane was a wondrous street filled with romance and adventure. Their circle had grown to include a cougar, an elegant French woman, and a baby girl. What a wonderful year this had been for all of them.

Their reluctance to accept love when it was offered was unquestionably a thing of the past.

Not everyone was sleeping peacefully tonight behind the closed doors on Lily Court Lane. Behind the yellow door, Simon was valiantly trying to work up the courage to propose to Dallas. He still didn't deserve her, he thought, but he didn't want to go through life without her.

In the house with the red door, Maryann and Alex shared another sleepless night with a baby who awoke at three a.m and decided she wanted to coo and play. Emilie Rose was so adorable they couldn't resist her. They hoped, like all new parents, they would be able to sleep late in the morning. They'd be disappointed.

Sarah and Marvin cuddled under the covers behind the blue door. Sarah felt supremely happy and so relaxed. The heat had flared between them once again. Age wasn't a barrier to their passion. As she fell asleep that night in his arms, Sarah thought about the year. So many weddings. First there was the New Year's Eve wedding of her brother Alex and her best friend Maryann. Then her own wedding to the beautiful man who now was snoring so peacefully beside her, and just recently her son Craig's wedding to Jane.

Sarah was hoping for yet another wedding—Dallas and Simon's. They were both so deserving of happiness. Afterall, Maryann had such a difficult time which she was able to overcome with a little push from Sarah. Oh, yes, she smiled, she was a very persuasive person after all. In the darkness of the night, Sarah shifted in Marvin's arms and gently stroked his balding head. Moments later she fell into a deep, contented sleep.

Once her green front door was closed, Carolee turned to Max, "Don't you think it's time you saw my bedroom?"

"It would be my honor," replied Max throwing his cowboy hat and bandana on the sofa and following Carolee up the stairs. He'd spend his first night not sleeping on Lily Court Lane.

Behind the purple door, Craig took great pleasure in removing Jane's witch's costume, slowly, one piece at a time. Making love to a witch can be a lot of fun.

A house at the end of the street stood empty. The house with the indigo door had a "For Sale" sign in the front yard. It was waiting.

Who would be the next resident of Lily Court Lane?

Epilogue: The Painting

One cold and snowy December afternoon, a ten-year-old girl stood in front of a painting. Her parents, dressed in their warmest winter coats and boots, stood back a little, watching their daughter. The Louvre would be closing soon.

Despite her parents' reminders, the child seemed reluctant to move, and Maryann and Alex didn't want to rush her. The family had traveled to Paris especially for this moment. Their daughter, Emilie Rose, would remember this day forever.

Her adopted grandmother, Emilie, had often shown her the faded photo of her own family and retold the story of the painting of the mother and child, and how it had been stolen and later returned to her.

Grand-Mère Emilie had been right, Emilie Rose was thinking. *This painting is truly special.* She could almost feel the soft curls on the baby's blond head and the rosy cheeks beneath. The mother was so pretty too, not in the modern way like her own mother, but in an old-fashioned style with her long hair coiled over her ears and her flowing blue gown.

The painting had been placed at the end of a long hallway and was beautifully lit so that visitors could experience its beauty as they approached the work. All afternoon, tour groups speaking many different languages had passed by listening to the guides tell the story of how the painting, a Flemish masterpiece, had been stolen by the Nazis during World War II. It had been recovered in California, and finally returned to France.

The little girl lingered in front of the painting. She knew that story better than any guide. This was the painting that had been donated to the museum by her *Grand-Mère* Emilie in memory of her family who'd perished at the hands of the Nazis.

The painting, although unsigned, had been authenticated and attributed to a master and was today worth millions of dollars. But Emilie had not wished for money. Emilie was very specific when she met with her attorney, Marvin Miller.

"*Monsieur* Miller, please make certain it is very clear to the Museum. My painting is never to be sold. I also want Papa's letter to be displayed on the wall next to the painting. It is to be translated into many languages for all to read."

That letter later became a memorial for Holocaust survivors and their children. Many tears were shed for the young girl who'd lost her family and for their own losses as well. It became a place of healing and remembrance.

Emilie had also directed Marvin to add sizeable bequests in her will for Pearl and her children, and Mathilde's family, as well as items of sentimental value to her friends on Lily Court Lane. She knew Carolee would appreciate her collection of designer handbags.

Then touching the pink gold wedding band on her finger, she added with a fond smile, "And this is to go to Emily Rose for her future children."

Following Emilie's instructions, Marvin made the arrangements to transport the painting to Paris. He was accompanied by Sarah, Craig and Jane. Craig oversaw its installation at the Louvre.

Maryann and Alex arranged a video conference so they could share with Emilie, and Pearl this emotional moment. Emilie smiled through her tears as she held her namesake Emilie Rose close to her heart.

Closing her eyes, Emilie could see her father's face. He was smiling at her in approval.

"Papa is so happy to have his beloved painting returned to France, the country he loved so much and died for," she had said.

When Emilie had passed away in her sleep the previous year, she was found with a smile on her face and a copy of her papa's letter tucked under her pillow. She had enjoyed her final years with her Lily Court Lane friends, watching her namesake grow into a beautiful and lively little girl.

Maryann leaned against Alex's shoulder remembering their dear friend. Emilie Rose had been close to the French woman spending many Saturday afternoons with her, drinking tea from her delicate cups and hearing about life in Paris before the War. Emilie often retold the story of her birth and with a twinkle in her eye, teased the child about how red and wrinkled she had been and how loudly she had cried that day in the hospital.

Maryann stepped forward now and whispered to Emilie Rose.

"Dear, the museum is about to close. It's time for us to get back to the hotel. Your brother, Bryan, will be ready for his dinner and the babysitter will be wondering where we are.

"It's hard to leave, Mom," she said looking up into her mother's face. "I still miss *Grand-Mère* Emilie. She was so much fun and she understood me so well. I wish she could come back to us," she said with tears forming in her young, bright eyes.

"We all miss her, darling. She was a very special person. "

"You know, Mom, *Grand-Mère* Emilie was right. The painting does look so much prettier in person." Emilie Rose hugged her mother, as she said, "Thanks for bringing me here."

Taking one last long look at the painting, Emilie Rose said, "Bye bye, Baby Emilie." She looked at her own mother for a moment. "Mom, don't you think the baby looks happy?"

"She certainly does. She looks like all the babies the world over who are loved by their mothers just like I love you."

The girl smiled and took her mother's hand as the two headed toward the entrance where her father stood hailing a taxi for them. Soon it would be time for them to return to San Diego and Lily Court Lane.

As they stepped outside, it was beginning to snow.

Mah Jongg: The Game as Played by the Ladies of Lily Court Lane

The game of mah jongg originated in China, but it underwent many changes as it spread to other areas around the globe. It is played by picking and discarding tiles, much like the card game Gin Rummy. There are now many American versions of the game with different combinations of winning hands and rules of play. Under the authority of several mah jongg associations throughout the United States, the winning hands are changed yearly and printed on a card each player uses during the game.

The 152 tiles of a standard American mah jongg set are identified by the picture on the front of each tile. There are three suits named **craks** (red Chinese characters), **bams** (green bamboo), and **dots** (colored circles). Then there are **winds** (north, east, south, and west); **flowers** representing seasons (winter, spring, summer, autumn); **dragons** (red, green, white) and eight **jokers**.

Craks, bams and dots are numbered from one to nine. There are four tiles of each number in each suit, and additional tiles for winds, flowers, dragons, and jokers. A joker may represent any needed tile except it may not be used to complete a pair and it may not be picked up from the discarded pile in the center of the table.

Only four people may play at a time. To start the game, the tiles are mixed and placed face down in the center of the table. Each player selects 38 tiles, 4 at a time, building a wall 19 tiles long and 2 tiles high. The player, who is declared **East** for the first game, moves the **wall** into the center of the table, and takes the first 4 tiles from the end of the wall. Each succeeding player, going in a counter-clockwise rotation, takes 4 tiles until each player has 12 tiles.

East then selects 2 additional tiles totaling 14 tiles. The other players select one final tile for a total of 13 tiles each. Everyone then arranges their tiles on their racks. Each player has a card with possible combinations for that year's winning hand. These are the only hands that can win.

Consulting their card, the players select a possible combination of tiles to play. Players then open the game by exchanging tiles with each other hoping for a more favorable hand. Three unwanted tiles are passed to the player on the right, and 3 tiles are received from the player on the left. This process is repeated with the player across the table, and then with the player on the left. So it's right, across, left. That completes the first go round called the **Charleston**.

A player can request the passing to be stopped after this if the player has a really good hand. The next go round (left, across, right) is optional. For the final movement, called **courtesy**, each player asks the player seated opposite if that player would like to exchange any number of tiles up to 3.

East then starts the game by discarding a tile into the center of the table. If no one wants the discarded tile, the player seated to the right of East selects a tile from the wall in the center, and either decides to keep it, placing it on the rack, or discard it. This continues until the players have drawn all the tiles from that wall, and then the next wall is pushed into the center.

The first player to complete a hand by matching one of the hands on the card announces "mahj," and displays the hand to the other players. Each winning hand is worth a designated amount as listed on the card and each player pays the winner. The player who discarded that tile has to pay double to the winner, but if the winner drew the tile from the wall, the winner is paid double by everyone. If no one wins, it is called a wall game.

Many groups like to play with five players. At the end of each hand, the designated East player for that round gets up and that seat is taken by the fifth player. The player to the right then becomes East and this is repeated around the table for each hand.

The player who is sitting out for that hand has the option to bet on which player will win. If correct, the player collects the same amount of money as the winning player. If incorrect, the player sitting out has to pay the winning player. Observing the other players provides a way to learn more about the game, as well as the other players' strategies.

Secrets have been exchanged, and friendships made and lost while playing mah jongg. The many thousands of players who love the game are committed for life and enjoy meeting for weekly games as well as taking part in the many tournaments and cruises built around mah jongg.

An interested reader can learn more about playing mah jongg simply by searching on-line. Some particularly helpful websites are: *www.nationalmahjonggleague.org* and *mahjonggfederation.com*. There is even a video on Youtube.com.

About the Authors

Susan Chan was a school guidance counselor in New York City. Carol Polakoff was a teacher and worked in high-fashion retail sales. The two met during a mah jongg game after they moved to San Diego, where they both currently live with their husbands. Inspired to write their own novel after a book club discussion, this is the first book for each of them.

www.ingramcontent.com/pod-product-compliance
Lightning Source LLC
Chambersburg PA
CBHW032207190626
46810CB00019B/2170